DAUGHTERS OF ANARCHY

SEASON 1

C.A. HARTMAN

5280 PRESS

ISBN: 0-9903919-5-7
ISBN-13: 978-0-9903919-5-1

Cover design by Chris Voeller (chrisvoeller.com)

EPISODE 1
NICE TO MEET YOU

"Invest in our youth, for they are the future."

Stevie stared at the platitude glaring at her in dull gray typeface, paid for by the supremely expensive private university nearby. She sighed, swiping the irritating message away so she could check the news.

Dianthus man found dead.

She sipped her double espresso, which seemed to go down too quickly that morning. Maybe a triple would've been better. She pressed a button on her white cafe table to place the order.

"I was so fucking wasted," a voice drawled from the adjacent table. He spoke in a low, slow, but still-too-loud style, the one commonly found among young men making a valiant attempt to sound cool. "I must've had six AirBombs... I puked everywhere in the Miashi lobby. Everywhere, man. I just left it for the janitor to clean up."

His two friends laughed and slapped hands in celebration of his triumph, his having imbibed with such derring-do that his limited human physiology finally rejected the bacchanalian onslaught. He wore a faded DeWitt University t-shirt and wrinkled pajama bottoms, his mop of dark curly hair disheveled from drunken slumber.

DeWitt. Educating the children of those who profited from decades of war.

Hungover Hero erupted into a hoarse whinnying laugh, also louder than necessary. Then his friends began the wasted youth's game of one-upmanship, offering their own stories of drunken misdeeds. Stevie took a surreptitious image of him, able to get a full frontal because he was too absorbed in his bragging to notice her eyes on him.

Why are you out and about so early, Hero?

As if on cue, he groaned about an important exam, one he'd tried to postpone but for an uncorrupted professor who'd refused.

When her extra shot of espresso arrived, Stevie smiled at the yellowy-blonde barista, produced her ID to scan for payment, and drank the hearty beverage before getting up to leave. Out in the chilly damp air, the sidewalk teemed with dark-suited folk heading to work and the occasional underdressed student scurrying to an expensive class. A train drifted past, nearly noiseless compared to the electro-taxis that whirred down the narrow street at velocities beyond what the law desired. The morning sky offered plenty of drear but no hint of impending rain.

Stevie walked through Dianthus, past closed bars and open chem shops, past shiny new buildings and the occasional vacant lot, a few with gleaming steel beams rising from the ashes of the past. When she reached the shuttle grounds, the gray sea rested in the distance. Once through security and on the shuttle, Stevie sat down when she saw no one else standing. She shifted in the stiff white seat, next to other preoccupied folk reading or chatting with an unseen other. Out the large windows, the City grew smaller and smaller. How orderly it all looked from that vantage point. How simple the gridded streets appeared, how tidy the buildings, how still the river, how verdant the few green patches sprinkled throughout. And how well the distance obscured the chips and chinks, the remnants of past pain and the seedy goings-on that lingered.

She checked her watch, her bladder speaking more loudly than usual to her, under pressure from the effects of precious 1,3,7-trimethylxanthine. But she needed that third espresso shot... after the weekend she'd had. When the shuttle finally arrived at the Disc, Stevie waited for the others to exit before making haste for the restroom, reminding herself not to drink a triple *and* a full glass of water before her morning commute.

On the way to her workstation, she peered out the window that circled the Disc, the elliptical station that floated far above their City. The City was only a sprawl of concrete blocks now, surrounded by recovering farmland, charred Earth, and, to the south, gunmetal gray ocean. When she passed Seth's workstation, she spotted a glimpse of his tightly cut blonde hair. She took a quick glance around before setting down her things and flipping on her red Do Not Disturb light.

After firing up her computer and monitors, she transferred Hungover Hero's image from her device to her computer and ran an image match. With a good frontal at close range, a match would take little to no time under normal circumstances. And within moments, two new images appeared onscreen, both with very high percentages. She took an image of his personal data before clearing her screen and search history.

Stevie stepped away from her standing desk and screens filled with lines upon lines of what Seth called "gobbledygook." Her feet were tired from supporting her during many hours of data analysis, of searching for the evil needle in the indifferent haystack. A yawn escaped her as she left her workstation.

Machine loomed in the distance, a shiny black beacon across the sea of other workstations. She headed that way, halting first at Seth's station. No red Do Not Disturb sign. She knocked on the tall partition and entered.

"Need some coffee, Captain?"

Seth turned around and looked at her with deep-set blue eyes surrounded by blonde but impossibly long lashes. "Yes. Please." He eyed her for a moment. "Did you change your hair?"

"No." She smiled. "I thought men didn't notice even when we *do* change our hair."

He shrugged. "You know me. I don't miss much." He glanced at her short dark hair again. "It looks lighter."

"It's all the sun I've been getting," she quipped.

He laughed at her jest. "So, did you hear the latest?"

"Only a headline."

"You still don't watch the news? The Oakenfold Killer... he struck again. Some Financial from Dianthus. Bullet to the heart, and another between the eyes."

"Like the others."

"Yep. And still no suspects." He shook his head. "Who uses an antique revolver? You can't find them on the black market anymore. You can't even find the specs to print one anymore."

She smiled again. "How would you know?"

A devious grin reached his face. "I collect antique weaponry. It's legal as long as they're disabled. I've been looking for an Oakenfold .357 Magnum for years."

"What do you do with them?"

"Display them, at my place."

"And what happens when you bring a woman home and she sees all that?"

Seth shrugged. "You'd be surprised how many of them like it."

She shook her head, chuckling, before she grabbed Seth's Army mug.

As she resumed her stroll to Machine, she glanced out the window. Clouds had begun to roll in, obscuring the City below. It didn't look like a notable system, though, which would make her evening plans a little easier.

Machine had no line. He stood waiting for her, like an old friend who secretly liked her more than his other friends. She acknowledged that for the small victory it was. "Double espresso, please."

She placed her clean black mug beneath the spout, and Machine dispensed the steaming dark liquid into the cup, the rich odor already filling her with renewed purpose. When the display indicated that she could, she replaced her mug with Seth's and spoke again. "Khaki, please."

You had to say "please." Machine refused to respond if you didn't. Stevie, trained to use the word since she'd learned to talk, never knew of Machine's distaste for poor manners until some of her coworkers received a lesson in good ones. When Stevie returned with both coffees, delivering the fairer of the two to Seth, he thanked her and gave her a wink.

Back at her station, she escaped into the privacy of her space and sipped her espresso, immediately feeling better. She spoke a couple of commands and her desk lowered to a position that would allow her to sit for a while. Just as she retrieved a new tidbit of information from her personal tablet, she heard Herbie's booming voice in the distance. She quickly hid her tablet.

Herbie said hello to everyone he passed, asking them how they were. Such a change from the socially disabled icicles she used to work with, who rarely managed eye contact much less the uttering of a greeting. Herbie's deep voice grew louder; he headed her way. It was the end of the month, and Herbie would want to discuss monthly security reports, to see the preliminaries before presenting them to the executives.

"Good afternoon, Miss Stevie!" he said, his large build towering over her, his navy suit buttoned over a pink checked tie.

She smiled. "Afternoon, Boss."

"How's my Big Data expert? You're looking a little tired today, even for a Monday. Exciting weekend?"

"I wish."

"So... let's talk about those reports..."

Once Herbie left, Stevie flipped on her red light, pulled out her personal tablet again, and retrieved her new data. After a search, an image appeared. A professional shot. Pushing 40. V-neck wool sweater over a white collared shirt. Hands in the steeple position, the one that still managed to lull citizens into an injudicious admiration. Address: 1840 Riverside Street. Rosa neighborhood. Right on the Milagro River. Stevie placed a track on his ID. Color: red.

Found you.

Stevie stepped off the shuttle and left the secured area, immediately heading into the heart of Dianthus. A bright light flashed, briefly illuminating raincoated citizens making their way home from work. She looked up, preparing herself for the clamor of thunder that soon followed. She might get wet, but it would be worth it.

She strode up the steep part of DeWitt Street, the pungent odor of cannabis wafting out from a chem shop as dark-suited men and women formed a long line outside. Even before she crested the hill she could see it: a sleek, dark edifice with glass sides that had no balconies, no windows that opened... only shiny blackness that reached the sky. Then the bright purple Miashi sign appeared, casting its royal glow over restaurants and clubs with six-week waiting lists. She put on her black polyester hat, donned her dark eyeshades, and buttoned her coat all the way to her neck.

The doors silently parted as she entered. The dark lobby enveloped her, its only illumination from purple pendant lamps and numerous mirrors set within the black velvet cushioned walls. Black epoxy tables and neat black couches dotted the nearby bar, where young couples sat quietly, their faces obscured by perfectly straight black hair and black drinks in their hands. She went to the front desk.

"May I help you?" said a thin man, his accent floating out from beneath a curtain of purple hair.

"Good evening," Stevie said. "The janitor who worked the graveyard shift last night... is he on duty yet?"

"Why do you want to know?"

"A friend of mine was rude to him last night. I want to apologize next time he's on duty."

The thin man's eyelids fluttered, an attempt to disguise a set of rolling eyes. "He'll arrive in an hour."

She smiled. "Thank you. I'll wait over there," she added, pointing to the epoxy chairs.

Stevie sat down on one of the seats, which were even less forgiving than those on the shuttle. She pulled out her tablet and read, glancing at her watch from time to time until she felt someone approaching. She looked up; an older man with a limp drew near, his custodial uniform neat and tidy, perhaps even pressed. He eyed her suspiciously. He'd served once. She could almost always spot a vet.

"You speak to me?" he said in a thick accent.

"Hello," she said, standing up to greet him. "Did you have to clean someone's vomit last night, here in the lobby?"

His dark eyes clouded over and his lip twitched. "Yes. I clean."

"What happened?"

"I don't know. I clean office, I clean bathroom, I go to lobby, and it is there, in four or five place."

"I know who did it. If you get me access to the fifteenth floor, perhaps we can ensure he never does it again."

His eyes narrowed. "Who are you?"

"A concerned citizen."

The vet shook his head. "It is risky. I need job."

"If you remain on the first floor when it happens, you'll have many alibis. Just get me access tonight, and I will take care of everything."

Back at home, Stevie changed into her tights and running shoes before heading to the lobby.

"Where to tonight?" Manny the doorman called out from behind his desk.

"To the bridge," she replied.

Manny gave the nod and returned his attention to the couple who stood before him. Stevie went out into the chilly evening, uncomfortably cold until she built up adequate heat from running. The rain had ceased for now. She weaved in and out of dark-coated citizens going home or heading to dinner, dodging the occasional sidewalk hole and making her way east. Out of Artemisia, through Rosa, and to Blackwood Bridge. Her bridge. Where she could run without obstacles and forget herself for while.

The electro-taxis relegated to the bridge's lower level, she ran along the upper, subtle movements of the suspension bridge under her feet. How quiet it was up there, how dark and peaceful. Only the occasional hum of a passing train could disturb the stillness that finally found her. Once at the bridge's midpoint, she stopped, lights shining at her from the east and west banks, the breeze from the Milagro chilling her and wiping away the stench of the City.

Time to head back. There's work to be done.

That evening, Stevie sat in the Miashi lobby bar. Patrons clad in black suits and tight, minimal dresses filled the place, the latter seeming to gather in unified defiance of the damp, cold weather. Black-glassed drinks were had, as were inane conversations and the occasional raising of voices over an already overstimulating hubbub. She nursed her bubbly water with lime, watching the women negotiate their high-heeled parade through the gauntlet that all bars seemed to have, with chairs on either side where men sat and gazed. Despite her long black wig, no one noticed Stevie tucked away in a quiet corner, her black suit and shades allowing her to blend in with the velvet.

Finally, opportunity came: a woman, whose loud flirtations and laughter had called more attention to her than even the other over-exuberantly vocal women. The voluptuous-hipped, large-bosomed woman negotiated the gauntlet with a sway, half-lidded eyes, and perhaps a certain haste, more preying eyes than Stevie's upon her. *Rosa queen.* Stevie followed her to the restroom. As she entered, the woman paused for several moments, recovering what little remaining equilibrium she had before she made for one of the black doors. Stevie removed her eyeshades and placed them atop her head before she approached the woman, putting her black-gloved hand lightly on a bare shoulder.

"Are you okay? Are you going to be sick?"

The woman turned and stared at her for some time, her capacity for processing such an inquiry, much less answering it, on significant delay. She turned away again and reached for the gilded handle.

"Don't go in there," Stevie said, almost pleading, grabbing the woman's shoulder again. "You don't want to get sick where others go to the bathroom, do you?" She produced the black bucket she planted beneath the vanity and set it on the countertop, nudging the addled woman closer to it. "Here."

The woman peered into the bucket. And without argument, she began to vomit. Stevie held back the woman's golden hair, hair so thick and lustrous that it smacked of genetic tampering. The woman paused, heaving with deep breaths and the unburdening of herself of the toxin with which so many poisoned themselves. When the woman underwent another round and the odor wafted up, Stevie focused on the hair, the soft beautiful hair, attempting to ignore the retching and splashing of stomach contents into the bucket. When it was over, the woman leaned over the sink.

"Here," Stevie said, handing her a small bottle of water. "Just sip it."

The woman complied, her expression taking on a greater lucidity.

"Do you need me to call you a taxi?" Stevie said, concerned about her safety.

She shook her head. "I'll call my driver," she replied, her voice tiny and weak for such a curvaceous woman. She pulled out her ID. "Where's your tip card?"

Stevie shook her head. "I lost it. Don't worry about me."

And the woman left.

Stevie put her shades back on and placed the lid upon the ice bucket, exiting the bathroom just as a group of giggling young women sidled in. She paged the janitor, whose eyes widened at the sight of her before they shifted to the bucket. He gave her the nod. She tucked the bucket into her arm and placed a hand on his shoulder.

"Thank you... for your service."

When she arrived at the 15th floor, she walked down the dark, dimly lit hallway, lined with mirrors that reflected her dark wig and dark eyeshades and narrow face back to her. When she arrived at apartment 1503, she set her package down and pulled out a device from her pocket, running it over the console. After the brief tinkling of electronic doings, the door unlatched. She coaxed it open slowly, seeing only the entrance to a kitchen and a hallway that led to another room, out of which lights flashed and muted sounds drifted.

She removed the lid and dumped the bucket's contents onto the floor, its shiny blackness marred by the splatter of the pink-red elixir of alcohol, dye, and hydrochloric acid. She set down the bucket, quietly shut the door, and pattered quickly to the stairwell, quietly taking her lightweight body up two flights to the 17th floor. She exited and shut the door gently, proceeding down another mirrored hallway as if she belonged, as if the many Stevies reflected in those mirrors belonged in such a place. She stood in a corner, waiting, a handful of excuses at her ready if anyone came by. Finally, she went to the elevator and pressed. Soon, the doors opened to a black-haired, black-clad couple pressed against the velveteen wall. He crushed her with such force that Stevie questioned whether the woman had offered full consent.

"How are you both tonight?" Stevie said in her best whiny drawl.

When the woman glanced at her, appearing mostly annoyed, Stevie got the reassurance she needed and said nothing else. When she exited, she half expected to see the wild-haired Hungover Hero waiting for her, as if knowing she must emerge at some point, that no matter how much black she wore or how she carried herself, she would never fit in with the Miashi crowd.

But he was nowhere to be seen. As she headed to exit the building and escape the noise and stink it came with, she spotted the janitor in the shadows. He gave her an almost imperceptible nod as she left.

A lot of trouble to go to, Steviansa, for a spoiled kid who will never learn.

He'll think twice next time.

It solves nothing in the long term.

There's no solving, Mom. Only management.

Go home, where it's safe.

I am, Mom.

Friday, when the shuttle arrived at the Disc, Stevie hurried to her desk. Herbie had already messaged her that he would keep her busy that day. More analyses to run, more charts to make for the executives. That year, the Federal Watch program had collected a prodigious amount of data after completing the surveillance installations in the west, and managing and analyzing that volume of data had stretched them all.

She was still tired from working late for Herbie last night, so much so that she'd overslept a little. Then she'd encountered another demonstration in Dianthus, forcing her to take a five-block detour. More wealthy citizens protesting the City's restrictions on the number of cannabis licenses allotted to the area, somehow guided by the misbelief that more was always better. The delay left her no time for coffee, not even a lesser-quality but quick espresso from one of Dianthus's takeaway joints.

Just as she started up her computer, Herbie came around the corner, his gray suit buttoned over a green polka-dot tie.

"I need you, Stevie," he said. "The executives have some questions about the phone data numbers from the southern regions." He peered at her. "No coffee yet today?"

She shook her head, glad she wore one of her better suits.

"I need you to look alive." He beckoned her to follow him. "This won't take long, and you can visit Machine afterward."

The meeting was brief. The navy-suited bureaucrats had straightforward questions that Stevie could answer even without coffee. Before paying her visit to Machine, Stevie returned to her workstation and checked on the red dot. It remained in the expected place, near the Circle. He was downtown, at work.

Seth appeared, startling her.

"Sorry," he said. "Didn't mean to sneak up on you."

She approached the doorway, ensuring Seth didn't come in. He held her black cup, steam rising from its shiny darkness. She took the cup, almost sighing with relief. "How'd you know?"

"Just a hunch."

She sipped the hot beverage, the smell of nearly burnt coffee beans already perking her up. "Thank you, Major."

He grinned, never minding the occasional promotions she gave him. He looked at her for a moment, the expression in his long-lashed blue eyes changing from their usual vigilance to something altogether different. "We talked about meeting for lunch a while ago. What are you doing this weekend?"

Stevie hesitated, taken aback by Seth's offer, never having expected him to follow up on that previous exchange. Her mind went to her own long-considered weekend plans, wishing she could say yes but knowing it was impossible, and unsure what would serve as a good excuse.

"I'll take a no over a half-hearted yes," he said, appearing a bit nettled.

"It's not a no, Seth. This weekend isn't good, but next weekend works for me."

He gave a half smile. "Good. Sunday?"

She nodded as Seth disappeared.

A man who's interested invites you to dinner, Steviansa, not lunch.

He's a friend, Mom.

A man like him—successful, served in the wars instead of staying here to profit from them—he'll have many options.

I know, Mom.

By the end of the workday, cloud cover obscured the City's lights. She glanced at her watch. If she hurried, she could catch the next shuttle. It wasn't too late to begin the proceedings that would consume much of her weekend. She ran past the mostly-emptied workstations, including Seth's, to the stairwell where she descended the metal stairs, her footsteps echoing off the walls as she clamored down to the waiting area.

"Shuttle will depart in one minute," an electronic voice said. "One passenger seat open."

Just as Stevie went to claim the seat, she saw Marianne Mulroney, Herbie's pregnant assistant who was rapidly approaching her due date and carrying an awkwardly overfilled bag. Marianne halted, looking at Stevie with a mixture of envy and acquiescence, knowing Stevie had beaten her to it. Stevie hesitated.

"You take it, Marianne," Stevie said. "I'll wait."

Marianne looked like she would burst into tears at the small kindness, and hurried through the doors to the shuttle.

Stevie sat down in the waiting area, checking the time again before peering out the large window at the darkness. The moon gazed at her, a waxing gibbous, about five days from reaching its fullness. As a child, before she learned the proper term in science class, she always referred to a gibbous as a potato chip moon. Its shape resembled that of the potato chips her mother would buy her, but only on special occasions. *Too much salt is bad for one's blood pressure, Steviansa,* she would say.

Stevie chuckled. If only her mother had known that with the exception of her most stressful moments, Stevie's systolic blood pressure never saw the triple digits, much less figures that would require caution with partaking in sodium chloride. She must have inherited that trait from him, the one who'd supplied the other half of her genome.

Steviansa. The kids had knocked her about her name in school. Teachers would often stumble over it and make a face, the sort of face one made when believing that a mother had been too earnest in her desire to make her child seem slightly less ordinary than other children. When Stevie told her mother about the kids' razzing and the teachers' contempt, her response was, "Stupid people make judgments. Smart people ask questions." Stevie never minded the name; it seemed to bother others more than her. Yet, she went by Stevie because it was shorter and easier.

Others began gathering in the waiting area, until the next shuttle arrived. Stevie stepped onto the shuttle, remaining standing so that the others could sit. When the doors shut and several seats remained, she let herself take one. After descending into the cloud cover, rain pelted on the shuttle windows, leaving droplets that streaked down their sides until the wipers cleared them away. Twenty-five minutes later, they landed on the surface. Stevie waited until everyone exited before she followed them into the station.

She glanced at her watch. There was still enough time.

When she arrived at her building, she waved to Manny and got into the elevator, its pseudo-wood paneled interior lacking the poshness of the Miashi elevator but having a more organic feel that pleased her. Seeing no one coming, Stevie let the doors shut. But before the gap reached full closure, the doors reopened. A dough-faced man stood in a tailored navy suit, his dark hair neatly cut and pomaded into place as perfectly as every time she'd seen him. He held the button while the doors gaped, motioning to two similarly dressed men in the lobby.

"You coming or not?" he shouted to them.

Stevie cleared her throat, hoping he would turn and see her there, waiting. He didn't.

He continued pressing, gesturing to his friends but showing no real concern at their dillydallying. Finally, they approached the elevator and Stevie moved over to make room for the three men. The dapper men talked amongst themselves, discussing which establishment they would patronize that evening. For numerous floors they bantered with the gaiety of those who benefited from the economic realities and resulting social mores developed over decades of war.

"Rosa tonight," Pomade said. "Pink ladies and pink pussy."

"Nah, man. Dianthus. Young Yellows with good knees and bad boundaries. I can probably get us into Miashi's second level."

At the 34th floor, Stevie waited for the men to exit, holding the door for them as they prattled on, the contentious mixture of testosterone and florid entitlement seeping into the hallway. They left, Stevie following until Pomade and his companions disappeared into the apartment next to hers. She continued to her own door and entered her code.

Solitude. Quiet. The smell of coffee lingering from yesterday, and the day before.

The window shades, made of manufactured but natural-looking bamboo, had already closed at sunset, blocking her southeastern view but offering her necessary privacy. If she didn't have her two tall cacti, whose photosynthetic needs demanded unfiltered light, she would keep the shades down most of the time. There were people out there who scoped, who peered into the lives of others through the windows of tall buildings, with instruments that grew more powerful with each passing year. They worried her more than the surveillance did. With surveillance, she knew where the hidden cells were, and thus where the dead zones were. Her job gave her that power. And no one could know what went on in her apartment. Not ever.

Stevie glanced at her espresso machine, but resisted temptation. *This isn't a difficult one. And you need your sleep tonight.*

In the master bedroom, she shut the door and unlocked her cabinets, their shelves lined with paraphernalia that would bore, or perhaps even frighten, the average person. Clean glassware rested quietly upon two shelves. Vectors and other biologicals, each in its own container that provided the environmental needs it required, sat on another. Potions lined the final three shelves. "Potions" wasn't exactly scientific, but she liked the word nonetheless. To most, what occurred in that room would seem magical, if they knew. But it wasn't. It was nothing more than science, at its very best.

She turned on her computer and ran through the genetic therapy's specs one more time. She'd used this one before, and it only involved modifying the regulation of ten genes. The work of a youngster. Once she checked everything, she created the therapy, filled the syringe, and injected herself.

Later, Stevie stepped upon her white looped rug and sat down on her white fleecy couch to eat the squash and kale casserole she'd prepared. And after a couple of hours, she took herself to her soft, clean sheets in the smaller bedroom, and fell asleep.

Saturday evening, just as it got dark, Stevie peered at the device she'd installed near her door, allowing her to monitor the hallway. She saw no one, heard no voices or rattling of door latches, and heard no hum of an approaching elevator. She opened the door and quietly closed it behind her, stationing herself near the elevator.

In the lobby, where Manny merely nodded as he would to a stranger, Stevie sighed when she saw that the rain fell in sheets, much harder than the forecasters had predicted. She would have to take a taxi, lest she mar her considered appearance. A taxi wasn't ideal; however, it would mean not having to walk numerous blocks in heels, an effort she would make only for special occasions, for special people. She reentered her building, left through a rear exit, traveled through a vegan cuisine joint, and exited to Perry Street, where she stepped into a sleek black vehicle. She sat against smooth black vinyl as the taxi began humming its way toward the Circle.

The driver eyed her in his mirror. "Going to the Science Museum, Miss? They say there's a big party there tonight! A big party, indeed!"

She smiled. "Yes, my fine friend," she purred. "How did you know?"

"A beautiful party for a beauuuuutiful lady, of course!"

When they arrived at the museum, Stevie paid the driver in untraceable currency, leaving him a large tip, to which his face lit up with surprise. Most, especially west bankers, disliked the inconvenience of currency. But currency meant no absurdly high and unregulated fees to pay ID Corp, a reality that impacted the many who struggled financially. And, untraceable was always a good thing. The driver rushed out of his seat and came to her door, taking her umbrella and opening it for her, allowing her to exit the cab unbesmirched by even a drop of water. She put her hand on the driver's shoulder and issued her thanks before entering the museum lobby. After removing her headscarf and shades, Stevie exited the lobby and began to walk.

Within minutes, a wall of rain surrounding her as her umbrella offered its intrepid service, she arrived at the south end of the Circle and stood before the edifice of all edifices: the main branch of the

City Library. The library, like all the stately buildings of the Circle, retained the old pre-war architecture: stone from top to bottom, with stained glass windows carefully restored by the few remaining craftspeople who knew the trade. Once under the awning, she collapsed her umbrella. She glanced over at a man nearby, a little girl in a blue satin dress holding his hand and looking forlornly at the deluge. The man studied the rain with concern before he began removing his long black coat, revealing a prosthetic arm.

"Stay close to me and protect your dress, Sweetheart," he said to her. "You ready?"

"Excuse me," Stevie said.

The man and girl turned to her, startled.

"Take mine. My friend is inside and he has another." She handed her umbrella to him before entering the giant doors, hearing a high-pitched "Thank you!" just as the doors shut.

Once inside the alcove, she smoothed her hair before entering another set of doors. She stood in line to be scanned as the floor dryers evaporated the rainwater that she and others had tracked into the beautiful building. Beyond security, the smell of books flooded her, that strange blend of paper and glue and dust, the smell that one could get nowhere else. Today, assault and battery would get you six months in the clink, at most. A stolen book would get you at least a year.

She headed to the stairs, the grand staircase in the center of the entire place that rose up, up, up to numerous other floors, each floor promising more paperbound knowledge and adventure. She put her gloved hand on the ornate banister, made from real carved wood, another wonder one rarely saw in such times. She paused upon reaching the fifth floor, the floor with the botanical books, where her mother would take her as a child. She checked her watch; she was early. She went to the shelves and picked out one of her mother's favorites, Harvey's Plant Identification Manual. She hauled the beast of a tome to a table, setting it down as gently as possible, a small fluff of dust exuding from between its hard covers.

No one cares about plants, her mother would say. *It's all animals and farming now. But without plants, there would be no animals or farming.*

Stevie carefully opened the manual to a random page, which happened to feature the *Salvia* genus. Thoughts of Seth encroached, but she shooed them away as she read about the various *Salvia* species, recalling the ones her mother had taught her were edible or medicinal, turning the crisp, delicate pages with great care. She glanced at her watch again, and returned the heavy manual to its proper shelf. She resumed her climb up the magnificent stairs until she reached the eighth floor, where she headed to a corner that had a few small tables. She'd always liked that spot; it was quieter than the others. On a Friday night, the tables sat empty... but for one. A familiar-looking man with thick dark hair and a handsome face waited quietly, his knit sweater neatly covering his pressed and collared shirt. No books in front of him. Just as she removed her coat to reveal her tight black dress, he spotted her.

Stevie gave a large smile and he offered half of one in return. He remained seated, looking her up and down, his expression showing perhaps a wisp of disappointment.

"You must be Brittany," he said, putting out his hand.

She walked over and shook it. His hand was warm, a brief moment of pleasure on a cold, rainy night. "Nice to meet you."

He gave her another brief onceover before deciding to stand. "You're... you aren't quite what I expected."

"Is anyone with this kind of thing?" she said, walking closer to him, smoothing the yellow locks that cascaded over her breasts.

He chuckled. "I guess not." He looked around, shrugging. "What do you say we get out of this place and go get a drink?"

"I'd love that."

As he turned to grab his jacket, Stevie retrieved her remnant of history from her coat and pointed it at him. When he faced her again, he'd barely begun to show surprise before she pulled the trigger on her Oakenfold .357 Magnum, the explosive din of the round muted to a mere pop by her carefully constructed silencer. He stumbled back until he fell to the slatted and scratched wood floor, blood seeping onto his sweater. She stood over him, following up with another shot between the eyes.

Tucking her weapon away, she donned her black overcoat and pulled out a damp black cloth, dabbing her face and neck briefly before stowing the cloth in her pocket. She made her way to the staircase, descending with no real haste. Once on the ground floor, she put her eyeshades back on and left the majestic library, embracing the rain that drenched her.

EPISODE 2
GOOD TASTE, GOOD MANNERS

A success.

With one hitch... he'd shown ambivalence. Not enough to make him reject her, to make him say "no thanks" and move on to better quarry... but enough to indicate that the model for that therapy might need more adjustment. It hadn't mattered this time—they were alone and she could have done her duty whether he liked her or not. But in another scenario, it could have meant a costly loss.

Were the lips not full enough? The hair not long enough? She was certainly skinny enough to look like the young Dianthus coeds before they matured and packed on the coveted womanly curves that men so valued. Yet, some men preferred a girlish look, especially the financially bloated and socially inflated Downtown types.

But perhaps her physical attributes had proven adequate, and what had given the handsome Financial pause was something else altogether. No matter how she trained herself to speak in an affected manner, move in an alluring way, to make strong eye contact and smile with rosy enhanced lips, she could never be a Dianthus girl. She could never convey the privilege, the lightheartedness, the eyes free of vigilance and protectorship. The average man couldn't tell the difference... but this one could. Yet, in the end, boredom trumped wisdom.

Another reason to remove him, and his genetic and social contributions, from the population.

In her large closet, a dead zone if she shut the door, she hung the black coat that looked like every woman's black coat, allowing the water-resistant material to dry. She pulled the wig of absurdly long, ironed-straight, yellowy-blonde hair from her bag, removed in a dead zone on her way home, to be placed upon the female form that stood in her closet. How inordinately cheap it looked. But it was popular among the Dianthus crowd, among those who desired the satiny, golden, genetically engineered blonde but didn't want to pay for it. And many men of varying stations loved the Yellow look. Stevie peeled off her black dress, the tight synthetic fabric chafing her light brown skin. She inspected the dress—with a good cleaning, it would prove its usefulness the next time she must become a Dianthus Yellow. She took out the black heels she'd changed out of, higher than heels should ever be, feeling less confident in the repurposing of those pointy tortures.

High heels are luxurious, Steviansa. Beautiful, even. But they impede the most essential safety mechanism a woman has at her disposal: her feet, and their ability to run.

I know, Mom.

Finally, on her bathroom vanity sat her Oakenfold, safe from the ever-present eyes. Shiny perfect metal, engineered to be much more than the sum of its parts. The Science Museum would clamor for such a relic, but it was one of the only things she could never part with. She emptied the remaining rounds from the chamber and began cleaning it.

Afterward, she turned on her steam shower, her bathroom quickly filling with a comforting humidity. She washed her face, streaks of black exiting the drain along with her misdeeds. When she finished and dried herself, she defogged the mirror and gazed at her reflection, glad to jettison the look of a Yellow but still disgusted at the few alterations that remained.

In her fluffy ivory robe, she went to her fridge, found the B therapy, and injected it. Previous experience told her that the reversal process would complete itself by tomorrow night. Just in time to return to work on Monday.

After heating her squash casserole, she sat down at her computer and logged into a secure portal. Twelve new reports today.

She shook her head, glancing through all of them. Most were too vague to be useful, despite the portal outlining step-by-step instructions for how to file a report. The rest offered, at best, only circumstantial evidence against new and familiar alleged offenders, to be filed away for potential future use. But she hesitated at the last of the bunch, three keywords leaping out at her.

Rosa. Drug. Rape.

Another report for Mr. red dot with the steepled hands. That was three now. Stevie shook her head and turned off her computer.

Monday morning, Stevie woke refreshed, glad to see her own face staring back at her in the mirror. When she left her apartment, she caught a glimpse of her perfectly coiffed and pomaded neighbor entering the elevator. She made haste and followed him, glad to catch the elevator this quickly during its busiest time of day. Just as she approached the narrowing gap of the doors, she smiled and made contact with blue eyes. It was very poor form to press the "open" button if the doors had begun to close. However, any decent-mannered person inside would call for them to open, especially for a neighbor.

The doors shut, leaving Stevie standing alone on the 34th floor.

Even the smile didn't work.

True, her attractiveness quotient wasn't up to the level that her gallant neighbor commanded. Yet, one would think such a sought-after chap would take pity on his beautiful admirers' less luminous sisters and call for the open door. After all, it was perhaps the only male attention such a plain-wrap would receive all day. She laughed at that.

With still plenty of time before she needed to catch the shuttle, Stevie sat at the Oak Cafe, sipping her double espresso and eating her oats and fruit. She could easily make coffee and oatmeal at home, but she preferred supporting the small businesses as much as possible. She could afford to, and they'd suffered enough during the wars. They were a positive contribution to the rebuilding of their pummeled City, unlike many businesses in the financial district, or the genetics salons that charged a fortune for alterations that Stevie could do in a few minutes. Today, she'd managed to score a seat near the window.

Something across the street caught her eye. A man lay face down upon on the sidewalk, engaged in a grim struggle to get up. *Another drunk.* But upon closer inspection, she saw that the man was elderly and had fallen. A mere few feet away stood a young woman with yellow hair, a very long leash stretched out from her hand, at the end of which stood a yellow dog with an obviously but cheaply enhanced mane. Stevie watched closely, waiting for the woman to offer a hand as the old man struggled. But she only milled about, gesturing and speaking to an unseen other as her dog sniffed some unseen odor.

Stevie left her coffee and rushed outside, looking both ways on Greenway Street before darting between the electro-taxis that whizzed by. By the time she got across, the elderly man had just reached a standing position. He wore a pinstriped suit, like his generation wore before the wars, the front of it sprinkled with gray dust from his fall. He was older than any man she'd ever seen.

"Are you okay, Sir?" Stevie asked him, putting her hand on his arm. "Did you take a fall?"

"I'm afraid so," he said, his voice faint with advanced age. "The sidewalk got me." Stevie looked down at the pavement, its once-smooth concrete squares revealing a foot-wide hole, leftover from the war. He produced his hand, his pinky bent at an unnatural angle. "I think it got my finger, too."

"Do you need me to call you a medic?" she said. "I think you broke it."

"Oh, no." He grasped his pinky with his other hand and gave it a quick jerk, a light crack emanating from it.

She smiled. "You're tough, aren't you?"

"I have to be, my dear... to survive in this Hades we call a city."

Yes.

"Will you be okay?" she said.

"I will, dear." He continued on his way.

Stevie watched him walk away for several moments before turning back toward the yellow-haired bystander. But she was gone.

On the shuttle, as the City grew smaller and more orderly, she felt a little better. Her mother had loved that view as well, the few times Stevie had taken her to the Disc. Herbie had been so kind to her mother, even insisting on giving her a tour of the executive floor and its supreme views, which even Stevie hadn't yet seen. That was before Seth had begun working there. She stood, staring out the window and putting on her headphones to tune out her seated neighbors blathering about which bars served the cheapest drinks. She would talk to Seth, if he were here. But he preferred an earlier schedule, a holdover from his many years in the Army. Her regular late nights preluded such hours.

At her workstation, she'd barely started up her computer and screens before Seth appeared, his beefy build contained within gray pants and a crisp button-down. "Did you watch the news?"

"No. What happened?"

"The Oakenfold Killer... motherfucker struck again. Some Financial got zapped just last night... at the old library of all places."

"The Downtown branch? In the Circle?" He nodded. "Same pattern as the others?"

"Yep. Another male, this one about my age. Same round... one to the chest, one between the eyes. The BPA showed high-velocity blood spatter, and signs the shooter got really close to the victim. And, he must have known that the City turned off the juice for the library and the other Circle landmarks a month ago. They barely have enough resources to manage their external cameras as it is." He glanced around, lowering his voice. "You think our cameras got him?"

She smiled. "You tell me."

He scoffed. "I don't have that level of clearance. Not that it would matter... unless you call flattening a handful of Financials a terrorist activity."

"Not by definition."

"And there's more," he went on. "The victim... he was a member of one of those girl sites, one for Dianthus girls. His account showed that he was supposed to meet her at the library. Eighth floor, where he bought it. The City's eyes showed a Yellow in a black coat enter the place and leave a while later. It showed other people too, but now the news is going on about the possibility that the Oakenfold Killer could be a woman."

Nothing more than speculation to make their biased, downtrodden news seem more valuable than it is.

"What's the matter?" Seth said. "Does all this serial killer stuff upset you?"

She shook her head. "Not at all. Something happened this morning... it shook me up a little."

"What happened?" he said, his eyes narrowing.

Her eyes began to water.

"Stevie!" called out Herbie's booming voice. A moment later, he appeared in a brown suit and his pink-checked tie.

"Morning, Boss," she said, relieved for the interruption.

Herbie glanced at Seth. "You harassing our Stevie again, Captain?"

"Always." Seth saluted and left.

"What can I do for you, Boss?" Stevie asked.

Wednesday, Stevie turned onto Greenway Street. She wore another suit, this one navy and perhaps slightly more cheerful than the black one she'd worn yesterday. The cloud cover had thickened and the air seemed denser, reassuring her that her trench coat was a wise choice. Just as she went to cross the street and find a seat at the Oak Cafe, she stumbled and almost fell.

The hole. Where the elderly man had tripped and fallen.

She shook her head, reminding herself to contact the City about getting it repaired. One person had injured himself there, which meant more had. And that meant the City would have someone out to fill the hole in six to eight months, tops. Stevie gaped at the hole again, bigger than most and near a large retirement community. When she looked up, she saw something that surprised her even more than the hole had.

The yellow-haired woman, with her yellow dog.

Stevie retrieved her tablet and took an image of the woman, whose professional suit did little to offset her dry, straw-like hair. Straw Hair didn't notice her, didn't notice anything other than her yellow dog weaving to and fro on a leash that was way too long for city living. Stevie approached her, briefly grimacing as a cloud of perfume assailed her. "Excuse me."

Straw Hair looked at her with dull eyes.

"Good morning," Stevie said, gazing at her through dark eyeshades. "Weren't you here the other day, when that elderly man fell down?"

She blinked a couple of times. "Yeah," she said in the nasally voice of someone who'd clearly never heard a recording of herself. "I asked him if he was okay. He said he was." She reached back and brought her straw hair forward, letting the over-processed and over-ironed locks take their place of honor along the front of her suit.

A well-dressed man passed Stevie, halting just before tripping over the lengthy dog leash. He scowled at the inconvenience, his eyes following the leash to its executor. He hesitated, his expression changing as he gave Straw Hair the up-and-down. He then glanced at Stevie and decided to move on.

"I was concerned for him," Stevie went on. "It took him so long to get back up, so I ran over to check on him. He broke his finger... and he looked shook up."

The woman said nothing, her expression unchanged.

"Anyway... have a good day," Stevie said. She walked away,

escaping the straw hair, the toxic cloud of cheap perfume, and the stench of apathy. She skipped the Oak Cafe and found another place she liked on the next block, ordering a triple espresso but no food.

At the office, Stevie immediately flipped on her red light and transferred her new image to the computer. Not a full frontal, but enough to run an image match, even with that ubiquitous yellow hair.

Never go yellow, Steviansa. Dye it the color of little girls' dresses if you must, but never yellow. Yellow shows poor taste. These men of today, they prey upon women with poor taste because they perceive them as having lower value.

Don't worry, Mom.

The search produced one image: a university ID. Not from DeWitt... but from City University, where Stevie had completed her education. Stevie shook her head and took an image of the data. Then, she conducted a separate search: internal surveillance data for 1840 Riverside Street, in Rosa. She copied the data before clearing all signs of her activity. Finally, she turned off her red light.

A few minutes later, Seth poked his head in. "We still on for Sunday?"

"Absolutely."

After work, when Stevie stepped off the shuttle, rain came down in a deluge. She would have to skip her usual stroll up Greenway Street, through Dianthus and to her home in Artemisia. With a sigh, she hopped on a train and grabbed a metal pole. Youth sat yammering away on their phones, their legs stretched out before them, while the old stood grasping the poles. She gritted her teeth. Perhaps the train was a bad idea. Still, it was somewhat better than getting her suit ruined by taxis splashing through flooded holes in the streets. And it was better than seeing Straw Hair, her bleached mutt, and the gaping hole that had started it all. Besides, running into Straw Hair once was chance... but twice was suspect.

Back at her building, the elevator ride included several familiar faces from other floors, some of whom gave her a nod. However, the ride was terribly unhindered by the ebullient conversation of Pomade and his moderately educated and grossly overpaid friends. At that very moment, Pomade was likely courting an entry-level Yellow from his firm, feeding her aged meats and old wines she couldn't afford, with the expectation of bestowing his considerable sexual prowess upon her.

Once back in the quiet of her home, Stevie sat down at her computer. She selected one of her portals and logged in.

Mobius: Scintillations, my fine lady. It's been a while. How are you?

Artemis: I'm well. How's the job?

Mobius: Eh, same story... post-war cleanup with limited resources from a corrupted government. What can I do for you?

Artemis: Two things, please. One, if I put in a request to fill a sidewalk hole, will you move it to the front of the list? East side of Greenway, 2600 block, midway. An elderly man took a bad spill there this week.

Mobius: Shit. Is he alright? I know that hole. We've had a lot of requests to repair it because it's near that retirement home. ID Corp won't sponsor it, though. They're too busy repairing the holes in Rosa.

Artemis: What a surprise.

Mobius. That's done. What else?

Artemis: The resident who lives at 2501 Greenway, apartment 1266. Shut off her heat and hot water for two weeks.

Mobius: Ohhhh, someone kicked the wasp's nest! Is that all?

Artemis: That's all. Thanks much. You know where to find me if you need anything.

Mobius: Be careful out there.

Stevie pulled her tights and other running gear from her closet, dressed herself, and headed down.

"Bridge?" Manny called out to her.

"Bridge. What can I get you for dinner on the way home?"

He waved a hand at her, shaking his shaven head.

She crossed her arms and waited.

"Fine," he relented. "Just nothing with tofu."

She giggled and stepped out into the cool night. To the middle of Blackwood Bridge she ran, to the quiet, the darkness, the fresh air. On her way back, she stopped near a host of familiar eateries. Before choosing one, she hesitated, gazing across the street at a restaurant she'd run past many times, its warm lighting and faux wood-paneled interior giving it a cozy look. Couples sat inside, sipping their wine and eating vegetarian or modest meat dishes from plain brown earthenware, engaged in the unaffected conversation that came not from a first date, but from really knowing someone, from feeling comfortable in their presence. One time, she'd come over to examine the menu; the host had invited her in, paying no mind that she was alone and in her running gear. Stevie had merely smiled, gave her thanks, and run off. She ate dinner alone all the time... but not at a place like that.

Stevie glanced at the pizza joint a couple of doors down. Manny was probably hungry by now.

Sunday, Stevie strode past a multitude of citizens, their suits replaced by slacks and shirts, their coats slung casually over their arms, and their umbrellas unopened. She shimmied past the glut of cafe tables that appeared on the sidewalks overnight, each filled with poached eggs and baskets of buttery croissants as patrons sipped flutes of fizzy beverage.

As she rounded the corner onto 10th Avenue, giant sculptures loomed ahead, glimmering ebony and reaching as high as some of the buildings. The black sentinels rose above the Circle that encompassed the City's oldest and most revered buildings: City Hall, the Courthouse, the Science Museum, and the City Library. The only thing more impressive about the Circle was what lay in its center: a park, with manicured bluegrass and graceful native maple trees with their bright green, newly formed leaves.

When Stevie drew closer to the Circle, she spotted Seth. He stood with iron posture, his all-seeing gaze scanning the crowd. He searched not only for her, but for anything problematic. He looked more military than usual, despite his tasteful checked oxford shirt tucked neatly into dark slacks. Men didn't have to dress well... not these days, not when women outnumbered them. Yet, there were two types of men who did: older men from a bygone era, and those who had a better-than-average understanding of women.

Seth was early. No matter when she arrived anywhere—work, a meeting, the annual office party—Seth was always there first. She used to tease him about that. He'd shrug and say, "You're late in the service, you get punished. You learn to be early."

He smiled as she approached.

"You got here early again. But I saw you before you saw me."

"Nope." He looked over. "See that old brick building on Tenth? I saw you when you came around that corner."

She made a face, acknowledging yet another defeat against Seth's visual acuity. "How did you know I'd come that way? It's faster to take Broad if you're coming from Artemisia."

He shrugged. "Broad's noisy. You like quiet."

"I could've just as easily come down Eleventh, after buying sodas from the market." She held up her bag.

"But you didn't. You came down Tenth."

She shook her head, laughing. "Okay, Major. You win for good logic."

He grinned, the lines around his eyes crinkling in that way she'd always liked, the way that reminded her of her mom, the rare times she smiled. So many underwent various procedures—from injections to epigenetic regeneration—to eradicate their smile lines, attempting to make themselves look younger or smoother. Stevie never understood such idiocy. Smile lines were the best part of people's faces. And whom did these biological tinkerers, these wasters of scientific resources, believe they were fooling? She could recognize nearly anyone's real age without even seeing a face.

"So," she said. "Where to for lunch?"

He reached behind a planter and picked up a bag. "Right here. Gotta be outdoors on a day like this."

A small euphoria came over her. But when she looked around, the black benches and tables were packed with fellow citizens enjoying the fair weather in one of the few green zones left in the City. Before she could worry, Seth marched them upon the turf grass, passing a patch of bright purple flowers. *Salvia.* He stopped near the fountain, set down his bag, and pulled out a neatly folded blanket, which he unfurled and spread over the grass. Stevie stared at the blanket in wonder for a moment, before helping Seth straighten it. Memories flooded her, and for a moment her eyes blurred with tears before she blinked them away. She removed her ankle boots and socks, tossed her trench coat aside, and sat down.

"Do me a favor?" Seth said. "Scoot over a bit and let me sit there?"

Stevie moved over on the blanket, remembering that Seth would need to sit with his back to the fountain. He didn't like not knowing what was behind him.

Seth pulled out a small slab of cured ham, some sliced cheese, and a loaf of freshly baked bread, which he sliced with a knife he'd stowed in his pocket. Stevie opened her bag and took out two sodas in glass bottles, handing Seth the tart lemon, his favorite, and keeping the sarsaparilla for herself. Seth made a sandwich from his goods, while Stevie popped a slice of ham into her mouth. It was just the right amount of salty... and unreasonably delicious.

"Where did you get this ham?"

Seth finished chewing. "A little joint in my Hood. I don't think it's going to stay in business though, with what's happening with the pork prices. You like it?"

"More than you can imagine. I can't remember the last time I had pork, and I don't think I've ever had pork this good."

"Really? Not even for a special occasion?"

She shook her head. "I don't really have special occasions. And I try to avoid meat when I can... out of respect for my mom."

"She's an activist?"

"Sometimes... but mostly just an environmentalist."

"Does she live nearby?"

"She passed away, almost two years ago."

Seth stopped chewing for a moment. "Sorry."

"She used to bring me here, when I was a child. We would sit on a quilt, one of those really old handmade ones, with all the patches. She would feed me bean salads and strawberry tarts and teach me the scientific names of the trees and flowers." Stevie chuckled, shaking her head. "I hated it... but over the years I learned to appreciate it, and to appreciate greenery."

"That's why I like coming here," Seth said, looking around. "I grew up on a farm. It's not the same as a green zone, but it's still... nature. What's left of it."

"What kind of farm?"

"Dairy. I was up at zero dark whatever milking cows as a kid. I hated it too. But at some point, I'm not sure when, I grew to appreciate it."

"I wouldn't have guessed you were a farm boy. You seem so... military, like you came from a military family. But if your parents were farmers, I suppose they couldn't enlist."

"Right. They're still alive... and somehow I am too."

"You saw action?"

"Too much of it." His face grew a bit more shadowed as he took a swig of his lemon fizz. "What about your dad? Did the war get him?"

She hesitated. "I never had a father."

Seth's eyebrows went up. "You're a donor kid?"

"I am. You're having lunch with a donor kid."

"I'll be damned," he said, appearing more impressed than disapproving. "I didn't think that was as common back then."

It wasn't.

Stevie took another bite of her porcine pleasure, savoring the deliciousness of it, knowing it would be some time before she ate it again. The pig farms still struggled to recover from the war, and feeding a populace that wanted to forget the past wasn't helping.

"I wouldn't have picked you for a denim girl," he said, gazing at her jeans. "They'll love you in Crocus."

"I do love my denim. I'd wear it to work if they'd let me."

He glanced at her shoulder, bare where her shirt hung off it, before shifting his gaze to her hair. "You ever thought about growing your hair long?"

She looked down, playing with her piece of bread. "No. No long hair, no yellow hair."

"I can't stand Yellows... but I think you'd look good with longer hair."

His dislike of Yellows is a sign of good taste, Steviansa. But a man with good manners wouldn't insult you for having short hair, for being different.

He didn't insult me, Mom. He merely revealed his personal preference. He knows I'll have trouble attracting men with hair this short, in this social climate.

Stevie gave no reply. There was little purpose in discussing something she had no intention of changing, and for reasons she could never share with Seth.

"What happened the other day?" Seth said. "You said something upset you, but Herbie interrupted us."

"Oh, yes... that." She told Seth about the elderly man, and about Straw Hair.

Seth shook his head. "What the fuck? What's wrong with people? Did you say anything to her?"

"I ran into her a couple days later and asked her about it. I told her about his finger, how much he struggled... a little guilt can be more persuasive than a lecture."

And two weeks of cold showers, perhaps.

Seth scoffed. "You're a lot goddamned nicer than me, that's for sure."

They finished eating and talked more, lounging on Seth's blanket and enjoying the meteorological respite and the resulting rise in collective serotonin levels across the City. But eventually, the clouds darkened and the air cooled.

Seth looked up. "That's our cue."

Stevie reached for her socks and boots, begrudgingly putting them back. They packed up their belongings and shook out Seth's blanket. When Stevie began folding it, Seth gave her a disapproving look.

"You have to make your first fold the other way. Then again on the same axis."

"Yes, Sir."

He smiled as they folded the blanket and packed up. A raindrop hit her cheek.

"Thank you for a nice lunch," she told him, putting on her trench coat.

"My pleasure."

Stevie hesitated, unsure what to say or do next. Finally, she hugged Seth. His hard chest felt warm against her as he put his free arm around her. He smelled good, like sandalwood.

"See you tomorrow?" she said.

Seth nodded, and Stevie turned and made her way toward 11th Avenue.

Stevie stood on the crowded shuttle, peering out at the City below. No clouds that night, just the sparkle of all those lights, clustered tightly together like data points on a scatterplot, growing less dense as they drew closer. When she was a girl, her mother had taken her to visit the Disc once, before the Feds took it over and began requiring clearance to visit. Her mom wondered at the sprawling lights, remarking upon the uncontrolled population growth and the strain it put on the plant and animal life. *We can't keep this up*, she'd say. Now, there were fewer lights... and fewer people.

After stopping at Tarragon Noodle Bar and eating a quick bowl of buckwheat noodles with vegetables, Stevie headed home to review the data she'd gathered and begin planning her weekend. First was a video of Steeple dressed down in slacks and a shirt to seem relatable, his hands in their signature steeple while he pontificated onstage. "You deserve to be rich!" he said with conviction. "You deserve to have all you want in life! And you can, *right now*." She loaded the surveillance data she'd pulled. A beautiful home in Rosa, with a view of the Milagro. A pretty platinum-haired Rosa wife, and two pretty platinum-haired Rosa kids. She skipped over the daytime footage, when the cashmere prince would be downtown, utilizing his vast financial knowledge to serve others, to better their City and the people in it. The steeple guaranteed it, as did the cashmere sweater. The first evening's footage yielded nothing, nor did the next four. But on the fifth night, Steeple returned, on his arm a young blonde woman with an ample bosom and lustrous hair. Gold, not yellow. He sat her down on his couch, prepared a drink... and within ten minutes she was unconscious.

Stevie covered her eyes with spread fingers, hoping the filter would render what she saw less repulsive. Afterward, to ease her disgust, she got to work.

A Rosa queen, Steeple? A carbon copy of your wife, but younger, unprotected, and with an impaired sense of caution? Perhaps with pink dappled cheeks and hair that would make your wife's look like bleached hay?

This would require an upscale appearance, which meant wigs and minor genetic enhancements wouldn't do. She needed more extensive changes... the kind that few others could accomplish. Stevie retrieved a genetic design that she'd used previously and made some modifications to it. Then she ran a series of simulations, after which she examined her model fit estimates. They were too low. She made a few more modifications, but still didn't get the estimates she needed.

She sat back to think. The large breasts and the full lips were easy. The beautiful platinum hair too, as long as she started early enough on Friday night. It was the cheeks—the full, round cheeks—that caused problems. Too much fullness in the tissues and she'd look like she'd taken too many steroids. Yet, altering her narrow facial structure to look apple-faced like new money was extraordinarily intricate work from a design standpoint. She could do it, but the physical changes would take more time than she had. She would have to compromise with a mixture of structural and tissue alterations, and hope it was enough. She adjusted her model and reran it. Her fit estimate came out moderately high, high enough to move forward.

Friday night, Stevie pulled out some of her potions, created the therapy, and injected herself. But when she woke Saturday morning, the changes hadn't fully manifested. Nor did they that day. She rechecked the model; given its complexity—involving 44 genes—it was possible she'd underestimated the alteration time. She would have to delay her plans until tomorrow.

They were huge.

Stevie marveled not at the size of her breasts, but at their weight, like two swollen burdens that would genuinely threaten her sense of balance. Her lips felt heavy too, inflated to what felt like twice their size, two pillows with no other purpose than to display an embarrassingly bright pink lipstick. And the cheeks? Not bad, really. Fuller, without looking puffy. The shapewear gave her the ample hips she would need to ensure her oversized breasts didn't have her teetering like a poorly engineered doll. Her black dress, wool blend and mightily expensive, barely fit in the bust due to her very localized weight gain. With a face full of makeup and her neck adorned with a choker of engineered diamonds, she smoothed any flyaway strands of her shiny platinum hair, itself another heavy burden to lug around.

At last, she donned her wool coat, immediately feeling guilty for wearing it, for partaking in the conspicuous display of a rare commodity. The sheep population was most affected by the wars, and only the hard work of the farmers and ranchers had allowed them to recover even as little as they had. With the post-war demand for fine woolens, scientists had already begun seeing signs of overgrazing and encouraged citizens to minimize wool consumption. Some proposed temporary regulations on the wool market, but the Financials ensured they failed. Again.

It was Sunday. Sunday nights weren't ideal, but she would make it work. She left her transition place and headed east. To Rosa.

Some men gaped at her. Others raised an eyebrow. Women waffled between envy and disgust. No rain fell, something for which Stevie felt grateful. Perhaps the only thing, right now.

This isn't for you. This is for the City. For everyone.

The landscape began to change as she approached Rosa. The buildings stood shiny and new, the street lamps lit softly instead of bright enough to see anything, and countless flowerpots displayed garish artificial roses. The sidewalks had no blemishes and were swept clean. Restaurant windows showed blondes in tight dresses and men in expensive woolens, instrumental music playing to those who paid no attention to it.

She came upon one particular restaurant. She stood outside it, gathering her thoughts before she set down her ostentatious sheepskin handbag and removed her heavy coat, letting it rest upon her arm. Inside, she squeezed through the throng of people, brushing against fur and wool, the smell of roses and leather rising to nauseating levels. She ordered her pink sausage lips to smile.

Men turned to stare as she pranced through the gauntlet to the bar, their eyes lingering upon her cleavage, upon the swollen organs that would serve as commodities that evening. But before she could search for her quarry, she spotted a less pleasant face: Pomade, sitting next to a Yellow she'd seen him with before. They looked somewhat out of place in the posh surroundings, perhaps living vicariously and imagining their future if Pomade managed to rise within the financial pyramid. Pomade's blue eyes lit up as he gaped at Stevie, impervious to his Yellow's disapproving look. Stevie scowled at him, and his face reddened in anger as he looked away. Fortunately, their glasses sat empty and they got up to leave.

Stevie disappeared deeper into the woolen den, finally spotting him and his cashmere sweater. He stared right at her.

Scintillations, Sir.

She gave him a pink puff smile before veering off to the bar, breaking eye contact and allowing him to gaze at the rest of her... to decide. He wouldn't come to her. He wouldn't need to.

Stevie ordered her drink, a divine pink cocktail for divine pink people. When she turned back around, he looked elsewhere but every other part of his body pointed toward her.

Feign casual disinterest if you will, Sir. Three seconds.

His gaze found her once more, starting with her face and traveling downward to her engineered bosom. She sauntered up to him and said nothing. That's what did it: the fact that she would wait for him to speak, instead of initiating conversation like most women. It always intrigued them, always made them wonder if perhaps she were a little less desperate than the rest to obtain whatever resources he wanted to bestow.

"Good evening, Miss."

"Good evening, Sir," Stevie said, keeping her eyes locked with his.

He motioned to the open spot on his red cushioned chair. She carefully placed her coat and handbag upon the smelly leather that was too soft to be sustainable. She sat down next to Steeple and sipped her sugary drink. Suddenly, she thought of Seth, who would give an incredulous mocking laugh, and perhaps a pointed slur, at her drinking such a concoction. Then again, Seth wouldn't recognize her. Even his hawk eyes wouldn't see her underneath the scientifically-derived circus that she called an appearance.

"Are you having a fine evening?" Steeple asked.

"I am."

"What's your name?"

"Pepper."

"A top notch name, to match your excellent taste," he said. "And what do you do, Pepper?"

He didn't care what she did. He merely wanted opportunity to talk about what he did.

"I'm an administrative assistant," she purred. "For a very talented commodities trader. And you?"

He leaned back against the stinking leather. "I guess you could say I'm a bit of a financial healer. I used to be a trader... but it was soulless and cutthroat." He paused, his hands instinctively steepling. "I prefer helping people, so now I write books and hold seminars to teach others how to recover financially from the war. Especially those who suffered most."

Oh, believable, Steeple! Pepper would never suspect anything about the steep price of your seminars, the number of expensive properties you own, or how many Financials you've helped into office.

"That's wonderful," she gushed. "I could probably use that kind of help. My poor mother... the war took everything."

"Why doesn't your father take care of her?" he said, feigning concern.

"He passed away when I was just a girl. He had a heart attack."

He sipped his drink. "I'm sorry to hear it, but I'm glad to know he didn't die in the wars. A man should lead his family, not abandon them for a war that good financial sense could have prevented."

Stevie smiled. "I couldn't agree more. I'd love to know more about your seminars."

He nodded in self-satisfaction. "Pepper, how would you feel about going somewhere quieter, where I can learn more about you and your mother's situation?"

"Oh... where to?"

"There's a quiet restaurant upstairs. It's busy, but I know the maitre d.'"

"That sounds lovely."

"Excuse me while I make the arrangements." He got on his phone and spoke a few quiet words. "It looks like they're too busy tonight.

However, they offered to deliver a nice meal to my apartment instead, which is just around the corner."

Of course they did.

She looked down. "I would love to, but I don't think I should."

"I'll be a perfect gentleman. I'll even have a taxi waiting, for when you're ready to leave. And there, I can give you files for my books and seminars. That will save you and your mother a lot of money."

She hesitated, fidgeting a little for extra effect. Then she smiled. "I can't resist."

Steeple's apartment smelled of roses. Lots of them. *Genetically engineered.* He offered her a seat on his gigantic leather couch, a fire already roaring in the fireplace and a vast view of the east bank's lights across the Milagro. She sat down, trying not to touch anything, even with gloved hands.

"May I get you a drink?" Steeple said.

"Yes, thank you."

Steeple disappeared and returned with another pink concoction. She thanked him and pretended to sip it, keeping her eyes on him as she set her glass down, placing it too close to the edge and causing it to topple over. Pink liquid splashed all over the woolen rug.

She stood, her hand on her heart. "I'm so sorry!"

Steeple stared at the pink carnage, a fleeting look of irritation making the briefest of appearances before he smiled and reassured her. When he left for the kitchen, Stevie pulled a handkerchief from her dress and wiped the rim of the glass, where her lips had been. Steeple returned with a mini-steamer to clean up the stain.

"Let me do that," she purred, walking closer to him and placing a gloved hand on his shoulder.

Before he could respond, whether with a breezy platitude, another glance at her breasts, or a quick exit to make another concoction with which to exert his already considerable power, he looked down.

Stevie pressed the barrel of her irreplaceable rarity against his cashmere sweater, against the soft chest beneath it.

He gasped.

EPISODE 3
MAN'S BEST COUTURE COLLIE

A waste, really.

Such a beautiful sweater, gleaned from an unsuspecting animal, from an unsustainable industry. Steeple's cashmere had a hole in it now, covered in blood and a hint of gunpowder. But at least his hands were arranged in his trademark steeple. That would give him a modicum of respectability to those he mattered to.

Stevie carried herself, along with her absurdly long hair and expensive woolen attire, out of the riverfront building. Her feet hurt from her heels. Her back hurt from transporting the extra cargo stored in her breasts. Her lips were chapped, unused to being painted. But such inconveniences were temporary sacrifices, and such discomforts couldn't compete with the relief she felt.

The chilly air felt dry. No rain for two days. She walked a few blocks to her preplanned destination, a bar where she would fit right in. She went straight to the restroom and into a stall. One of several surveillance dead zones, known only to a privileged few. Cameras, but no juice. Perhaps the brainchildren behind the Federal Watch program felt that witnessing people urinate and defecate would be an invasion of their privacy.

She stripped down to her skivvies and changed into black pants and a white shirt, just like the waitstaff wore. Then she pulled out her scissors and cut off her mass of hair, its sheer volume laboring the scissors and fatiguing her hand. Into the toilet the shiny platinum locks went, along with a solution to dissolve them into nothing but protein fragments. A wig to cover her chopped up hair. A cloth to remove the paint from her face. The rest of her stupid ensemble—shoes, coat, dress, shapewear, hosiery, diamond choker—stuffed into a student's self-locking pack.

She left the restaurant and headed west, the shiny buildings, kept sidewalks, and plastic roses fading away as she escaped Rosa and returned to Artemisia. She walked quickly, dodging a few torn-up patches and checking the occasional empty lot for signs of cleanup or restoration. None yet. When she arrived at her building, Manny nodded at the key card she flashed, never recognizing her. Knowing where the hidden eyes were in her lobby, elevator, and hallway, she averted her gaze to make facial matching nearly impossible, in the unlikely event that someone decided to peruse the Watch footage for her building. She looking forward to getting home, to becoming herself again.

At her apartment, she unpacked in her closet. Shoes put away. Wool coat hung up. Shapewear and hosiery put aside for laundering, along with her black wool dress and any back spatter that hid within the luxurious fabric. Her Oakenfold, in all its alloyed glory, carefully cleaned and stowed away. She undressed and stepped into her steam shower, closing her eyes and letting the steam consume her. Afterward, she trimmed her hair until it looked like it had, a task she'd gotten better at with time and the addition of two mirrors. But she still looked ridiculous with platinum hair.

Back in her soft ivory robe, Stevie went to the kitchen. The cold black tiles refreshed her misused feet as she opened the refrigerator and took out a glass vial of cloudy liquid. She removed the lid and dumped it down the sink. That B therapy was for Saturday night, with 32 hours maximum reversal time. Now, she needed the 8-hour version, the one that could make her suffer, but would reverse the changes in time for work tomorrow morning. She prepared the new B therapy, ignoring the software's warnings before she loaded a syringe and injected her leg. She disposed of the needle in her biowaste canister—to be taken to one of many depositories—and lay down on her soft sheets.

When the fever came, it seemed to arrive all at once. Heat that soaked her in sweat. Aches in her temples, her arms and legs, and her hands, beginning to spread. Her eyes stung as sweat dripped from her forehead. Suddenly, a wave of nausea hit her. She ran to the bathroom and kneeled on the white tile. Nothing but dry heaves. She hadn't eaten or drunk anything yet. She knew better.

After the nausea passed, she stood. Bright lights flashed before her eyes, like the fireworks of her childhood, the white ones she loved so much. She grabbed the countertop to keep from toppling over. She began to shiver, her sweat like a cold compress covering her body.

Deep breaths.

Back in her dark bedroom, she climbed into bed, burying herself under the covers, trying to get warm.

Hours passed, where sleep came and went, bringing her restless dreams of running through Rosa, arguing with Steeple, fighting with some unseen other. She endured it, shifting from one position to another, trying to find a cool spot in the sheets, then covering herself to get warm.

Try to sleep. When you awaken, the worst will be over.

A woman. High-pitched yelling.

Stevie leapt from her bed, put on her robe, and grabbed the energy weapon stowed nearby. But before she could get far, wooziness came over her and she sank to one knee in the hope of recovering herself. More high-pitched cries. She stood more slowly this time, taking small steps as she left her bedroom. The yelling faded.

The noise hadn't come from the hallway. It had come from behind the wall of her bedroom. From Pomade's bedroom. Pomade and his Yellow. Fighting.

She returned to her bedroom and glanced at the clock. Just past two. Just after the clubs had shut down for the night.

"You didn't have a good time tonight?" Pomade demanded, his voice turning strangely nasal in his indignation.

"No! You ruined my night!"

"I didn't ruin anything. Stop being a Rosa queen!"

"You barely talked to me. I came all the way to Rosa to be with you, and you talked to your friends all night!"

"Ohh," he crooned. "Didn't get enough attention, did we?"

"Stop it! You said you were in the mood!"

"I'm not having sex with you!" he bellowed. "I'm not fucking touching you!"

And on they fought.

Yes. Have this conversation here, in the one room that borders mine, and have it now. There's no one else around, no one sleeping, taking repose in their quiet space, or preparing for the next day's work. It's just you two, your consequential problems, and a hearty dose of dolled-up ethanol to remove what little capacity for rationality either of you have.

Stevie waited, her head beginning to pound as another wave of wooziness came over her. When the voices finally quieted down, she got back in bed and closed her eyes. Everything hurt. She fell into a chaotic sleep, only to be awakened again by more noise. Squeaking. Repeated squeaking.

Pomade's bed.

The squeaking got louder and more rapid. She heard nothing at all until a grunt... Pomade in his finale. The squeaking ceased. Stevie's nausea returned. She hurried to the bathroom and endured another round of dry heaves as sweat poured from her. Everything quiet again, she lay her achy, feverish body down and shut her eyes.

The next morning, bright lights awakened her before sending shooting pains through her optic nerves.

"Lights off."

Darkness again. She slowly crawled out of bed, lightheadedness assailing her when she stood upright. Her body still ached. She shuffled to her kitchen and sipped some water. When her stomach grumbled, she took out some sliced fruit and ate it with a few salty wafers.

Better but still unwell, Stevie returned to her bathroom and peered into the mirror. Her breasts had shrunk, but one far more than the other, and her face looked like she'd suffered at the hands of an uncertified cosmetic geneticist. She shook her head, went to her computer, and put in a call to Herbie, squinting at the screen's bright light.

"Morning, Miss Stevie!" Herbie boomed. "What can I do for you?"

Stevie cringed at the volume of Herbie's deep voice, which seemed to resonate throughout her body. "I'm not feeling well, Boss. Would it be acceptable for me to take a sick day?"

"I can't see you, Stevie."

"I'm audio only. Still in bed."

"Ah," Herbie said. "Yes. Of course. Feel better and we'll see you tomorrow."

"Thank you, Boss."

She'd warned Stevie... the scientist who ran the genetic engineering lab where Stevie had volunteered during graduate school. She'd said that the faster one tried to reverse the changes, the more one's physiology rebelled. Stevie had pushed the limits before, but this one had taken an unprecedented toll. She hated using up a sick day, but she couldn't go anywhere until she recovered.

Never toy too much with Mama Nature, Steviansa.

You're right, Mom.

After another glass of water, Stevie went back to bed.

Ah, there you are.

Small breasts, narrow face, dark hair, coffee and cream skin. And physiology that functioned properly once more. Relief came over Stevie when she examined herself in the mirror after her night of febrile suffering. Now she could return to work. It would be a long day; whatever Herbie needed from her yesterday, he would need today, and then some.

When Stevie finished getting ready and stepped into the elevator, it was already half full. Right away, she sensed tension.

"Maybe the dogs wouldn't bother you if you got a job and left your apartment once in a while," a 40-something woman with a blonde bob sniffed, tightening her trench coat around her.

"I have a job, lady," a similarly-aged man insisted. "I work at home. And I can't work when your dogs bark and cry all day long because you ignore them."

"What do you want me to do?" she whined. "I don't have the luxury of working at home, like you do."

"Hire someone to walk them! Why do you have dogs, anyway, if you're just going to leave them cooped up all day?"

"I can't afford dog care, not that it's any of your damned business."

"You can afford couture collies, but not dog care? That makes no sense, lady."

The elevator stopped two more times to let in others heading to work. The squabbling duo went quiet until they reached the lobby, where Stevie held the door as everyone exited. Blonde Bob tried to sneak away, but her neighbor followed her.

"Hey," he said. "I'm your neighbor. I need to do my work in peace."

Blonde Bob stopped. "They're dogs, Sir. Dogs bark. And I know for a fact they don't bark that much. They're only noisy when someone gets off the elevator because they're protecting their territory."

"They bark all the time! And how would you know? You're never there!" When she began to turn away, he spoke again. "Look. They seem quiet when you're home. If they're lonely, maybe I could watch them for part of the day."

She made a face. "I would never trust a stranger with my dogs. They're mine. I worked very hard for them."

He rolled his eyes.

"If I had a colicky baby that cried all day long, you wouldn't complain about that, would you?" She stomped off.

"Who leaves a baby at home to cry all day?" he shouted after her.

Stevie shook her head, waiting until they cleared out of the lobby before she headed to work.

That afternoon, Stevie stepped away from her standing desk and stretched. Machine beckoned. She could almost hear his steam rushing through his dark espresso beans, could almost smell the roasted essence trickle its way into her black cup. The remnants of yesterday's fatigue began to lift.

"Hey!" a male voice barked.

Stevie started and turned to face the offending voice. Seth.

"Why so jumpy?" Seth asked, surprised by her reaction.

"You of all people should know not to sneak up on others, Lieutenant."

Seth raised his eyebrows. "I didn't sneak. I just said hey."

She realized that everything still sounded too loud to her, like Herbie's voice had. Another holdover from her B therapy adventures. "I apologize, Seth. I am jumpy today."

"And what's this Lieutenant bullshit? Last week I was Major."

She smiled. "And you'll be one again if you get me some coffee."

"That's why I'm here."

When Seth returned, he handed her black cup to her and took a sip from his. "What happened to you yesterday?"

She shook her head. "Some bug. I'm better, but still not a hundred percent."

Seth watched her, almost as if noticing something about her. She felt self-conscious suddenly, like she'd worn an outfit more revealing than her usual dark suit.

"Did you hear the latest?" he said.

"No. The shooter again?"

"Yep."

"Same thing?"

"Same thing. The victim was a Rosa Financial, some guy who writes financial advice books and runs those big seminars... you know, charges a fortune for them and gets rich off vets and single moms. He seemed like kind of an asshole... but still, it's sad. He had a wife and two young kids. They say he was seen with a blonde woman just before it happened."

"Didn't they say that about the last one?"

"Yep. But the City's facial recognition software said it's probably not a match, and they haven't made any arrests. I guess this one was a Rosa queen type, and they didn't say that about the last one." He shook his head. "I think these women are bait, not killers. I don't think the perp's a woman."

"How come?"

"No woman would do this. I knew some pretty mean women in the Army, and even they wouldn't do this." He waved his arm dismissively. "Anyway, what do you think about grabbing some pastry and coffee one of these days?"

She smiled. "I never say no to coffee... or pastry. Where do you want to meet? Maybe not Rosa..."

He chuckled. "Nah. I hate Rosa and those wool-wearing motherfuckers. There's a good place in Salvia, if you don't mind coming my way."

"Sure. Sunday?"

He hesitated. "Uh... Sunday isn't good. What about next Sunday?"

He has plans with another woman this Sunday, Steviansa.

I know, Mom.

"Next Sunday should work, Captain."

Near the end of the workday, Stevie checked the shuttle schedule, ensuring it still ran on time. She peered out the window, the City completely obscured by clouds that glowed orange from the setting sun. So peaceful it seemed, as if the City and its dirty cracks didn't exist. Then, charred earth would give way to pioneering flowers and grasses, which would give way to shrubs and fast-growing trees, only to allow the kings of the forest to take their place and restore final balance, clean the air, and provide home and sustenance for the animals. No humans to muck with it, to pull it out of kilter through well-meaning and not so well-meaning intentions.

"Looks like someone's ready to go home."

Stevie turned around. A middle-aged man stood before her, his suit dark and fine, his hair salt-and-pepper, and his eyes a soft brown that Stevie had always liked. "Good afternoon, Mister Carr."

Ronald chuckled. "It still amuses me greatly when you call me that."

She smiled at the man she'd known since she was ten, glancing over at the other dark-suited executives milling about. "Meeting?"

"Of course. We received more bad hits from that phone data than we anticipated. I don't know if we have enough resources to probe them all."

She shrugged. "In my experience, one's as likely to be a terrorist as another. But, if you get me the list, I can gather ancillary data for them and run some odds ratios. That might help you choose whom to investigate."

He raised his eyebrows. "Would you mind?"

"Not at all. If you get the list to me today, I'll do it tonight."

"Thank you, Stevie." Ronald shook his head. "When they hired you, I knew you would work hard, but I had no idea what a good analyst you'd be. Herb speaks highly of you."

"Thank you," she said, looking down for a moment. "How is Miriam? And Minnie?"

"Miriam is well. She's been volunteering at Minnie's school, and she's still with Social Services part time."

"When did you take in Minnie again?"

"Three years ago, when she was six. She had some attachment problems, but she's made great strides and even has some friends."

Of course she has. A stable family, a kind foster mom at home, and you as a father figure.

"And how's Kira?"

Ronald cocked his head a little. "Kira is also well. She's still at Social Services, but we don't see her as much since she transferred to the Acacia office." He checked his watch. "Stevie, I'll send you that list in the next hour. Thanks again."

After Ronald left, Stevie peered out the window once more. The orange glow had faded as darkness set in. Her thoughts went to Kira, her friend since they were ten, after Stevie moved to Artemisia. She recalled their being sequestered indoors when the City had issued warnings of bioterror threat, their talking at great length about how they would make the City strong again after the war ended. The rare times Ronald came home before her mother finished work and picked her up, he would listen to their ideas, encouraging their lofty plans and offering suggestions. Perhaps it was time to call Kira.

Kira stopped calling you, Steviansa, not the other way around. And with some of the things she did... you don't owe her anything.

She went through a difficult time, Mom. It happens.

An hour later, she got the data she needed from Ronald. She finished up the task and sent Ronald the results, heading out to grab a late dinner.

When she arrived on the surface, rain drenched the streets. She gritted her teeth and took the train. At least it was past rush hour and a bit less crowded. When she boarded, she remained standing, allowing others to scramble for the two or three open seats. She looked around—a sloppily dressed student slouched in his seat, stretching his legs out in the isle and causing the unsuspecting to trip; a Yellow talked loudly to some unseen person about how much her yellow hair had cost her; another dark-hooded man spit his chewing tobacco onto the floor. As the train headed north, Stevie left her secure pole and found another whose location offered a more promising sampling of humanity.

When her stop came, Stevie opened her umbrella and made her way to the Tarragon Noodle Bar. She sat down at the counter, the place half full with a smattering of Artemisia folk: couples in cotton and synthetic clothing, women with hair that was neither yellow nor enhanced, a young child with his mother, a tattooed band around her left wrist. A war widow. Stevie ordered rice noodles with tofu and broccoli. Rice, soybeans, and cruciferous vegetables had recovered well post-war and were reasonably plentiful. As she waited, two women entered the joint and took a seat near the window. One of them stared at her.

The watcher was tallish and thickly built, with a tawny mohawk. The other, skinny and shifty-eyed, only gave a brief sidelong glance her way. Both were clad in blue jeans and brown pleather jackets. Brownies, as west bankers called those from Crocus. Probably passing through for an evening out together. The taller was likely a cop, given her sharp eye, and a lesbian, given her extended gaze.

Stevie looked away. She had no problem with lesbians, or cops. But she had no desire to attract either.

When she arrived at her building, Stevie pressed the elevator button as people began lining up behind her. Once it arrived, she held the door as others filed in silently. Pomade joined them, his eyes fixated on his tablet. When the gap between the doors shrank to a mere sliver, the doors suddenly reversed themselves while a collective groan emanated from the group.

A familiar face stood outside the elevator, no shame in her expression. Blonde Bob, the woman who'd ardently defended her barking canines to her irate neighbor. She pranced in, three purebred labradors in her wake, their feet and tails wildly furry, their blonded coats impossibly shiny, all of it clearly enhanced by scientific means. *Couture collies.* Everyone made way for her and her brood, their irritation at her poor manners somewhat muted by their envy as they gawked at the rare, expensive creatures. The creatures that had mostly perished during the second war, when the enemy launched the bioterrorism that had proven more fatal to canines than humans. Pride spread across Blonde Bob's face as if the sun shone upon it, and she soaked up the admiration like vitamin D as she attempted to herd the dogs.

"Come on, Goldilocks," she cooed to the most errant of the three, who sniffed at something just outside the elevator. "Goldie," she cooed again. Goldie sniffed away. Again she repeated the polite request.

"Come on, lady," Pomade groused, his tenor approaching a whine. "You shouldn't keep people waiting."

True, Pomade. Except when you're causing the delay. Then, it's acceptable.

Blonde Bob, impervious to the rebuke, continued coaxing Goldie. "Come on, Goldie," she said again, her tone even more sugary as she lightly tugged on the leash, as if guiding the dog would harm it in some irreversible way.

In Goldie came and the doors shut, many a narrowed eye darting to Blonde Bob as she talked to her dogs like they were infants. Stevie surreptitiously pressed the button for one of the highest floors. At various stops, residents wove their way over leashes and past enhanced fur to exit. At the 34th floor, Pomade left while Stevie remained, until Blonde Bob and her couture collies got off on the 39th floor.

A quarter pound of cured ham says she takes more than ten seconds to exit.

It took her eight and a half seconds. No ham this week.

Once home, Stevie read through the messages she'd received over the last couple of days. Thirteen of them, eight of which voiced complaints without following the clearly outlined protocol. Two offered tips, both circumstantial but worth filing away for potential future use. Two more reported the secret wrongdoings of two different Feds—one accusing a senator of sexual assault on an adult female, another accusing a Revenue Department officer of misappropriating funds. She read them over and filed them away. The probability of her receiving a useful lead on the average citizen was small; the probability of receiving one for a Fed was negligible.

When she created the portal two years ago, she'd paid the most attention to reports on Feds and City government officers. She'd received complaints about several, some of whom worked at the Disc. The complaints indicted only executives and other management, of course. Never a drone, never a janitor or an administrative assistant. She would carefully research them, using every tool she had, both legal and otherwise, leaving no stone unturned. After all, who better to get away with clandestine offenses than bureaucrats and elected officials, infiltrated by the greedy during the wars and part of an imbalanced system that struggled to right itself? And what better way to restore balance than to remove those who weighed too heavily upon the system through their positions of power? So much work on her part. Tedious, painstaking work.

And nothing. Other than a couple of minor embezzlements, some extramarital affairs, and several soliciting all kinds of services in the sex trade, none were guilty of the sort of missteps they were accused of, the missteps she cared about. The messages came from passionate citizens who assumed any government official who didn't support their ideology was crooked and destroying their struggling City or country. The accusations included those that appeared like truth on the surface but didn't hold up to scrutiny, as well as bald-faced lies that lacked even misleading evidence to support them.

When she would probe further, she found that the accusers themselves weren't especially stellar citizens, and merely utilized the portal with the hope of exacting "justice" for perceived wrongs through a bureaucratic scapegoat. Feds, if powerful, were easy targets. Far more so than Financials. It was easy to mistrust the government, who some saw as the cause of the wars and other ills. But it was the Financials who had the real power, whose promises of economic growth and the regaining of their nation's former strength got them into elected positions, where they turned the economic tides their way.

The subject line for the final message said "Thank you."

No one woulda believed me. They'd say I wanted revenge because he rejected me and because I'm not on his level. They woulda blamed me for going to his house and for trusting him and for wearing a dress and they woulda said I invited it because I was on the site. It woulda been simple if he was ugly or some Viola guy in one of the container homes. But people only see he's a Financial and goodlooking and goes to the big library to read paper books and stuff and they never believe he'd hurt a woman because why would he when he could fuck any woman he wanted and when he's goodlooking and successful and all that. They don't want to believe he's just the same as all the bad ones in Viola and Crocus and everywhere else. So if you had something to do with him gettin' shot up in the library, thanks again.

Stevie stared at the message. A thank you for Library Guy. She rarely got a thank you, or any acknowledgement. She didn't need it; but she appreciated it nonetheless.

Never be alone with a man you don't trust completely, Steviansa. The more powerful the man, the truer that is. Power only wants more power. And the less a woman has, the more easily he can justify harming her.

Stevie turned off her computer.

Stevie made her way to Herbie's office, where Marianne sat looking more tired than usual.

"How are you feeling these days?" she asked her.

"Beat," Marianne said. "No matter how many books you read, it just doesn't prepare you for the back pain and the fatigue and the hemorrhoids!" She shook her head. "Do you plan to have children, Stevie?"

"Oh... perhaps someday," Stevie said.

Perhaps never.

"Did you need to talk to Herb?"

"Just for a quick minute?"

Marianne pressed a button. "Sir, Stevie needs a minute."

"Send her in."

Stevie entered Herbie's office—small, quiet, and with plenty of natural light from the window behind his desk. She glanced at his painting, three men with jazz instruments, likely created and purchased in Crocus.

"Miss Stevie! What can I do for you?"

"Would you mind if I left early today and completed the rest of my work at home tonight? I have an errand to run."

He checked his watch. "That's fine."

"Thank you, Boss."

Later, back at her building, Stevie took a ride to the 39th floor. She heard them before the elevator doors opened. Raucous barking, at times in stereo when the barks of three dogs quit competing with one another and joined together. Once the doors opened, the barks downshifted into whines. They'd heard the elevator, probably hoping it was Blonde Bob with her sensible suit and scarf. When the whines morphed back into barks after smelling someone other than their doting owner, Stevie traversed the short hallway and entered the stairwell. She stationed herself on the metal stairs until five o'clock, when Bob and the other professionals would begin making their way home. During those two hours, the barking ceased for no more than a few minutes at a time.

At her apartment, Stevie pulled up the City Police site and searched for complaints about dog noise. There were many, most of them in Rosa and Dianthus, where citizens not only had the income to afford dogs, but often the character necessary to desire the benefits of dogs far more than the realities they came with. When she cross-referenced her own building's address, there were eight complaints total, seven of them for Blonde Bob, who'd moved in less than six months ago. Six of the seven came from her next-door neighbor, the man who'd confronted her in the elevator.

She pulled up the surveillance footage she'd copied from work, sat back in her chair, and began with the living room and kitchen area. However, when it appeared onscreen, she stared. It was the wrong home. She must have pulled footage for the wrong address by mistake.

But just as she went to turn it off, she realized she'd made no mistake at all. Upon closer inspection, she recognized the layout. The emergence of two blonde dogs only confirmed that it was Blonde Bob's apartment. Her pleather couch and chairs were torn along the edges and sides, their innards leaking out. The walls had scratch marks and the windows were blurred with layers of paw prints and slobber. There was no other furniture, revealing numerous yellow and brown stains on the once-white carpet.

What's wrong with these dogs? But after watching several days' worth of footage, she saw exactly what was wrong with them. Blonde Bob was gone nearly every day, often until late at night, sometimes not returning until morning. When she was home, she looked nothing like the neatly groomed woman who had entered the elevator in her couture collied splendor. Instead, she had messy hair and a sour face, and she sounded annoyed as she ordered the dogs to behave. Once she was groomed and gone, the dogs barked for much of the day, finally ceasing when she came home and fed them, whether at 5:30 pm or 2:30 am. She rarely took them out of the apartment, and when she did, they returned quickly. Stevie now understood why she'd never seen the dogs until that week.

She pulled up the other data she'd retrieved. Blonde Bob worked for ID Corp as a processor. Her tenure with the financial giant meant she was paid well enough to afford to live in that part of town, but not enough to afford even one, much less three, purebreds. And she was a 40-hour per week drone... not management or anything that would require such long hours. A further search indicated debt... lots of it.

Stevie contacted Mobius.

Mobius: Scintillations, my fine lady.

Artemis: Hi, my friend. How's life on the east bank?

Mobius: The best, as always. What can I do for you?

Artemis: How much control do you have over dog noise complaints?

Mobius: Not much. Unless a dog attacks someone or sets fire to a building, we don't have enough resources to bother.

Artemis: What about neglect?

Mobius: Same thing. Do you have a dog problem?

Artemis: Nothing you need to worry about. Is there anything I can do for you?

Mobius: I was about to contact you. I do need something.

Artemis: Name it.

Mobius: I'd prefer to meet. I'll contact you soon.

The next day, Stevie stood up from her desk and began her pursuit of caffeinated pleasure. She knocked at Seth's workstation and poked her head in.

"Coffee?"

Seth turned and looked at her through his lengthy lashes. "Sure." He glanced at his watch. "Make it decaf, though."

"Will it keep you up if you imbibe too late?"

He shrugged. "Kind of. Gives me nightmares."

Stevie nodded, wondering what Seth's nightmares were made of but knowing not to ask. "Decaf it is." She grabbed his Army mug and made her way to Machine, a tiny smile reaching her lips at the mere sight of him.

"Khaki, decaffeinated, please."

She placed Seth's cup under the spout while Machine performed his magic. As she waited, a group of dark suits headed her way, probably heading to the conference room for a meeting with the managers. Ronald was among them. When they passed by, Ronald gave her the thumbs up.

"Excellent work, Stevie," he said, his brown eyes gleaming with approval.

She smiled. She'd always liked that look, a look she'd rarely received from her mother. Stevie requested her own beverage, the dark liquid exuding its delectable odor as it filled her cup. "Thank you, my fine sir," she said as she took a sip. Machine didn't require a thank you, and certainly not a Crocus-style one, but it couldn't hurt to issue an expression of genuine gratitude from time to time.

When she gave Seth his cup, she lingered at his workstation. "Do you have a minute?"

"Sure. Decaf, right?"

"It is. But let me test it, just to be sure." She set down her cup and went to grab a tiny pipette from her desk. When she returned, she took a drop or two from Seth's mug. The light at the top turned green. "You're all set."

"Thanks," he said, sipping his coffee. "What's up?"

"You're a veteran. You live in Salvia. I'm guessing that you know your share of vets."

He nodded. "I do."

"Do you know any who are single?"

He raised his eyebrows. "Uh... yeah. You looking for a date?"

She laughed. "No. I have an idea... and I need your help."

Stevie glanced at herself in the mirror.

Not bad for a quickie.

Yellow hair... a wig for a quick job, of course. Pale blue eyes... contacts. A few alterations to the face and skin... pointier chin and some depigmentation. A tight skirt, a DeWitt tee, a trench like everyone else's trench. Pretty believable, really. Some DeWitt students, those whose parents at least pretended to teach responsibility to their children, took side jobs, including dog walking. She took the elevator to the second floor and exited through the rear of the building, skirting down the alley until she reached Perry Street. She donned her eyeshades, rounded the block, and reentered her building.

"Dog walking for 3901," she said in her highest nasally voice, flashing a key card. Ian, the morning doorman, nodded and looked her over briefly. At the 39th floor, she heard barking, followed by whining, then more barking. As she decoded the console and entered the apartment, the barking ceased.

The stench. Dog urine, dog poop, and dog smell. The blonde creatures came up to her and nearly knocked her over in their exuberance. With gloved hands, she petted each of them briefly before searching for their leashes. Once she found them and began attaching them, the dogs began whining and shaking with excitement. She pulled the trackers from each of their collars and let them fall to the stained carpet. Out they went, to the lobby and onto the street, making their way north as Stevie engaged in a battle for control between her slight self and three enthusiastic canines.

Others oohed and ahed, offering chortles of admiration and caressing hands as they passed. After walking north for some time, far enough that even neglected labradors had a chance to calm down, they entered a dog grooming hut, one that would understand what she needed and not ask too many questions. Stevie gave them instructions and informed them that the dogs' new owner would pick them up the following day.

Sunday, Stevie's normal appearance restored other than a platinum wig, blue contacts, and large eyeshades, she returned to the dog hut. And there, waiting for her, were three purebred labradors, their coats restored to their original short black hair. They were cleaned and groomed, their brown dog eyes filled with wonder. Stevie smiled at them.

"They look great without all that genetic enhancement," a shaggy-haired woman in a white lab coat said. "That shit ain't natural."

"I agree, ma'am." She thanked the woman and paid her in currency.

"Come back any time!"

Stevie took her newly energized canines out to the street, again working hard to manage their eagerness to take in every odor the City had to offer. She surveyed the area for Blonde Bob or anyone staring at her with an unnatural gaze. But no one looked at her; they only noticed the dogs, smiling at their dark coats and friendly faces. About halfway to her destination, she snuck into an alley and removed her wig, contacts, and eyeshades with her one free hand, stuffing it all into her pack.

Soon, she arrived at Seth's building, a plain but sturdy brick edifice with balconies that were large enough for two chairs. One rarely saw balconies anymore, what with the new sleek builds and their shiny glass windows that didn't open. Her acts of service required the space and amenities of a modern building. But Seth, he could live in the sort of place she preferred, a better version of the tiny apartment she'd shared with her mother once they moved to Artemisia.

Stevie entered the building, keeping her three leashes tight. Fortunately, people made way for her, several of them cooing at the newly groomed dogs and asking to pet them. Once inside, she stood out of the way, the lobby's faux wood chairs and neutral tile clean and unassuming. Soon, the elevator sounded.

When the doors opened, Seth emerged in gray slacks and a white t-shirt. Before he said a word to her, he stared at the dogs. "Holy fuck. Are those purebred labradors?"

Stevie looked down at the smoky black dogs, whose tails wagged with great merriment at the prospect of another new friend. "I think so."

Seth began scratching their heads and ears, their tails whipping everything in their wake. "We had a dog at the farm... a border collie. He was the best dog in the world." He paused, staring at the dogs for a moment before glancing at her. "Let's head up."

Stevie followed Seth to the elevator, taking up the slack in the leashes and keeping the dogs close. When the dog formerly known as Goldilocks stopped to sniff something, Stevie gave the leash a gentle pull and ordered her to follow. She did. At the 11th floor, Seth led Stevie and the dogs down a hallway until they stopped at a door. Seth gave a couple of hearty knocks.

When the door opened, a man in his 40s stood before them. He wore plain pocketed pants and an Army t-shirt, his clothing not fully obscuring a prosthetic lower leg, burn scars on both arms, and a vigilant eye not unlike Seth's.

"Harry." Seth put out his hand, and Harry shook it. "This is my friend, Stevie."

Harry offered his hand to her. But the handshake lacked any sort of vigor, and Stevie realized it was because something else had hijacked his attention. He stared at Goldie, who'd squeezed her way between Seth and Stevie and gazed up at Harry with earnest eyes. His weary expression completely changed. "Holy fuck. Is that a purebred lab?"

Seth laughed. "Harry, meet your new dog."

EPISODE 4
THE PASSAGE OF TRUTH

Stevie stood on the shuttle, a peep of sunlight warming her hair and neck. The shrinking City below didn't give her the peace it usually did, as today's forecast called for no rain, and even hints of sunlight. Days like this made her want to remain cityside... to head to the Circle and stretch out on a quilt upon the soft grass, sipping a large espresso and munching on an even larger cheese sandwich with tomato and eggplant. She sighed as the shuttle returned her to the world of spying on her fellow humans, all under the guise of preventing more war.

Never listen to such propaganda, Steviansa. They engaged in "bulk data collection" back in my day, too, in secret. A lot of good it did them. The enemy came for us anyway and we let them because we'd overextended ourselves to maintain an inflated economy. Federal Watch is still in its early stages, but you wait... they'll begin infringing upon your civil liberties.

Stevie did listen to the propaganda—she had to—but she never believed it. She'd dreaded telling her mother about landing the analyst job with the Federal Watch program. It had taken a year to get hired, for her to stand out among the other highly qualified applicants. She'd faced tests, interviews, and extensive background checks, along with any other unknown methods the Feds used to select their employees.

It had helped that she kept her hair short and dark. As one rose from low-level assistant to high-ranking executive, the ratio of males to females shifted from low to high. She'd heard other Disc employees joke about the "testosterone up top and estrogen down below" structure at the Disc. As if it were different anywhere else. Her appearance, and its lack of overt sexual attractiveness, wouldn't work against her here. Her mother told her that more women had occupied positions of power at one time, but the wars and resulting economic strain had shifted the zeitgeist in the wrong direction. *It's never good when leadership lacks a strong female presence*, her mother would say.

To Stevie's surprise, her mother hadn't gotten angry about her job at the Disc. She'd seemed almost... relieved. For better or worse, being a Fed nearly guaranteed lifetime financial security.

Perhaps you're more pragmatist than idealist after all, Mom.

When the shuttle arrived, Stevie waited for the others to exit before she did so. She climbed the stairs and headed to her workstation, passing Ronald and Herbie on the way. She waved but said nothing, not wanting to interrupt their conversation.

"Stevie."

She halted.

"Ron here tells me that report you ran for him yielded a couple of useful data points," Herbie said.

"Yes, it did," she said.

Herbie turned to Ronald. "Didn't I tell you? Didn't I tell you she was my best analyst?"

Ronald smiled. "Stevie, I need you to run a similar analysis, but for the western region. However, be aware that the seed sample I'm going to send you is considerably larger due to the population size."

"Of course," she said. "I'll get started as soon as I hear from you."

The two men resumed their course and Stevie went to work.

Saturday, Stevie made her way to the train station as rain pelted her umbrella. She tried to ignore her dread, wishing she could just run to her destination instead. But even she wouldn't take to her running shoes in rain this heavy. At least she could celebrate casting aside her dark suits in favor of jeans, a City University t-shirt, and her trench.

Lots of seats today. No yapping young women or groups of young men puffing out their chests like a flock of frigatebirds. She sat down, knowing she robbed no older person, vet, or single mother of a seat, of a short period of repose. The train hummed its way into Rosa as Stevie focused on her tablet, not wanting to see the garish flowers, the impossibly smooth sidewalks, or the efficient construction of new gleaming buildings. The route included several stops in Rosa, but no one got on or off. Rosans also avoided the train, although for different reasons than she did.

When the train began its journey over Blackwood Bridge, Stevie put her tablet away and peered out at the gray Milagro River. The river widened into a bay there and appeared even wider from all the rain, water taxis transporting citizens up and down its length before it spilled into the ocean. Her mother took her on river cruises when she was little, back when it was still affordable, before ID Corp bought all the taxi companies. They'd sail north, Rosa's expensive waterfront properties to the west, and Crocus's bright but worn buildings to the east, to be followed by Viola's warehouses and row homes, before they fell.

As they drew closer to Crocus—Krokus to those who called it home—street art began to emerge. Murals of dark and light heroes and heroines, messages of antiestablishmentarianism, symbols of freedom and love and war, all in gorgeously garish shades. And the giant blocky purple letters painted across the windowless concrete train station, spelling out KROKUS, a tall yellow-orange crocus flower painted next to it, upside down. Stevie smiled at all of it. The train halted at the station and a group of new passengers boarded. When a young male sat next to her, she stifled a frown.

She felt him staring at her. She turned, her eyes meeting a set of even darker ones, peering out from a brown face and accompanied by a brown pleather jacket. He grinned.

"You have a nice smile, Brown Sugar."

She produced a half smile, the result he'd sought. "You're lucky my mother didn't hear you use that phrase."

"She a tough one, huh?"

"You have no idea."

She resumed looking outside. But she still felt his eyes on her, and turned to face him again. "What?"

He gazed at her hair. "Why you keep your hair so short?"

"Why does anyone do anything?"

He seemed perplexed by her answer. Then he shrugged. "They want to, I s'pose."

"Exactly."

"But why? Why you want to? You ain't half bad... long hair make you damn good."

"I don't want to be damn good."

He made a face. "Why not?"

The train stopped. "Have a nice day," she said before stepping off the train.

Denim, everywhere. And brown pleather. People with varying amounts of melanin, but with generally more of it than one saw on the west bank. Noise—chattering neighbors, someone playing the electric cello on the corner, the whizzing of brightly colored electro-bikes as they sped down the street, reminding her why they'd been banned west of the Milagro. She crossed the busy street, sidestepping a series of holes and hoping a pleather-clad biker wouldn't run her down. Best of all, it was dry. No rain in Krokus today.

Stevie smiled again, glad to be there. To be home.

She arrived at the Sassafras Cafe, hoping the dry conditions meant they could sit outside for lunch. But when she saw the throng of denim skirts and overalls among the sidewalk tables, she sighed, knowing their chances were slim.

"Stevie!"

She searched until she spotted a woman in a denim jumper that exposed her dark arms and legs, her big natural hair standing out among the others. Mobius already sat at a patio table, her pleather bag guarding the other seat. Stevie squeezed through the crowd just as Mobius shooed away a couple who wanted the empty chair.

"Scintillations," Mobius said in her throaty voice, the Krokusian greeting containing just the right amount of irony. She gave Stevie a big hug, the softness of her full breasts reminding Stevie of her mother. "How are you?"

"I'm good, now," Stevie said, sitting down in the coveted chair. She glanced at her friend's hair, an afro that had expanded to a very respectable loft. "Your hair's grown. I love it."

"Thank you," she said, patting her hair with both hands, as if pretending to fluff it. "You look thin. You running more?"

Stevie shrugged. "Probably."

"Coffee? Double or triple?"

"Double. It's a Saturday."

Mobius pressed the button for a double espresso. "Thanks for coming... I know you hate the train. But consider this: you wouldn't have to make that odious journey if you moved back to where you belong. Your mother isn't around anymore." Mobius cocked her head, in that way she did when she said something that might get under someone's skin.

Stevie wagged her finger in warning.

"And no serial killers here," Mobius added. "Mister Oakenfold won't cross the Milagro and risk dealing with one of us east bankers."

"I would love to come back, believe me. But my commute to the stratosphere is long enough without adding a river taxi ride."

"True. We shan't cut into your extracurricular activities, shan't we?" She winked.

Stevie smiled.

"Speaking of which," she said, lowering her voice. "You're being safe, right? I don't like you out there late at night, stalking people at the Miashi building or taking images of Viola garbage selling junk to kids. Especially with a murderer on the loose."

"Don't worry. Most of my extracurricular service work gets done sitting at a desk, like yours does."

It wasn't a lie. Her service involved extensive research and preparation before she acted. And while Mobius knew of her petty acts of service, she didn't know about her grand ones. No one did.

After the braided barista delivered her espresso in a bright mosaic cup, Stevie scanned her ID over the barista's handheld and thanked her. She and Mobius sat for a few minutes, watching Krokus's citizens come and go on the street. After ordering vegetarian fare for lunch, Mobius took another swig from her cup and glanced around. "Speaking of the shooter... I've heard scuttlebutt around here. Some people think the DOA is behind those shootings."

"The Daughters of Anarchy? They don't exist anymore, do they?"

"Some say they're back. Others say they've always been here. Think about it... who else would use an antique firearm? Who else could get *access* to an antique firearm? Those things lost what little value they had left when handheld energy weapons took over, and everyone sold them off to the Feds as part of the war's metal recycling program. But the DOA... I betcha they stowed a few away, just in case."

"I could see that."

"And consider this: who's taking a bullet to the head? Financials, that's who. The people who've corrupted our society and turned our economy from unstable to fuck-all. If the DOA does what it swore it would do—protect society from selfish, corrupt rats—why not start there?"

Stevie smiled. "Sounds like someone's been doing her homework."

Mobius waved a dismissive hand. "You have to admit... it makes sense. The DOA was always political, you know. They focused on the white-collar criminals, the people embedded in the system, the people we trust and would never suspect. That's what made them so genius."

"I can see what intrigues you," Stevie said as their meals arrived. "It's more meaningful than some serial killer knocking off rich men just because."

Mobius's eyes narrowed. "But you're skeptical. Of course you are. Ah, I can't help it. I get excited about shit like this. About social change and the people who do more than talk about it. It's probably not them, but I admit I like the idea that it could be."

"There is one flaw in your argument," Stevie said, taking a spoonful of her butternut squash soup. "The DOA always left their insignia when they acted. No one's seen it for, what, the better part of two decades? Not to rain on your ideas, but I'd guess the DOA probably died off during the second war."

Mobius took a bite of her sandwich. "Eh, what fun is that?"

"Is that why you asked me here? To talk about the Daughters of Anarchy?"

"No," she said, wiping her mouth with her red-checked cloth napkin. "I have a real request... but it's easier to show you."

When finished, Stevie paid for their lunch and followed Mobius deeper into Krokus. They walked past throngs of people, past the cafe tables with people sipping everything from coffee to fermented lemongrass, past art galleries and handcrafted furniture stores and street musicians warbling out tunes with varying degrees of skill. A pack of bright orange electro-bikes raced by, men and women pushing the speed laws beyond their limits.

Finally, they arrived at very familiar ground, the concrete passageway with walls that stood tall on each side of them and stretched south for a quarter mile. Both walls displayed an array of street art and murals... some new, some old, some famous. The upside down crocus flower. A series of faces slowly graduating from light to dark and hair from straight to kinky. The powerful first and second war murals, depicting the City's people rising from the ashes of destroyed buildings and blackened trees. And the infamous depiction of a giant man with a woolen v-neck sweater over a crisp pink shirt, his hair perfect and his watch expensive, holding his penis as he stood over their City and urinated upon it.

She knew them all well, well enough to recreate them from memory if she'd had any aptitude for the visual arts. She'd grown up near the Passage of Truth, and even after they moved away her mother made sure to bring her back every few months to teach her about the art and to appreciate any new creation that had materialized.

But something was wrong. The mural portraying the second war, with a dead dog curled up on the sidewalk to represent bioterrorism, had slashes of color, ugly and misshapen and stupid, painted over the famous piece. Stevie put her hand to her mouth.

"Now you know why I brought you here," Mobius said.

Who would do this? Who would deface the art of the people, the allegory of our surviving the worst attack we have ever known?

The ignorant, Steviansa. The useless, the attention-seeking, the ungrateful. If they don't have something to create, they'll find something to destroy.

"You work for the City," Stevie said to Mobius. "The Passage is heavily surveilled. They must have footage..."

"They claim it's missing."

Stevie scoffed. "Right."

"The Hood's up in arms over this, Stevie. They're outraged." She lowered her voice. "You're the only one I know who might be able to help."

"When did it appear?"

"A couple of nights ago, late. Still not watching the news, huh?"

"Only when I need to." Stevie paused, unable to tear her eyes away from the vandalism. "We communicate about this only through the portal from now on."

Mobius nodded.

Stevie headed west on 32nd Avenue, making her way to the old concrete and brick buildings of Salvia. She passed a man in his late 20s, his gate somewhat awkward from two prosthetic limbs as he dodged the occasional blemish on the sidewalk. She passed another man, middle-aged and with a teenaged daughter, scars marring his right arm and disappearing up his shirt sleeve. A few others displayed telltale signs of war as well, the sort of signs that many City-dwellers didn't want to see, as if avoiding them would erase the impact of two long wars on their society. She'd also learned to recognize the not-so-telltale signs: the no-nonsense way they strode, the rigidity of their posture from years of standing at attention, the keen gaze that saw everything, and, sometimes, the less keen gaze that saw things that weren't there.

As she strode though Salvia, she searched for condemned lots, looking for one with small buildings that, ideally, had mostly crumbled. This meant less demolition and cleanup, which meant lower cost, which made it easier for the City to approve a proposal to convert the lot into a green zone. Salvia had no green zone. And Stevie had long decided that it needed one, that it needed a natural, quiet place for the vets, a respite from the noises and triggers of the City.

When she arrived at Sage Bakery, the smell of fresh bread made her stomach grumble. Seth was already inside, sitting along the room's perimeter, his back to the wall. Where he could see everything. He'd probably arrived some time ago to ensure he got the seat he needed, or to wait until it became available. Indifferent to the cool weather, Seth wore a short-sleeved Army t-shirt, the sleeves snug around his muscled arms.

She sat down in the other chair. "Funny seeing you here, Major."

He grinned at that, his smile lines crinkling in that way she liked. Before she could say anything else, the barista arrived with her espresso.

She stared at it. "Let me guess; you saw me coming long before I saw you."

"A double, to start with."

She pulled out her ID.

"Too late," the shaven-headed woman said. "Captain already took care of it."

Stevie giggled as the barista sauntered off. "Thank you, Major."

Seth winked. Yet, despite his brief grin and his generosity, a crease rested between Seth's eyebrows and his blue eyes looked murky.

"How's Harry? And the other vets?" She hoped such a promising topic would get his mind off whatever troubled him.

"Giddy. I thought a lot about who to gift those dogs to, and now I know I made the right choice. Thomas, the second one you met... he served in the first war. No family, he loves dogs, and he believes in dog training. Marcel... he did nothing but talk about his old dog during our entire deployment. Widower... wife killed in the line of duty." He shook his head. "I was so tempted to keep one for myself. But those guys... they need it more. And I can afford a mutt when the time comes."

"Thanks again for finding homes for them. All you need now is a green zone in your neighborhood."

"Yeah, not holding my breath on that. A bunch of us have applied... and nothing."

"There's a good double lot at Charlie and 30th. I spotted it on my way here. Good size, condemned property, crumbled structure. It helps if you get people to pledge that they'll volunteer their labor for cleanup and landscaping. If you like the lot, let me know. I have contacts at the City, and it's better to do it now, before some Financial builds a glass monstrosity on the lot."

He raised his eyebrows. "Learn all that from your mom?"

"I did."

"Thank you... for the info. And for the dogs. I'm surprised it worked out; in my experience, most purebred owners use their dogs as status symbols and don't give three fucks about the animals themselves." He shook his head. "Harry... it's like he found the love of his life. One of those matchmakers couldn't have done a better job."

No, they couldn't have.

"Not a fan of matchmaking?" Seth said, somehow reading her thoughts.

"No."

"Why not?"

"They treat women like commodities, not people."

He shrugged. "It's just to meet people. What's the big deal if you can afford one?"

"If that's all it was, I'd have no problem. But those matchmakers order women to wear extremely tight clothing and really high heels. They require them to go to salons for genetic enhancement, salons they get kickbacks from, which they don't reveal to the women. They don't like dark hair, curly hair, short hair, skinniness, or small breasts... if you have any of those, they send you to the salons at your expense, just so you can parade in front of a bunch of Financials who are mostly there to find the best looking woman they can lure into their beds. Love, indeed."

"It's that bad?"

"It's that bad. I did recon with Madame Rose once, after I heard reports from women."

"I assume they wanted you to change pretty much everything about you... since you have a lot of the traits you say they don't like."

"Absolutely. I'm happy with my appearance, but I'm concerned about these women who are willing to go to such lengths in the vain hope of landing some rich guy. Oh, and they only represent men with lots of money... and no visible war wounds."

Seth shook his head. "Fuck. I had no idea. I just thought they rounded up cute girls and set them up on dates." He shrugged again. "Well, if a guy needs to pay someone to find a date in this town, he's probably a fucking loser anyway." He sipped his coffee.

"So," Stevie said. "What's in the basket?"

Seth smiled a little as he opened the gingham napkin. Baked goods: plain and chocolate croissants, a raspberry danish, and two frosted donuts. He nudged it toward her. Stevie chose the plain croissant. It was still warm, and she took a bite of its buttery goodness. Seth reached for the chocolate croissant.

"You like chocolate," she said.

"Yep... it's that time of the month."

Stevie stopped chewing. She suppressed a smile. "I can't believe you said that."

"Ah, it was worth it, just to see your face."

She giggled.

A loud crash interrupted their mirth. An explosion of metal on metal, far too loud for a Sunday morning. For any morning. There was a collective cry as everyone turned their attentions to the window. Another electro-taxi collision. Stevie stood, along with a few others.

It's a bad one. They'll need help.

She turned back to Seth. But instead of standing and surveying the wreckage like everyone else, he was still seated. His sat with his elbows on the table, face resting in his hands, eyes staring at nothing. He breathed rapidly and blinked several times.

"Seth," she said quietly.

No response.

She pulled her chair close to him and sat down. His eyes shifted toward her without fully looking at her. "Deep breath," she said, her tone neutral but direct.

He blinked a couple more times as he inhaled, letting out his breath slowly.

"What do you see, Seth?" When she got no response, she picked up the basket of baked goods and held it in front of him. "What do you see?"

"Pastries." His voice lacked its usual vigor.

"Yes, pastries for us. Another deep breath." He inhaled again. "You're safe. You're here, at Sage Bakery, with me."

He nodded. His eyes shifted beyond her.

"What do you see?"

"People."

"The noise... it was a taxi collision. You know they always drive too fast."

She glanced outside to ensure that someone had responded. Several people milled around the ravaged taxis. She wanted to go outside to help, but she couldn't leave Seth. Others would have to take care of it. When she turned back around, Seth looked calmer.

Mild reaction. Quick recovery. He's had at least some treatment.

Seth finally looked at her, his eyes still clouded. "I'm alright. I just need to sit here for a while."

"Okay." Stevie took her cue and scooted her chair back to its original place. She nudged Seth's chocolate croissant toward him before she took another bite of her own croissant. Seth gazed at his pastry for a moment before he picked it up.

She looked outside again. The cops were there by now, shooing away the bystanders and erecting a temporary blockade around the scene. The bakery's patrons went back to their delectables. Just when Stevie went to sip her coffee, two women clad in denim pants and brown pleather jackets entered: one tall and proud with a thick mohawk, the other thin and morose, a gray streak in her otherwise dark hair. Both wore dark eyeshades. Even with the shades, Stevie knew they looked at her. Fear shot through her.

They were the same women she saw last week, at the Tarragon Noodle Bar.

Could be a coincidence. But probably not. Not in the City, where most didn't venture far from their own Hoods. Two Brownies didn't show up at a noodle house in Artemisia and a bakery in Salvia in the same week. Perhaps not lesbians after all. Cops, possibly detectives, somehow tracking her. Or, worse than cops... those who would try to catch her alone in some vacant lot, or follow her home to see where she lived. If they didn't already know. She couldn't take an image of them, not without giving herself away.

Stevie turned back toward Seth, taking another sip of her espresso and coming up with an excuse for her inattention. But Seth's usual vigilance was on hold, his own attentions focused on soothing his inner turmoil. The next time Stevie turned around, the two women had taken a seat near the window.

"What's the matter?" Seth said, his eyes sharper now.

"Nothing. I just feel a little off from that collision."

He pushed the basket toward her. "Have another."

She smiled and took one of the donuts. They sat for some time and eventually resumed conversation, talking about work, about dogs, about anything that wasn't upsetting. But when they stood up to leave, the two women, both finished with their coffee, remained at their table. Waiting.

Make sure Seth is safe. They're probably not interested in him, but make sure anyway.

"Can I walk you back to your place?" she said.

Seth gave her a look. "I'm fine."

"I know you are. But it's nice out, and I thought I would search Salvia for more lots... for your green zone."

"Sure," he said, appearing not entirely convinced.

When they left, Stevie made no eye contact with the two women. Let them think she was unaware or unconcerned. Let them be that much less careful in their pursuit. As Stevie strolled with Seth, she checked behind her whenever they turned a corner. The two women didn't pursue them. She breathed a sigh of relief.

Paranoia?

Possibly. There's one way to find out.

Soon, they stood outside Seth's brick building.

"I'd invite you up, but a nap will do me some good. I didn't sleep much last night."

"That's fine," she said. "I'm going to keep walking."

"See you tomorrow?"

She nodded.

After a few sips of espresso, Stevie flipped on her red light and began several new queries. The Sage Bakery in Salvia, internal and external. The neighboring businesses, external. Yesterday, time range 0930 to 1200. The files appeared onscreen and she scanned the external view of the bakery first.

The two Brownies stood outside, watching the wreckage from the taxi collision, perhaps waiting for her to come outside and lookie-loo before the cops barricaded the scene. When she inspected the earlier footage from nearby cameras, she saw what she hoped she wouldn't. Just around the corner, the two women stood waiting. For her.

The footage from inside the bakery yielded a decent frontal of Mohawk and a partial for Gray Streak. She saved the images and began a search. The eyeshades would complicate the search and lower the match percentages, but the mohawk and streak of gray would help compensate for that. Even a pool of 20 candidates would be easy to research. The search function continued its duty, mining through countless images until it finally ceased. No match. For either woman.

Not good.

They had connections among those who could render them blocked from searches, something as rare and privileged as her own access to Federal Watch data. Stevie closed her eyes, dread coming over her.

Herbie's booming voice pulled her from her brooding thoughts. He was nearby, greeting and engaging in small talk with those he passed. She sent the images of the Brownies to her personal tablet and cleared away her searches and search history before flipping off her light. Herbie's voice got louder as it made its way to her.

"Miss Stevie!" His tie had blue flowers today. A new one, probably from his daughter.

"Good afternoon, Boss. What can I do for you?"

"The directors are jazzed about that work you did for Ron. Would you mind running some initial analyses with the messaging data, all of it?"

"Sure. But the messaging data takes much longer to wade through, because there's so much more of it. It'll take me a few days."

Herbie nodded. "Put it at the top of your pile. The other reports can wait."

"Will do, Boss."

Once Herbie left, Stevie considered everything she needed to do. Begin work for Herbie and the executives. Research the Passage of Truth incident. And another idea to gather intelligence on the two Brownies. She stood up to pay Machine another visit. It was going to be a late evening.

Nearly six hours later, after the Disc had all but emptied of its devoted bureaucrats, the northeast segment of her messaging data query for Herbie had completed. She began a new query for the western coast, which would take far longer due to its larger population, a population that had faced less ravaging during the second war. The query would run at least 14 hours, and she initiated it with the plan of letting it run all night.

On another screen, her City-wide surveillance data scan for Mohawk and Gray Streak—using the Sage Bakery images as seed—marched forward with another hour to go. The search had taken numerous hours, longer than most, but would bypass the image match software that had blockaded her previously.

On her third screen, Stevie pulled up the data for all eyes that captured the Passage of Truth, beginning with Thursday. She scrolled quickly through countless electro-bikes coming and going, and numerous tourists gathering, taking images, and pointing with expressions ranging from boredom to awe. As it grew dark, fewer bikes came and the crowd thinned, until the Passage enjoyed a respite from its exhibitionism. Then, deep into the darkness, when even the drunks had left the streets and gone to pass out on their hideaway beds, she saw them. A group of individuals, all in black, all in hoods, all with face masks. Four stood by while one did the ignoble deed, artlessly painting stupid nothingnesses that no one except his useless friends would understand, upon which they would place some misguided value.

And the black. No one wore black in Krokus. You were looked down upon for it, for trying too hard to seem cool and for not embracing self-expression. Brown, on the other hand... brown was organic, the color of earth, soil, chocolate, beef, melanin. These feckless youth, they weren't from Krokus.

Gang activity? Possibly. They'd faced less of it during the wars, but some of the east bank Hoods still struggled to recover. More single parent homes that couldn't afford to live on the west bank, less money and resources, more kids seeking community from their fellow beleaguered peers.

Obscured in black or not, it was obvious by their quickness of step and the way they moved: they were young males. But that was it. Stevie could see no identifying details. No faces or hair, no exposed tattoos or scars, no war wounds. Nothing she could use. She shook her head. It didn't happen often, but there were times when even her level of access wasn't enough. With a sigh, Stevie cleared the searches and all signs of her activity.

Finally, the search for Mohawk and Gray Streak ceased. Typically, a search of that kind resulted in numerous images that were repetitive in nature: inside one's home, nearby one's home, commuting to an office, or at a nearby restaurant, club, or friend's home. There was little deviation from such patterns. For all their inventiveness and desire to explore, humans were remarkably routinized, living most of their lives within a few blocks from the tiny square footage they called home. But these two women, they showed up everywhere... always in pleather jackets and eyeshades, and always together.

"Hey," a male voice said.

Stevie whipped around. Seth.

"Sorry," he said, putting his hands up. "I think this time qualifies as sneaking up on you, since it's so late."

She put her hand on her chest, her heart pounding from the sudden demands of her sympathetic nervous system. "Seth, you scared me."

"Why are you here so late?"

"Herbie asked for some time-intensive analyses and I needed to make sure they ran. What are you doing here?"

He sighed. "I had some extra work to take care of. I'm trying to get real good and tired so I'll sleep through the night."

"Do you often have difficulty sleeping?"

He shrugged. "It comes and goes. The last few days..."

"Nightmares?"

He nodded, glancing away from her.

"What time are you finished?" she said.

"Whenever you are. I'll make sure you get home safe. A woman shouldn't be out alone at this hour."

Perhaps he was right. She considered the safety of other women... but often neglected to do the same for herself. "The next shuttle leaves in twenty and I'm about done. Just give me a few minutes to shut everything down and I'll come get you." She paused. "I have something that might help with the sleep, if you're willing to stop at my building before you go home."

"I've tried the sleeping pills. They don't help."

She shook her head. "This is herbal. Try it tonight. That's an order, Captain."

Seth gave a tired half smile. "Yes, ma'am."

Back on the surface, Stevie and Seth stepped into an electro-taxi. Stevie handed the driver currency, more than the fare called for, and told him which stop came first. After glancing at the currency and running the math, the driver perked up.

"Why currency?" Seth asked her.

"No fees for the drivers. Another holdover from my mom."

When they arrived at her building, Stevie ran up to her place and retrieved a small bottle of dark liquid, which she brought down to Seth. "Five drops, seven at most, in water. It tastes terrible."

"Thanks," Seth replied, looking unconvinced. "See you tomorrow."

Back at home and in her ivory robe, Stevie logged into her portal and contacted Mobius.

Mobius: Scintillations, my lady.

Artemis: You still awake?

Mobius: Not for much longer. How are you?

Artemis: A bit tired. Just got home. However, I did some research for you.

Mobius: And?

Artemis: Found the targets. Five young males. Possible gang activity. But no identifying information.

There was a long pause.

Mobius: Shit. Fuck.

Artemis: I have an idea. But it will involve a lot of time, and we'll need help.

Mobius: Hit me.

Artemis: Who's your best muralist?

The next morning came sooner than Stevie would have liked. She pulled herself out of bed and searched one of her drawers, ensuring her body blocked the ever-watchful eyes. She selected a small polymer cylinder and searched her potions until she found the correct one. After she finished getting ready, she placed the cylinder in her jacket pocket before leaving for work.

Stalk me if you choose, Mohawk and Gray Streak. But come near me, and you'll learn what a science degree can do for the more industrious.

Back at the Disc, a belly full of oatmeal and a hot espresso in her hand, Stevie turned on her computer.

"Hey."

She turned to find Seth standing there. He looked rested and refreshed.

"That shit tastes like rotting garbage. But it works."

She smiled. "Good."

Saturday, Stevie put on her running gear. She included a hydration pack this time, knowing she'd be out for longer than usual. Once outside, she headed east, quickening her pace through Rosa until she felt the Milagro's breeze cool her sweaty brow. She ascended the upper deck of Blackwood Bridge and took in the view of the gray river, the east bank, and the ocean beyond it all.

The quiet. Nothing but the passing hum of the occasional train or the footsteps of another runner. Up there, the bridge was free of chatty women, boasting men, and people cooing over a coddled couture collie. No rain, even. When she spotted the purple Krokus mural in the distance, she smiled a little. And when her positioning device read 7.14 miles, she stopped. She'd reached the Passage of Truth.

More people than usual, even for a dry Saturday. Peering, talking, speculating. She weaved her way through the dense throng, doing her best to quell her eagerness. Finally, she reached a hole in the crowd, one that parted enough give her a full view.

A new mural. A graphic style depiction of the Passage's east wall, with five young men lined up in front of it, their backs to the wall. The youth wore black masks, identical to those the defacers wore when they committed the infraction. But instead of cladding their bodies in all black, the artist had depicted them unclothed, skinny and hairless, each with two fingers holding a tiny penis, reminiscent of a boy learning to urinate standing up. The rightmost youth held a giant can of spray paint in his other hand, which stretched beyond normal capacity to aim itself at the wall and leave a pink message over the bright yellow background:

"Where's my mommy?"

Stevie burst out laughing. It was even better than she'd hoped. A challenge, a burr under the skin of the putatively audacious youth. And a searing insult that would pique any male of that age range, regardless of whether he was east or west bank, chocolate or vanilla, poor or new rich. Behind the safety of her dark eyeshades, she turned and glanced up at the place where someone would rotate keeping the watch, every hour of every day. Waiting. She turned back to the new mural.

Your move, fools.

EPISODE 5
FECKLESS MISSPENT PRIVILEGE

Men stared.

Stevie resisted the temptation to put on the hard face that would shorten their stares, instead donning some remnant of a smile. The smile was necessary. It matched the tight black dress that constrained her and the yellow hair that tangled as it rubbed against her dress. An unfriendly face wouldn't do tonight.

She strolled along DeWitt Street, her pointy tortures taking her up the hill until she saw the Miashi building looming above them all. She passed the black tower, recalling Hungover Hero and his soiled entryway. How many times had he puked since? Had he reconsidered his imbibing, or would he continue on to a lifetime of self-abuse, broken bones from drunken falls, and liver dysfunction, like too many of his misguided peers?

The nearby sign read "War Zone," its large typeface army green with a trickle of blood running through it. Stevie gritted her teeth behind her pleasant, full-lipped smile as she entered the dubiously named bar. Pounding music assailed her, as did the stank of cannabis vapor. Such connections the owner must have to pull off both cannabis and liquor licenses. The bartenders and waitstaff wore skimpy military garb, fake weapons tucked into the belts that stored their ID Corp handhelds. The electronic menu listed drinks with names like AirBomb and BioTerror, quaffed by the DeWitt students and faculty that filled the place. She could only imagine what Seth would think of it all.

She spotted him. Dark hair, olive skin, gleaming smile... the sort of smile that drew women in, much further than they'd bargained for. He didn't see her. Stevie reached over and retrieved a couple of peanuts from a nearby table, winking at the men who offered no protest to her petty theft. First one missed, second one landed... right on Olive's head. She'd found only one instance of hard evidence for Olive... but one was enough. Deal with him before he inflicts more damage, before he reproduces and transmits his corrupted genetic and social influences to the next generation.

Olive looked around for the source of the assault, his eyes landing on her. When his magnificent smile reappeared, she smiled back and headed his way. Just as she did, someone bumped into her, enough to make her stumble and grab a nearby table to balance herself. She turned to issue a quick apology... and found herself face to face with Herbie. Her stomach heaved.

"Oh!" Herbie exclaimed. He still wore a suit and tie, leftover from his workday, a day she'd called in sick. "My apologies, Miss! Are you alright?"

Frozen, she managed a small nod.

He patted her on the arm and went on his way, sitting down next to a 30-something man in a button-down. When she began breathing again, she glanced at Olive, the urge to continue her long-awaited mission nearly overwhelming.

He's right there. Even Herbie didn't recognize you. Do it. Otherwise all that time, effort, and impact on your body... wasted.

No. It will set off an emotional maelstrom for Herbie, knowing the murder took place only yards from him. That will tempt him to follow up on it, using his considerable means to do so. Leave. Now.

Stevie left the dubiously themed bar, trudging down the hill in her ridiculous heels, feeling as deflated as a Yellow who went to snag a guy she'd had her eye on and instead found him with another woman. Suddenly, a man in an expensive suit swayed too close to her, putting his hand on her shoulder.

"Plans for the evening, Gorgeous?" he said, his breath reeking of whiskey.

She inched her shoulder away, her surprise preventing any coherent response other than shaking her head.

His leer morphed into a sneer. "Oh, too good for me, huh? Yellow-haired cunt."

Anger flared through her. Before she could allow herself to think, she bent down and removed her high heels. And with one pointy torture poised in her hand, she smashed him in the face. He recoiled from the assault, and she barely saw his expression of shock before she took off running. An inebriated man in a suit couldn't keep up with her for long.

Did you just strike that man, Steviansa?

I did. I don't know what came over me.

What came over you? You lost control of yourself!

Blocks later, Angry Drunk nowhere in sight, Stevie slowed to a walk, the cold, gritty concrete strangely comforting to her bare feet. She continued on to her chosen dead zone, looking forward to changing out of her unlucky getup, heading home, and making herself some espresso.

"Out for a run?"

Stevie nodded, wiping the sweat from her brow as she joined Seth in his elevator.

"Did you hear the latest?" he said.

"Another shooting?"

He shook his head. "Not this time. Some piece of shit defaced one of those wall murals at the Passage of Truth."

She frowned. "I heard. I saw it for myself."

"Is it that bad?"

"It's bad, although still reparable. The problem is that the artists take all that time to fix it, and then the perpetrators just come back and do it again."

"Did you see the new mural, the payback?"

"I did," she said, smiling as she recalled the sight of the man-children tugging their little penises.

Seth chuckled. "That was fucking beautiful. That shit will hurt when they see it." He paused. "What were you doing in Crocus?"

"I have friends there."

"Really?" he said, genuinely surprised. "I didn't think west bankers associated with east bank types."

"I'm originally an east banker. I lived in Krokus until I was ten, before my mother moved us to Artemisia."

The elevator doors opened at the 19th floor. "I should've known you were a Brownie," he said, glancing at her. "With the denim and the food you eat and all..."

She lost her train of thought once inside Seth's apartment. It smelled like him, a mixture of sandalwood and rain from the fresh air that drifted in through an open window. It was the kind of window one opened by hand, like she remembered from childhood. Shiny black epoxy floor, black cabinetry in the kitchen, gray pleather furniture, neat and uncluttered. A single shelf with a small stack of paper books on it, protected by airtight glass to preserve them. But, most of all, the wall: Seth's antique weapons collection, displayed in an orderly fashion and also behind protective glass. Revolvers: short and long-barreled, small and large caliber. Semi-automatic pistols, their magazines proudly displayed next to them. Rifles, from single shot to automatic. About 15 in all.

From her peripheral vision, she saw Seth turn and face her, crossing his beefy arms and waiting for her reaction.

"Wow," she said.

They're gorgeous.

"Been building the collection since I was a kid. Got my first three from our neighbor at the farm... he was a casualty in the first war, so his wife gave me the .22, the .44, and the single shot rifle."

"Where did you find the rest?"

From the families of older dead vets. And the black market in Viola.

"Other vets. And the occasional trip to Viola." He glanced at the display again. "Notice anything missing?"

"Missing?"

"No .357. I've got the Oakenfold .22 and the .44 mag, but no .357."

"Why is that important?"

"It's iconic. Stopping power without too much kick. Easy to carry, assuming you have a J-frame with a two-inch barrel."

Exactly.

"Anyway... the cactus I need your help with." Seth pointed to a six-foot tall succulent, its many blue-green trunks covered in 2-inch spines.

"A Peruvian Apple. I love the color... it's bluer than either of mine." As she approached the cactus to get a closer look, she saw it. Brown spots along one side.

"Please don't tell me it's fungus. I paid a fortune for that fucking thing, and I like it."

"You're in luck. It's not fungus. It's sunburn. It can be hard to tell the difference."

"Sunburn? We don't get any sun here. I thought cactuses... I mean cacti... are used to sun."

"These aren't as much. Your window gets the southern sun, and it's more UV than the plant can take. I'd program your shade to lower about two hours before dark."

He nodded. "Thanks. How do you know so much about plants? Oh... your mom. She was a botanist or something..."

"Not an official botanist. Self-taught... more of a plant aficionado."

"Wait... is Steviansa a plant? I always wondered what the story was behind that name."

"It is. In fact, *Steviansa* is what I gave you when you had trouble sleeping."

His eyebrows went up. "I'll be damned. So botany... is that one of your degrees?"

"No. My degree is in genetics."

"Genetics? How'd you get a job at the Disc with a genetics degree?"

"I have a minor and a graduate degree in Information Systems."

"Graduate school, huh? You don't see much of that these days. Most kids go for the business degree and hope to go out and make a fortune."

She shrugged. "I love to learn. And you? University or straight into the service?"

"University after the service. It was tough, but it gave me something to do. Got the Disc job while I finished." Seth gazed at her, his expression a strange mixture of admiration and something else she didn't understand. "Shit," he finally said. "Sorry... I didn't offer you water or anything."

Stevie shook her head. "I'm okay. I need to finish running and take care of some things. I'm glad your cactus is okay. You have a nice home, by the way."

He opened the door for her. "Thanks. Find your way out?"

She nodded.

After a few more miles, two green zones, and a few groceries, Stevie headed back to her apartment. She ordered the window shades to close, cutting off the energy source for her own Peruvian Apples.

It's only temporary, friends. You'll be photosynthesizing again very soon, I promise.

She went to her office, turned on the computer, and found a favorite site. She began removing her clothing.

"Scintillations, Artemis," a male voice said. "Who is your pleasure today?"

"Lor, please."

She stood fully nude before putting on her body suit and headpiece. When she engaged the power, the visual interface appeared. And there stood Lor, in nothing but muscled male form and a crooked smile. He walked closer to her and reached out his hand, touching her just as the tactile interface engaged.

Showered and dressed, Stevie went to her kitchen and pulled out a new jar of garlic pickles, her mouth already salivating at the prospect of their crunchy sour deliciousness. She tapped the lid on her concrete counter before attempting to unscrew it. No luck. She tried again, her muscles burning and her hand aching from the strain. With a frustrated sigh, she grabbed the bulbous jar and took it to her lab bench, clamping it in place while she hugged the jar and tried to rotate it. Still nothing.

She looked around, searching for some other method of leveraging the metal lid. She tried prying it off with pliers, using a wrench that wound up being too small to fit around the lid, and turning the jar upside down and pounding it harder so the seal would break. Nothing worked.

She would have to do the unspeakable.

Stevie picked up the jar and left her apartment. She rang the bell of her only male neighbor, almost praying no one was home. But after a minute, the door opened. And there stood Pomade, in slacks and a t-shirt, more underdressed than she'd ever seen him. But his hair remained perfectly coiffed.

"Hi," she said, suddenly feeling a confounding mixture of annoyance and embarrassment. "I can't get this jar open. Would you mind lending a strong hand, please?"

A flash of amusement crossed Pomade's doughy face, the sort of face that would never be handsome, but would never hold him back given his perfect coif, tailored suits, and air of entitlement.

You think I'm flirting. That I barely tried to open the jar with the hope of allowing it to fall into your capable hands, just for the opportunity to talk to you.

Pomade took the jar. When it didn't immediately open with his first half-hearted twist, he walked to a nearby table and set it down for more leverage. He tried a bit harder for a mere moment, then returned the jar to her. "Sorry."

"Thanks anyway."

The door shut.

Down she went to the lobby, to the place and person she should've consulted in the first place.

"Stevie," Manny said, his short stocky body emerging from behind the desk. "I was wondering... do you have any extra pickles?"

She laughed. "I need your help with this lid, Manny, if you don't mind. I've tried everything. Do you have any tools that can accommodate a lid this big?"

"Probably, in the storage room," he said, taking the jar from her and setting it down. He grasped it and gave it a twist, to no avail. "Damn, it's on there good." He made a second attempt, hugging the jar a little tighter and twisting until his face reddened with effort. Whoosh. The sound of a broken seal.

"You got it! I knew I should have come to you first."

"Someone else tried?"

"My neighbor. Couldn't do it."

He grinned with pride, flexing his arms for her. She laughed, offered him a pickle, and left.

Several pickles later, Stevie checked her tracker for Olive's whereabouts and considered the rescheduling of their appointment. But it didn't show him at DeWitt or anywhere nearby. He was at Milagro Hospital. After breaking into the hospital's records, she discovered that Olive had suffered a beating from another male, sustaining a few broken bones and a head injury. A sweep through police records gave her no clue as to who'd done it.

Probably the friend or boyfriend of one of the women you swear gave her consent. You lucked out, Olive. I'll be watching you, and if you make one wrong move, you'll get far worse than a beating.

Stevie went to her portal and read through the new messages. It was the usual slew. Those not following directions for submission. A few with questionable evidence, to be filed for potential future use. Two with accusations against familiar targets, to be cross-referenced later to determine if they qualified for the next step... preliminary investigation. And finally, two more accusations against Feds.

The first was for a Federal judge. Stevie recognized the name, a judge known for being harsh and sometimes accused of disproportionately putting away the poor over the privileged when it came to sentencing. She'd never trusted Judge Delaney; Stevie had done her research and the numbers supported the accusation. However, while the sentencing discrepancy wasn't the vast one that people assumed, it was still unjust. But it lacked the punch to make headlines or to interest the disciplinary counsel, especially during times of scarce funding.

Today, someone accused Judge Delaney of corruption, of receiving incentives to alter her sentencing practices. The report included the data Stevie already knew about, thoroughly researched and explained in lay terms. The accuser had done some homework instead of merely tossing out accusations with no useful evidence. Yet, just as the local government couldn't afford to do anything about it, neither could she. Not when there were far worse people to hunt. Instead, Stevie logged into another portal and forwarded the carefully gathered data to Judge Delaney herself, adding a brief note that she should be more circumspect in her sentencing.

She moved on to the second accused Fed. Who would it be today? A politician? An exec at the Revenue Department or at Federal Intelligence? Reading through the report, it appeared to obey her guidelines. It was well-written, thorough, professional. She liked those. However, as enjoyable as they were to read, she'd found that, over time, the well-prepared ones produced no more fruit than the less professional or poorly written ones.

This time, the accused was an executive at the Federal Watch program. Someone she probably knew. Which of the nearly all-male cast of power players would serve as scapegoat today? And what egregious offense would he be accused of? She always read the evidence and other information first, leaving the name of the accused for last. Less bias, at least initially. When she read the name, Stevie blinked a couple of times.

Ronald Carr. A woman accused Ronald Carr of molesting her as a child.

She sat for a moment, too many thoughts competing for her attention. It was the first complaint she'd ever received about

Ronald. However, he'd received a promotion that year, placing him in the public eye and making him a more likely target. The complaint, written anonymously by a woman who claimed to have known Ronald and his family, stated that he'd molested her on multiple occasions when she was a child... and would likely do the same with their young daughter Minnie, whom Ronald and Miriam had adopted through Social Services.

Ronald Carr, Steviansa?

I'm as shocked as you are.

You slept at their home, vacationed with them. He never harmed you or behaved inappropriately with you, did he?

No, never.

Sexual abuse. A deed more than worthy of her services... but one of the most difficult to prove. She'd found that of the small handful of child sexual abuse accusations she'd received, many were false, used as a ploy to get her attention, while the rest didn't produce enough evidence to take action. Stevie knew such figures reflected the sort of people who utilized the portal, rather than the actual proportion of guilty abusers. She knew there were countless victims out there, too young to know about the portal or too afraid to speak to someone who might.

She ran through her preliminary analysis. On the one hand, this was her first accusation for Ronald. Also, the allegations, while serious, didn't have as broad an impact on society as others she pursued. The events occurred in the past and may or may not be occurring now, making it difficult to obtain evidence. Finally, the case would require a vast amount of research that had a low likelihood of success. But on the other hand...

Child sexual abuse. One of the most abhorrent of crimes, for too many reasons. It was an offense she found hard to turn her back on, especially when the accused held a position of power. Also, the accuser claimed to know Ronald personally, as do most victims. Teachers, coaches, family members, youth pastors... these trusted superiors had access to children with whom they'd built trust. A disgusting and insidious way to temporarily quench some unsated desire, without consideration of the damage incurred.

You pedophiles... you'd be better off putting a bullet in your head than continuing to convince yourself that you deserve to exist. And if you're too cowardly to pull the trigger, I'm happy to help.

She let out a long, tension-filled breath. Ronald or not, low likelihood of success or not, she would have to follow up on this one.

Stevie broke into the City's justice system and checked their records. Molesters often had numerous victims; once one spoke out, others followed. But she found no accusations filed against Ronald... for that, or for anything. Such a finding, mixed with her own experience growing up around a man who'd treated her almost like a daughter, helped put her at ease. Ronald probably wasn't guilty. But she still had a long journey ahead of her.

A new message appeared. From Mobius.

When you get to work on Monday, take a look at last night's footage from the Passage. Let me know what you find.

M

Stevie headed into Dianthus, encountering a bakery that often had tempting delicacies and a remarkably appetizing smell emanating from it. Almonds and bread. Her stomach already full, she ignored the fleeting temptation until she spotted a chocolate croissant. Seth might appreciate one, perhaps more so than the one from Sage Bakery, where the taxi crash had harmed his ability to enjoy the treat. She ducked into the warm cafe and got in line.

"That was such a hard exam," a young man behind her groused. "I hate essay questions!"

"I didn't think it was that bad," a yellow-haired woman replied.

"Too early, though. Classes shouldn't start until ten. And they should never end after four."

"We'd be fine if we hadn't been out so late," said another Yellow. "Five weeks we waited to get into Miashi's second level, and it was *so* dumb on a Sunday night."

"That didn't stop you from drinking six shots," the young man said.

"You had eight," she countered.

"I had nine," the first Yellow chimed in with a feigned casualness. "I have really good tolerance. I get it from my mom."

"You have the coolest mom ever."

"Whatever, I'm tired. My dad wants me to get a part time job, but I'm like, when am I supposed to have time for that?"

Just as Stevie reached for her earphones, her turn came. She ordered what she needed and glanced around the place with paranoid eyes, wondering if her two feminine stalkers would make an appearance. They seemed to like showing up at eateries, perhaps preferring to stalk on a stomach filled with good food from a small business. But there was no sight of them. She patted the cylinder in her jacket pocket and left.

On the shuttle, Stevie let others fill the seats as she stood holding her warm bag of pastries, the inviting odor wafting up not only to her olfactory sensors, but to others nearby who eyed the bag with envy. Once arrived, Stevie dropped her things off at her desk. As she went to offer her temptations to those she liked, she heard loud laughter. The kind that only occurred among men powerful enough to make an office ruckus without any sort of self-consciousness. The executives.

Ronald.

She hung back, knowing they would guffaw their way from the managers' conference room to the elevator that would return them to their offices above. Once the clatter died down, Stevie left her workstation... and came face to face with Ronald.

She started. "Hi... I mean, good morning, Mister Carr."

He smiled. "Didn't mean to sneak up on you, Stevie."

Friendly with good social skills? Or smooth and charming to disarm young victims, Ronald?

"No problem," she said. "I'm just used to hearing Herbie long before he makes it to my station."

Ronald nodded, acknowledging the truth of Herbie's booming voice. "I've got another meeting to attend, so I'll be quick. The western data produced some problematic individuals... people who shouldn't have been flagged. Will you look into them for me and see if the algorithm needs tweaking?"

"Of course. Just send me the IDs."

"And will you look into a few IDs from the northern region and pull their messaging and phone data?" He turned to find the other execs, who'd disappeared. "I'll need them tonight, but I won't be here after lunch or for the rest of the day, in case you have questions..."

"If needed, I can give you a call. Although I don't think I have your personal number..."

"I'll send it with the IDs. Thanks again."

She'd done it without thinking. Gotten his number. She didn't have access to phone data for the executives, and now she could track him.

She shook her head, uncomfortable with her role in turning Ronald into a target. But it was a necessary evil. Shaking off darker thoughts, Stevie headed to Seth's workstation, gently knocking first to avoid startling him. She opened the bag, encouraging the odor to make its way to Seth's nose. He grinned.

"Whatcha got?" he said, peering inside the bag.

"You get first pick, Captain."

He barely glanced at the other treats before selecting the chocolate croissant. She smiled.

"Thank you, ma'am," he said, taking a big bite. "What are you up to this weekend?"

"Not sure yet... but I'll probably take a trip to Krokus and visit some friends."

"Speaking of that... any news from the Hood on those assholes who defaced the Passage?"

"Not yet. But I'm told the neighborhood is looking into it. They won't let this go."

"They shouldn't." He paused. "You're probably due for your allotment of dead animal soon... there's a joint in my Hood that I want to try. Harry told me about it. He's given it up so he can afford food for the dog, so I said I'd help keep the place in business."

"Sure. When?" she added, careful not to suggest a day this time.

"Saturday? Noon?"

"Perfect."

Lunchtime. Still no dinner, Steviansa.

Mom, we talked about this. He's a friend.

Stevie proceeded to Herbie's office, her shock at seeing him at War Zone having mostly worn off. Marianne sat at her desk, looking even more pregnant than before, something Stevie hadn't thought possible. "Good morning, Marianne. Boss in?"

"Go on in," she said, eyeing Stevie's bag.

Stevie opened it for her. "Would you like one?"

"I'd love one, but Mario here doesn't seem to like sweets," she said, a forlorn look in her eye as she patted her giant belly. "If I'd known, I wouldn't have let James talk me into choosing a boy. All girls love sweets."

Stevie smiled. "I know I do."

After leaving a joyous Herbie munching on a frosted donut, Stevie went back to her workstation to eat the remaining donut. She flipped on her red light and pulled up the Friday evening footage for the Passage. After scrolling through for some time, eventually a group of black-clad, masked young men arrived on scene. Five of them. Within half a minute, two other men emerged from around the corner, one fair and one dark. They wore jeans and brown coats... and each carried something in his hand.

Rope.

The Brownies began rotating their ropes, swinging them round and round above until thrusting them toward the black-clad men. Lassos! By then, the masked men had begun to run. But the lassoes caught two of them and yanked them both to the ground. The Brownies rushed in and pulled off the black masks, fully exposing their faces. The other three offenders stopped and looked back, but when the Brownies pursued them, they ran off. By that time, the lassoed men had wrestled themselves free and taken off in the other direction. Even without sound, Stevie saw that there was shouting. A few other Brownies emerged, ready to help. But it was too late.

Stevie ran through that footage several times, and then footage from two other surveillance cells.

Come on. Give me something.

No full frontals of the lassoed youth, but very good partials for both. She took multiple images from different angles, as the matching program worked more effectively with more data. She began the search and waited. Who would it produce? Gang members from the periphery of Krokus, Viola, or the Outer Rim, eager to have their voices heard? Local teens lacking in parental supervision because one parent worked to put food on the table after the other parent left or perished in the wars? Angry Pansies from Viola, fed up with the Brownies looking down on them?

The excuses they had for the misdeeds of youth, particularly boys. Snips and snails and puppy dog tails, indeed. Where she came from, adolescents stayed out of trouble by working, serving the community, or learning a trade. By making themselves useful instead of expecting their youth to excuse them from responsibility. But now, post war, no one wanted kids to suffer more than they had, so nothing was expected of them. As her mother used to say, *if you don't involve youth in creating a better world, why should they care about it when they become adults?*

When the search ended, the first exposed youth produced several images, all of the same young man. Eighteen years old, brown hair, nice smile. More importantly, the search produced something even better: a university ID. He was a DeWitt student. The search for the other unmasked offender produced three possible matches, including one university ID. When she researched them, one relocated overseas last year and hadn't returned. The second had a very similar face to the third; however, despite their resemblance, the third was several years older than the second. And when she checked their data, the younger of the two was also a student at DeWitt... and lived at the same address as the young man she'd already ID'd.

Got you.

Stevie smiled. If two were from DeWitt, it was quite probable the others were too. But she had no way to identify the other three through those masks.

With one possible exception.

She went through all the footage again, this time attempting to get decent images of the eyes for the other three youth. Iris searches didn't work unless one of the images had good resolution. In most cases, images borrowed from surveillance footage didn't. However, university ID photos did. If the other men were also students at DeWitt, she would have enough data to conduct a successful iris match. When she ran it, she got hits on two of the three masked youth. Another DeWitt student and his brother, a DeWitt graduate.

At home that evening, Stevie logged into one of her portals.

Mobius: What did you find, my lady?

Artemis: I managed to ID four of the five.

Mobius: Four?? If I didn't know you to be utterly humorless, I would think you were frizzing my 'do!

Artemis: No frizzing. How do you want to proceed? I can pull the evidence and the IDs and have it all delivered anonymously to the City... or you and your people can decide how to handle it.

Mobius: Are they Krokus boys?

Artemis: No. Three DeWitt students and an alum.

Long pause.

Mobius: We can't go to the City. They've got a mole there who already sabotaged the City's eyes. But if we go after the perps, especially outside our territory... it could ruin everything. Let me talk to my peeps.

Artemis: Okay. But I just came up with another idea... a better one to run by your people.

The next day, after working late to finish up some work for Ronald, Stevie made her way home and changed into her running clothes. It was sprinkling out, but such drizzle couldn't keep her from taking her favorite excursion... to Blackwood Bridge. If anything, drizzle was refreshing, and it meant sharing the bridge with no one other than the occasional train.

The sprinkle came with an ever-thickening fog. Stevie ran, dodging holes and puddles and electro-taxis and people. Once at the Blackwood's midpoint, the fog consumed the bridge and the Milagro. All she could see of Krokus was the occasional light here and there, between patches of mist. What would become of her old Hood, if west bank youth were allowed to run roughshod over it?

When she got home, she had a message from Mobius.

The news. Watch it starting at 5:01 pm.

M

Four DeWitt students found responsible for Passage of Truth defacement, the headline read.

Two familiar news anchors appeared: an older man with sparkling blue eyes, distinguished gray hair, and a face enhanced by science to smooth the collagen breakdown that accompanied his years... and a decades-younger woman with gorgeous platinum enhanced hair and enhanced eyelashes and lips that accentuated her symmetric face.

The man spoke first. "In a startling development for the Passage of Truth defacement case, an anonymous individual has released surveillance data revealing not only footage of five masked individuals vandalizing the City's famous landmark, but a second visit to the Passage where the young perpetrators engaged in a confrontation with two neighborhood watchmen. During the confrontation, the watchmen managed to remove the face masks of two of the five perpetrators."

Edited footage appeared onscreen, showing the two Brownies and their lassoed catches.

"The anonymous report included names of four of the five perpetrators, who've been identified as three current students and one alumnus of DeWitt University. All surveillance data and information was sent to several organizations, including CityNews, the mayor's office, and City Police. In a statement made just minutes ago, City Police stated that they've corroborated the information supplied by the anonymous whistleblower."

The Chief of Police stood at a podium, a slew of reporters and other officers surrounding him. "With the help of the surveillance team, we have carefully checked the footage and run facial recognition and iris matching analyses. The four perpetrators were correctly identified, we have placed them under arrest, and we will pursue charges against these young men. We are making every effort to identify the fifth perpetrator."

Four images of smiling young men appeared, their faces still skinny with youth.

Chief Jansen went on. "We are a City in recovery from the devastations of war. We will brook no offense of any kind against our public art or landmarks. We have a great respect for the citizens of Crocus and will continue to work with them to ensure that these landmarks are given the respect they deserve."

The news anchors reappeared. "In response to this scandal, the president of DeWitt University also gave a statement."

A gray-haired man in an expensive suit stood in front of a crowd of reporters. "DeWitt University places high value on educating today's young men and women, with the goal that they will go on to contribute to the advancement of our City and become the leaders of tomorrow. We are greatly saddened by the actions of these four men, that they chose to cast off their pledges to be excellent scholars and deface our City's most valuable display of public art. These three men will be expelled from DeWitt University and the fourth, the alumnus, will receive no letter of recommendation for future employment."

The female anchor spoke. "The parents of these students issued public comment and have threatened legal retaliation for what they believe is unfair scapegoating of these young men and for the illegal use of Federal Watch data."

"There is nothing fair about these charges, which are based on illegally obtained data," said a wool-sweatered man in his mid-50s, his face red with sanctimony. "My son and these other young men are being unjustly scapegoated by the City and by DeWitt University, especially when there are far worse crimes being committed every day that will go completely unpunished. Young men often get into trouble; we should be guiding them, not punishing them. They're good boys from good families. They made a mistake."

The female anchor continued. "Many have raised questions about where this surveillance footage came from, and why no one came forward sooner. The City claims the data did not originate from their sources, asserting that their footage from the night of the original incident was sabotaged. An independent investigation has been initiated to examine why the City's surveillance data went missing, and to examine data from the Federal Watch program that is currently run from the Disc. Federal Watch was designed to protect our country from more terrorist attacks. And while the data cannot be used for other purposes, including non-terrorist-related criminal investigation, the Disc has agreed that it will investigate whether the footage originated from the program. CityNews will keep you fully updated on this case. Stay tuned."

You've put yourself and the hand that feeds you at risk, Steviansa. And for what? A handful of spoiled kids who will face no punishment because the evidence will get thrown out when they discover its source.

Punishment or not, people need to see the truth for themselves, Mom. If that brings heat upon the Disc, or me, then so be it.

I didn't raise you to take such risks, Steviansa. I didn't work to put you through university and graduate school, just so you could throw it all away.

Stevie turned off the news. Fear nipped at her, hovering like a giant shadow, a monster that threatened to overwhelm her. Maybe she'd gone too far. She'd covered her tracks, as always, but one never knew. Even cautious people made mistakes, and the right person looking at the right time could begin putting together clues that she'd done the deed. And if caught, she would face charges of her own and lose her job... and with it her power to do what mattered most. Yes, the defacement was important. She knew it was, otherwise she would've told Mobius no or found some other way to punish the offenders. However, faced with protecting the place she came from, where she felt at home... perhaps she'd risked too much.

She remained on her couch, beginning the long wait until tomorrow.

Stevie stood on the shuttle, wondering if others would watch her more carefully that day, if they'd take new notice of her light brown skin and dark hair, if they'd wonder whether she was the leak, the former Krokusian seeking to protect her own.

Of course they see you, Steviansa. What you did was stupid, and you deserve to pay for it.

Stop it, Mom.

Don't you mouth off to me.

Stop, Mom! I'm not a child anymore.

Stevie kept her face neutral as she made her way to her workstation. Before she could even start up her computer, Seth appeared unexpectedly, making her jump.

"I scared you again? I didn't say anything!"

She shook her head. "Sorry. Too much coffee today."

"Did you hear?"

"Hear what?"

"Hear what? They found those motherfuckers who defaced the Passage. Some bunch of rich assholes from DeWitt. Their parents got them all big lawyers and they're talking about suing."

She nodded. "I did hear."

"And? What does the Brownie in you think of all this?"

She let out a breath. "What kind of world do we live in, Seth, where parents defend the actions of their children as if they're three or four, rather than eighteen or twenty?"

"Beats me. If I'd done this even as a young kid, my folks would've whipped my ass."

"Me too."

"Well... the interesting thing is that those surveillance data came from somewhere. And there are only two potential sources, the City and us."

"Both illegally obtained. I don't see how it could be the City. DeWitt's a big tax base for them, which is probably why their data got sabotaged in the first place."

"I was thinking the same thing," he said, glancing around. "What do you think about their punishment?"

She looked down for a moment. *Tell the truth. He's your friend.* "To be honest with you, and I hope I don't seem cruel or callous here... I'm glad they got caught and I think they deserve what they'll get.

And it isn't because I'm from Krokus. It's because the actions of those young men... they represent everything wrong with us, with our society. A scandal like this... maybe it will help put us on the right path."

And with that, a breeze of calm came over Stevie. Then she knew... it was all worth it.

When Seth left, Stevie sat down and got to work. After an hour or so, someone knocked on her partition. When she turned around, Herbie stood there, navy suit buttoned over a red tie, the expression on his dark face serious.

"Hi Boss," Stevie said. "What can I do for you?"

"I need you to come with me, Stevie. Right now, please."

EPISODE 6
SLEEPLESS IN ARTEMISIA

No Miss, no greeting, no pleasantries.

Stevie stood and followed Herbie. Fear flooded her, despite her resolve about what she'd done. Instead of heading to his office, Herbie led her to the stairwell. Up they went to the executive floor, the place she hadn't been since Herbie gave her mother a tour years ago. The first thing Stevie noticed was the quiet. No voices or humming computers, and what little sound existed seemed to get lost in the plush carpet, the upholstered furniture, and the framed paintings that hung on the walls.

They knew. They knew by now that the Passage surveillance footage originated from the Disc and not the City. And they knew where she came from, where her loyalties lay. They shouldn't know that she leaked the data—she had ways of preventing that, ways even Technology couldn't detect—but it was always possible that some other source had identified her.

Mobius? No. She would never.

Stevie knew what happened next. Herbie would lead her to one of the conference rooms, where men in expensive suits would sit around the table and wait for her to stand before them, like the men sat lining the gauntlets at the bars. They would stare, sizing her up. Their minds would begin assessing whether her actions matched her appearance, if the intricacy of her corrupt act was commensurate with her attractiveness quotient. After that, they would begin feeling a misguided outrage that her actions didn't fit those expected of her gender, that she'd somehow reached the tails of the distribution of normal female behavior. And nothing she said would matter. Once you behaved outside of people's beliefs and expectations, you were guilty in their eyes, of far more than any crime you committed.

But instead of bringing her to a conference room, Herbie led her to an office with a familiar name on the door. Ronald Carr.

Herbie knocked before opening the door. And they entered Ronald's sizable office, with its black leather couch, large viewing screen, several tall plants, and an unobstructed view of their City. Ronald sat back in his tall chair, watching them. Stevie waited while Herbie, still silent, shut the door. They sat, sweat forming in her armpits.

"Stevie," Ronald began. "You've heard, I presume, about the Passage of Truth scandal."

She nodded. "Of course."

He watched her with brown eyes that lacked their usual warmth. "The surveillance footage that's all over the news... we had it analyzed this morning. It didn't originate from the City. It came from us." He paused, leaning forward. "Stevie, I don't need to tell you what a delicate situation this is, or what the repercussions are. But I've known you for a long time and I need you to be honest with me."

She nodded.

"Did you leak these data?"

She shook her head. "I didn't."

"Do have any information about how this happened?"

"I don't. I'm sorry."

Ronald's jaw tightened. "You worked late on multiple occasions, Stevie. Nothing Herb and I assigned you would warrant such late hours."

"Herbie asked me to analyze the messaging data for the entire population, and you requested some extra help. I don't often need to work late, but it's easier to run the more intensive analyses at night, when there are fewer distractions and fewer demands on our systems.

If you pull the logs, you'll see what I worked on those nights."

But you already checked those. You're baiting me.

"You were also seen in Crocus, at the Passage, twice after this incident occurred."

Ah.

Stevie remained still. "I have friends there, Sir. Friends I've known since childhood."

"You've known Kira since childhood. How often do you go to Acacia to visit her?"

Stevie noticed Herbie shift in his seat.

"We've lost touch, Sir. I'm sorry to say it, but we have. I had lunch with a friend in Krokus a few Saturdays ago. She's the one who showed me the vandalism. And I went back again after that."

Ronald gave a faint nod and stared at her for a moment. He turned to Herbie. "Would you excuse us, Herb?"

"Of course," Herbie said, glancing at Stevie before he got up and left.

Stevie absorbed Ronald's stare and waited for him to begin the real inquiry.

Go ahead, Ronald. If you have something on me, hit me with it. Threaten me, if you must. But don't be surprised when I come back at you with my own bargaining chip, one that keeps me working at the Disc. True or not, those allegations about you will hurt you... if they go public.

But Ronald merely sat there, perhaps hoping to discompose her before revealing what he knew. Finally, he spoke.

"I understand, Stevie. I understand why you might choose to do something like this. Although I see you as a fellow Artemisian, I know your Crocus roots are quite strong... perhaps as strong as your mother's were. I know how passionate you Brownies can be, and that the lens with which you view the ills of our society may be different from everyone else's."

Stevie went to speak, but Ronald put his hand up.

"Years ago, when I was with Federal Intelligence, I once leaked information to Federal Law Enforcement. I won't cite the specifics, but let's just say that the person I sought to punish paid a price... a price he deserved to pay. However, the incident led to an inquiry that lasted over a year, taking away from other important work. It harmed our reputation with Law Enforcement, with many of the other federal agencies, and with several foreign governments. To put it in your language, Stevie, it's like... it's like altering a line of code in the middle of a script. You think you're fixing one contained problem, but then you realize that small change impacts other portions of the script and can sabotage your end result. I never got caught, but the damage was far greater than the wrongdoings of the individual I punished. And I've had to live with that mistake.

"I'm not concerned about the leaked footage. Those spoiled DeWitt piss-ants can kiss my ass." Stevie smiled at that. "What concerns me is future leaks, and the erosion of trust in what we're doing here. If you tell me the truth now, I can mitigate the damage. If, however, you do not come forward, the consequences will be far worse down the road. In my experience, 'down the road' comes more swiftly than you can imagine. So, from a friend to a friend... did you leak that footage?"

Stevie sighed. "I understand why you would suspect me, why anyone would. And I admit that a part of me is glad this happened. But it wasn't me."

Ronald stood. He glanced out his sizable window for a moment before coming around to the other side of his desk and taking a seat where Herbie had been. His jaw was still tight, his eyes aflame with emotion. "It's just you and me here, Stevie. I know you, I know your character, and I can handle this for you, for all of us. What I can't handle is some unknown agent using Federal Watch data for his or her own agenda. I won't tolerate it. I won't let our reputation fall asunder. Do you understand?"

Growing more uncomfortable, Stevie nodded. "I do, Sir."

He stood. "You can go."

Bundled up in her soft robe and sipping her post-dinner espresso, Stevie sat down to watch the news. She searched for the latest coverage and selected it. After the perfect-faced blonde anchor finished her summary, Ronald appeared onscreen in one of his nicer suits. Miriam stood next to him in a blue dress, her light brown hair in a bun. Stevie couldn't help but smile at the sight of them, and could almost taste the potato chips Miriam would let her snack on during her visits to the Carr home.

Ronald spoke. "The defacing of one of our City's most iconic symbols has been an upsetting event for us all. Those who would show disrespect for our public art, and for the neighborhood of Crocus, deserve full punishment for their actions... and we are pleased that the City has taken this offense seriously. However," Ronald looked down for a moment, "it is problematic that these youth were identified using Federal Watch data. When the Federal Watch program began five years ago, we made several promises to all of you. We promised to protect our great City and country from those who would harm us. We promised that we would protect each and every citizen's right to privacy. We also promised that Federal Watch data would not be used for criminal investigations, with the exception of terrorist activities. And we have every intention of honoring those promises." He paused. "The program has been a great success. We have detained those who would plot against us, we have prevented more attacks, and this incident reflects the only time these data have been misused. We are taking every measure to investigate and contain this leak, and we will continue putting the safety of our people first."

Stevie turned off the news.

She'd had close calls before. Most were necessary. Calculated risks... but risks nonetheless. As satisfying it was to expose the perpetrators and to show people that an unfettered upbringing could prove destructive to society, Ronald was right about the manifold repercussions of such acts. The fallout impacted her too—because of this incident, everyone would watch her closely now. She would have to avoid personal use of Disc data for a while, severely curtailing her other acts of service. She would also have to postpone tracking Ronald or accessing his phone data. The dust needed to settle, and it would leave a mess to clean up. And there was nothing she could do about that.

From the corner of her eye, she saw movement. She glanced at her hallway surveillance... Pomade's yellow-haired girlfriend ringing at his door. She looked nice in her dress and black coat, her makeup freshly applied. Stevie turned away until a loud noise made her start. Pomade's door slamming shut. The neatly coiffed Financial had never learned that a door would shut if one merely closed it, rather than shoving it to a loud finish.

Late that night, Stevie was awakened by squeaking. Pomade's bed. Faster, and faster... then a loud grunt. And then silence.

Stevie shook her head and closed her eyes again.

"Double espresso, please."

Machine did his admirable job and poured the steamy goodness into her black cup. She ordered Seth's khaki and waited patiently for it, taking a quick sip of her own delicious pleasure.

"Did they come at you about the Passage thing?" Seth asked when she brought him his coffee. He spoke in a hushed tone.

"They did. I'm a natural suspect."

He shook his head. "What do you say this weekend, instead of going to the joint in my Hood, we go see the Passage? Maybe get some of those dumplings you Brownies are famous for?"

"Sure. Still noon?"

"Maybe a little later... head out there around three, look around for a while, then go eat afterward?"

Dinner.

"Um, sure. Perfect."

"I'll pick you up at your building..."

She nodded and returned to her desk.

But by the time she'd finished her espresso, something nagged at her. She headed upstairs to the tranquility of the executive floor. At Ronald's office, his young yellow-haired assistant looked at her.

"Hi. May I drop in on Mister Carr? It will only take a minute."

The Yellow got on the phone and spoke quietly before turning back to Stevie. "Go on in."

"Thank you."

Stevie gave Ronald's door a quick knock before she opened the door. Ronald looked up, his brown eyes still with a veneer of chill. He said nothing, merely waiting for her to speak.

"I don't mean to bother you. Seth and I... you know Seth... we're going to Krokus this Saturday, to see the Passage and to spend time there. I thought, with all that's happened, that I should inform you first. And make sure you're okay with it."

He gave a faint nod. "Thank you for letting me know." He turned back to his computer.

Stevie hesitated for a moment before she left. As she clattered down the metal stairs, Stevie felt something she hadn't in a long time.

Guilt.

Ronald trusted her. They all did. And she'd violated that trust.

That evening, when she got home, she had a message from Mobius.

Mobius: I'm worried about you. Are you okay?

Artemis: I think so.

Mobius: No evidence?

Artemis: Only strong suspicion. I'll have to keep a very low profile.

Mobius: Shit. Fuck. I shouldn't have asked for this from you.

Artemis: It's not your fault. The last part... it was my idea.

Mobius: Still... It's better if we don't talk for a while.

Artemis: Agreed.

Long after Stevie went to bed, she awakened to shouting. A woman. She sat up, her heart pounding.

"You take me for granted! I saw you looking at those girls tonight!"

Stevie glanced at the time. After two in the morning.

"I'm a man!" came the response, in a voice that was deeper but just as petulant. "All men look at women! Don't be so fucking insecure."

"No woman wants a guy who stares at every woman except the one he's with."

"Then fucking leave. Go find Mister Perfect. Good luck with that."

"You're such a jerk!"

"You're an insecure bitch. And I'm tired of this conversation."

And then silence.

Yes, Girlfriend. Leave. You can do better than him!

Stevie lay there, hoping that Girlfriend had the wisdom to make her exit, that she would recognize that the cost-benefit ratio of associating herself with Pomade was not in her favor. At last, Stevie fell back to sleep. Until she was awakened again... squeak, squeak, squeak, then a grunt. Stevie sighed, checking the time. After 3 am. And not long afterward, she heard muffled talking, which turned to shouting, this time about their sexual encounter. Stevie threw her covers aside. She dragged her comforter and pillow out to the couch, where she tucked herself in. Sometime near 4:30 am, she fell back to sleep.

Another yawn.

Stevie shook her head and raised her desk to its standing position. She considered paying a visit to her mechanical friend for an extra shot of espresso, but stopped herself. If she couldn't handle one night of poor sleep, she was a pitiful individual, indeed. And if she couldn't tolerate unnecessary noise from Pomade and his girlfriend from time to time, then she needed to work on her patience. Just like she would patiently wait until the noise from the Passage scandal quieted down.

After a long day and a quick dinner at the Tarragon Noodle Bar, Stevie looked forward to climbing into bed and sleeping off the jangling ups and downs of the past few days. She had research to do before work the next morning, so she set her alarm for earlier than usual. Without even checking the portal, she climbed into her soft sheets and fell asleep.

Shouting. Stevie didn't shoot up in bed this time, didn't feel the gut-level fear at hearing a woman cry out. She lay there, knowing exactly what she heard. She tried to ignore it, but on it went, Pomade and Girlfriend lobbing arguments at one another in the misguided belief that doing so would yield something valuable instead of a stubborn adherence to their own perspectives. Earplugs offered no real protection against the shouting. Just when it simmered down, allowing her to drift off, it boiled again. Irritated, she dressed herself and stood at Pomade's door.

When the door opened, a shirtless Pomade appeared. His midsection was surprisingly soft for a man of his age and swagger... but his hair was perfect.

She forced a smile, in the tiny hope it would help. "Hi. I don't mean to butt in to your argument, but would you mind taking it into another room? My bedroom is next to yours and you're keeping me up."

Pomade looked at her, his eyes flat and lifeless. "I do mind." The door slammed shut.

Stevie stood there, anger spreading through her.

You can't take that approach with Financials, Steviansa. They thrive on thrills, emotion... not reason. They often lack empathy, so you have to persuade them using other methods.

Ah, so I should be irrational and ill-tempered, like a child.

Stevie went back to her apartment. She stood in her bedroom, waiting for the racket to return. When it didn't, she got into bed.

She'd barely gotten comfortable before they started up again. Quieter at first, but inevitably loud. Stevie snatched up her comforter and pillow. But halfway to her couch, she knew she wouldn't sleep. Not while she was this agitated. She went back to her bedroom and pulled out her running gear.

In the lobby, Manny eyed her with disapproval. "At this hour?"

"To the bridge," was all she said.

When she returned, covered in sweat and far less angry, Stevie stripped down, took a brief shower, and settled in on her couch. When the lights awakened her what seemed like minutes later, she was tempted to order them off and sleep another couple of hours.

No. Get up.

She dragged herself out of bed, grabbed the bag she'd prepared, and left. She walked to a nearby cafe, a dead zone due to its delayed retrofitting, and went straight to the restroom to change.

Artemisia... so a wig of long, unadorned hair. Shapewear for her hips... moderate, not Rosa. A skirt, tights, ankle boots, and a black coat. Top it off with blue contact lenses and a black fedora. When she emerged from the stall, she checked the mirror. Yes. That was it.

Outside, it had begun to sprinkle. She opened her umbrella and headed south, then east, to a section of Artemisia with single-family homes, large stone mansions that had survived time and war. When she arrived at the Larkspur Diner, she claimed a seat in the back, against the wall, momentarily recalling Seth and his seating preferences. She sent in her order from the console, glancing at the salt-and-pepper-haired man seated several tables away.

Hello, Mister Carr.

Ronald read his tablet, sipping plain drip coffee with milk and eating a brand new stack of pancakes, just as he had nearly every morning during all the years she'd known him.

"Daddy, why do you like pancakes so much?" Kira once asked him, when school wasn't in session and he'd brought her and Stevie with him to the diner.

"Because they're delicious," he said. "And because the ingredients are easy to grow. We need to conserve our resources, honey. We're at war."

That had stuck with Stevie. It was the first time she'd considered that one's food choices impacted the world, that some foods had greater environmental and economic cost than others. Her mother had eventually taught her the importance of such things. But it was Ronald who'd brought it to her attention first, at an age when her mother only told her what she would eat, without explanation.

Ronald continued reading, glancing up only to thank the young female server for warming his coffee. He didn't steal a glimpse of her walking away. On a couple of occasions, he offered a brief greeting to a fellow customer, likely another creature of habit who liked the Larkspur Diner's particular brand of pancakes.

When Stevie's pancakes and khaki arrived, she thanked the server in a high, feminine voice. She sipped her Seth-inspired coffee in her Seth-inspired seat, wondering why he preferred the milky concoction. It was pleasant... but it wasn't coffee, not with the bovine adornment that masked the brilliance of the beans.

Soon, as she'd hoped, several parents entered the diner, toting their children with them to get a quick bowl of grains or some eggs and toast before going to school. And she watched.

Nothing.

No staring, no surreptitious look at a cute little girl with long curls or an older girl with a dark ponytail. He didn't even attempt the stolen glance, the one that gets repeated periodically, as if a series of brief looks somehow counted for less than one long one. But nothing. Ronald finished his meal, put on his trench coat, and left for work.

After cleaning her plate, Stevie paid in currency and left. She darted back to the dead zone cafe, changed back into her own clothing, and purchased an espresso before heading back home to get ready for work.

"I want to settle down!" Girlfriend whined. "Don't you want a family, and children?"

Stevie lay in bed, her cortisol levels rising upon being subjected to another conversation she had no interest in.

"Of course I do! I want all that, to have a family and a nice home. I want what my parents have. But I need more time to build my fortune first!"

"But you have plenty just on your salary alone!"

"Look, the market is unstable right now. I need a lot more saved before I'd even consider supporting a family. It's the responsible thing to do. Why do I keep having to repeat myself again and again?"

"If we got married, we could save together, before we have kids."

"It's better to save now. This place is cheaper than what I can afford and I can put money away."

"We could save money if I moved in—"

"You know how I feel about moving in together before marriage!"

"We could get married," she insisted.

"I don't want to get married until I have more saved."

Stevie groaned. She'd been out late, shadowing Ronald Carr again, in a different disguise. Between that and many days of her neighbors' late night feuds, sleep had become a rarity. She grabbed her conformer and pillow and thrust them upon her couch.

Why don't you just leave your bedding here, at least until the City's most dysfunctional couple splits up, gets married, or participates in a murder-suicide?

Nestled into her couch, after coaxing her sympathetic nervous system back into sleep mode, she heard shouting. They'd taken their squabbling into the hallway. She tossed her comforter aside, dressed herself, and opened her door to stare down the verbose offenders. They didn't notice her.

"Hey!"

Pomade and Girlfriend looked at her in surprise, as if she'd appeared by magic.

"I need you two to take your arguing somewhere else. You've kept me up all week long."

Girlfriend looked somewhat remorseful, but Pomade didn't.

"Mind your own goddamned business, will you?" he said in disgust.

"You make that impossible with your constant fighting, *neighbor*." She glanced at Girlfriend and softened her tone. "I can recommend a good couple's therapist."

"No one else has complained," Pomade went on, his voice more nasally than ever. "And you'd probably understand what it's like to have couple's problems if you could manage to attract a man." Girlfriend tugged at him, urging him to stop, but he shook her off.

"I need you to keep it down," Stevie said, more pointedly this time.

He scoffed. "Or you'll what? Tell your butchy girlfriend to come kick my ass?"

She shook her head. Pomade sounded like a snotty schoolgirl, but for the first time Stevie saw something else, something other than an arrogant, spoiled Financial with perfect hair. Something worse. Before Stevie could respond, Girlfriend spoke.

"It's okay... I'm leaving." She gave Stevie a look of chagrin. "Sorry."

Stevie shut the door. She stood in the dark, taking several deep breaths to calm herself, wishing she had a virtual experience program to deal with anger, like she had for dealing with other primal feelings. Pomade's comments about her attractiveness, or her being single, didn't bother her. But losing sleep did... as did the fact that the world rewarded the behavior of men like Pomade.

Men like him... they didn't murder, didn't rape. Most didn't even intentionally defraud the public, instead choosing to exploit a system where their avarice had free reign. But they created a ripple effect that spread far and wide, that impacted every girlfriend, friend, coworker, neighbor, barista, waiter or waitress, or electro-taxi driver they came into contact with. Florid self-interest was no crime... but it was a disease, an insidious cancer that no one detects until it's too late, until a tumor has developed and metastasized to all that surrounds it.

How many days in a row had this happened now? She'd lost count. It was all a blur of work, listening to fighting, tailing Ronald, more fighting, embarrassingly one-way sex, work, and more fighting. Couples fought. They had conflicts. But she didn't need to know about them. She didn't need her place of solace invaded by the scourge of such people.

After thinking about it for some time, Stevie knew exactly what to do.

Stevie woke to her luminescent alarm, only a mere three hours of sleep under her belt. Excuses for not rising for her day tempted her like whiskey poured near an alcoholic.

No. No sick days. You'll need them when the shakeup from the Passage scandal dies down, when you'll have to make up for lost time.

Stevie stood, the bright light doing little to awaken her. She bumped her toe on the glass coffee table, almost letting out an expletive as pain shot up her leg. In her shower, the steam did nothing to lift her fatigue, her tile beckoning her to lean on its whiteness for just a moment's rest.

One sick day. Sleep. You're too exhausted to be useful at work.

No. It's just sleep deprivation. Deal with it and stop complaining.

Stevie drank a triple espresso before she left, the dark elixir barely denting her exhaustion. Only walking to the shuttle and feeling the breeze from the gray sea gave her any sense of refreshment. She hoped it would last.

By lunchtime she'd paid two more visits to Machine, his kind service the only thing that allowed her to get any work done. However, her projects took longer than usual and she made mistakes, which required more time for corrections. By afternoon, she'd nodded off three times, even after raising her desk to a standing position. She considered flipping on her red light and allowing herself a nap. But she couldn't risk it, not when Ronald and others no longer trusted her. She left her desk and got in line at Machine.

"Triple espresso, please," she said, when her turn came.

She placed her black cup under the spout, her fatigue already beginning to lift. Once finished, she took a sip of her concoction and headed back to her desk. But a short while later, she nodded off again. The espresso seemed to have no effect on her. Had she reached some plateau, beyond which the effects of 1,3,7-trimethylxanthine were rendered moot? Or was she so tired that the stimulant had too steep a gradient to climb in order to impact her nervous system? She gave herself a light slap on each cheek and glanced at the time. Three hours to go. A strange hopelessness set in.

Seth appeared. He took one look at her and his expression changed. "What's wrong?"

"I can't keep my eyes open. I've had... loud noise... in my building all week long. I haven't slept much. I can't stay awake, and I don't know how I'll get through the day... if someone sees me falling asleep, they'll wonder. They'll wonder about me. They're already suspicious of me because of the Passage scandal..." She trailed off, knowing her words rambled almost as incoherently as her thoughts did.

"Why don't you grab an espresso?"

"I did!" she said, trying to control the snappiness of her tone. "It isn't working."

"Are you sure it's caffeinated?"

"Of course. I never order decaf." But then it hit her... Machine could have gotten it wrong. She pulled out her pipette and aimed it at the dregs of her cup. The indicator light turned green. Decaf. Stevie let out a breath. Damn him.

"How many have you had today, before the decaf?" Seth said.

"A lot."

Seth glanced at Machine in the distance, shaking his head. "I know it sounds crazy, but I'm convinced that motherfucker messes with people sometimes. But maybe he's right this time. You need sleep, not more coffee." He checked his watch. "I'm leaving soon. You can come to my place to sleep it off. It's quiet there."

She shook her head. "I can't. My leaving early looks bad."

"Just tell Herbie you're sick and that you'll work late tomorrow." When he saw her resistance, he went on. "You need sleep. I know all about sleep deprivation, Stevie. It's all downhill from here."

Too tired to argue anymore, Stevie nodded.

Once on the shuttle, Stevie sat down next to Seth, no longer concerned about allowing others to sit first. Not that it mattered; there were fewer people commuting at this hour, as most didn't have the inclination or the discipline to get up early enough to warrant leaving at 3:30. She leaned back and took a deep breath. Soon, she would get to lay her head down and shut out the world.

"Stevie."

She opened her eyes and sat up.

"We've landed," Seth said.

She looked around, momentarily disoriented. She'd fallen asleep on Seth's shoulder.

He chuckled. "You are tired. I started talking to you and when you didn't answer..."

Stevie gave a groggy smile.

"You need to get anything from your place?"

"I do. I'll be over in an hour."

After Stevie went home and collected her things, she left and headed west to the sturdy simplicity of Salvia and its mostly pre-war buildings. She passed a few vacant lots, including the one near Charlie Street that would make a good location for a green zone. She imagined Harry standing on the grass while the black lab formerly known as Goldie fetched a ball Harry threw for her. Or Seth, sitting on a bench, reading or perhaps watching the nearby children to ensure they were safe. She stopped off at a noodle bar to pick up lemongrass chicken for Seth and fried tofu for herself.

When she passed Sage Bakery, it reminded her of her two stalkers. She almost hoped they would've accosted her in some darkened lot, just so she could deploy her homemade method of defense and borrow a small sampling of DNA from both women. The things she could do with such information. But she'd seen no sign of the tawny mohawk or the gray-streaked hair. Maybe it was a coincidence after all, their showing up where she was on two occasions. Maybe the staring was nothing more than a recognition of a fellow Brownie who'd defected to the west bank. Or, more likely, the two women hadn't found sufficient reason to continue following her. Nonetheless, her little cylinder sat quietly in her pocket anytime she ventured outdoors.

When she arrived at Seth's building, she approached the swarthy doorman.

"Seth told me you were coming," he said. "Go on up."

"Thank you."

Seth opened his door and stood aside to let her in, his gaze shifting from her to the bag of food. "You didn't have to do that," he said, taking the bag from her.

She glanced around Seth's spotless home before her eyes settled upon his impressive collection of violent artifacts. His Peruvian Apple cactus stood watch nearby, and she went over to check that its sunburn hadn't worsened. It hadn't. Seth got out plates while Stevie sat down at the black, two-person dining table and unwrapped their dinner. He poured her some water, popped the top off a beer, and sat down.

"How'd you know I like lemongrass chicken?" he said.

"I've seen you eat it at work."

They ate in silence for a time, Stevie unsure what to say. She never ate dinner with anyone else. Finally, she had a thought. "Did you or Harry give any more consideration to sending in a proposal for a green zone?"

He nodded, swallowing his food before he spoke. "Yep. Harry's been all over that for a while now, scoping out locations and asking some of the other vets if they'll help out. I think the lot at Charlie and 30th looks good, and so does Harry. Like you said, less cleanup."

"Good. Let me know when he submits the proposal."

Once finished with their meal, she helped Seth clean up before she went to his bathroom to change into her sleepwear. When she came out, Seth had created a makeshift bed on his couch.

"I'll take the couch," he said.

She shook her head. "You're already doing me a big favor. I

wouldn't feel right." Before Seth could argue, Stevie settled onto the couch and pulled the soft blankets over her.

Stevie headed up DeWitt Street, tired from a day's work but feeling better after a good night's sleep and respite from Pomade and Girlfriend's toxic fumes. She passed another new chem shop, a line of men in button-downs and women in DeWitt garb waiting for their dose of temporary numbing. Soon, she found the place, hoping she wasn't too late: a pink and black bar filled with patrons sipping expensive pink drinks while women in little pink dresses flitted here and there. Stevie scanned the sea of yellow hair until she located her. Pomade's girlfriend.

She was with two other women, of course. Women like her never went anywhere alone. As Stevie approached their table, Girlfriend spotted her. Their chitchat ceased as the other two turned to stare.

Stevie smiled at Girlfriend, hoping to put her at ease. "Hi. I don't mean to interrupt your time with your friends, but can I talk to you?"

Girlfriend glanced at her Yellow friends. "Sure." She stood and followed Stevie outside to the relative privacy of the street. Before Stevie could say anything, Girlfriend spoke. "I'm sorry we kept you up the other night. We're doing much—"

"It wasn't just the other night. It was every night this week, and others in the past." Girlfriend's face fell at Stevie's curt interruption. "I know you two are struggling and I don't mean to make it worse. I didn't come down here to talk about the noise."

"Then why did you come?"

"To tell you something. You can do a lot better than him." Girlfriend looked down, weighing her own recognition of the truth along with the manifold arguments that kept her with him. "I've heard him and his friends talk in a disrespectful way about going out to pick up women to sleep with."

Girlfriend shook her head. "That's man talk. All Financials do that."

"Okay... but he also talks disrespectfully to you."

"Only when he's drunk. He can actually be very sweet."

"A man's behavior when he drinks tells you who he really is," Stevie said. "He's also rude to me, even when he's sober."

"He can be that way. But men like him... they always calm down when they're married."

"When they're the marrying kind." Girlfriend shook her head, glancing inside at her friends, who watched them through the window. "I hear things. I hear when you and he have sex. I hear him every time, but I never hear you."

She scowled. "That's none of your business."

"I don't want it to be my business. But I still hear it."

"What do you know about having sex with a man?" she said angrily.

"I know that a man who only pleases himself in bed is worthless. Financials can be hard to pin down. They live for their work and for the challenge. But if they can work that hard to make money and to outperform their colleagues, they can spend some time on their partners in bed. If they don't, it's because they don't want to and don't care."

Stevie waited for more head-shaking, for Girlfriend to walk away from the pain that Stevie doled out. But instead, her eyes filled with tears. "It's hard to find a good one, one that's successful and can provide for his family. I want that."

"I know," Stevie said. "But when you tolerate a man's bad behavior, even if it's only bad sometimes, you tell him and all other men that you aren't a high quality woman. You give your diamonds to a thief. You can call me a lesbian or make fun of the fact that I'm alone, but at least my diamonds are mine. Do you understand?"

Girlfriend nodded faintly, carefully dabbing at a couple of tears so her makeup wouldn't smear.

"You're pretty, with good manners," Stevie said. "Find someone better. And thank you, for talking to me."

Stevie turned and left.

The mural of blocky purple letters and the upside-down crocus welcomed Stevie and Seth's train to Krokus, a wee bit of sun warming them through the window. She glanced at Seth, who seemed to brighten at the sun's rays, like a sunflower opening its petals.

After stepping off the train, they strolled along the streets teeming with denim and pleather. A trio of brass musicians let out a rousing melody on the corner, and she thought of Herbie and the colorful jazz painting in his office. Three green electro-bikes whizzed by at daring speeds, enjoying the fairer weather for as long as it would last.

"I want one of those," Seth said, eyeing the bikers as they sped past.

"Really?"

"Oh, yeah. Just for weekends. I'd take it out of the City, on the open road."

"They aren't as fast as they look."

"I know. But it would still be fun."

They passed gallery after gallery of art, from the very affordable to the unimaginably expensive. The latter had potential customers ranging from lookie-loos who could never justify the cost, to more affluent west bank types searching for something to clad their personal spaces. When they reached a gallery filled with paintings of weaponry, including antique weaponry, Seth halted. Stevie smiled as she followed him inside, not having imagined a better place to encourage Seth's appreciation of Krokus's art scene. He hovered longest near a painting with a blood red background and a .357 Magnum revolver as its subject. It wasn't an Oakenfold, but it was still a nice piece.

They continued on until arriving at the concrete walls of the Passage of Truth, where a large crowd assembled as it usually did on the Passage's busiest day of the week. Stevie and Seth beheld the murals in the waning daylight. When they approached the war murals, including the one that had been tarnished, Stevie felt a flash of excitement. Someone had repaired its blemishes.

Seth eyed it. "I can't see where those little fuckers damaged it."

"I can't either. Hours of painstaking work, but it looks great."

They approached the newest one, depicting the defacers holding their minuscule penises. Seth laughed, just as he had when they'd first spoken of it, his smile lines bringing joy to his face. "This one's my favorite."

"Enjoy it... it probably won't last."

"Why not?"

She shrugged. "The Hood won't want to honor them. They'll want to move on to something more meaningful."

When they made their way farther down the Passage, Stevie spotted a crowd gathered at the far end.

"Is there a new one?" Seth asked, eyes scanning the crowd.

She smiled. "I hope so."

When they drew closer, the sight of three painted faces above the crowd told her Seth's suspicion was correct. They waited their turn, for those who blocked their view to scatter and reveal the new creation. What would it be this time? Finally, they got their view.

A portrait. The background had a building-lined street in perspective. In the foreground stood three people: a gray-haired woman, a dark-haired woman, and a curly-haired girl. All stood straight and proud, their eyes making strong contact with their audience. The elder held a book, the middle a weapon, and the child a set of ancient scales. Knowledge, protection, justice. Stevie gasped.

When she looked down at the mural's lower right corner, she saw it. Instead of the artist's signature, there was a symbol. A letter D, a letter O, and a letter A, in their familiar design.

The Daughters of Anarchy.

EPISODE 7

ROSES ARE RED, VIOLETS ARE DEAD

Stevie stared.

"I don't get it," Seth said. "What's the big deal, other than it's three generations of women?"

"Look at the signature."

Seth's eyes tracked down. "I still don't get it."

"Have you ever heard of the Daughters of Anarchy?"

He raised his eyebrows. "I thought they were a myth."

"They were real. But they've become myth because no one's seen that insignia since the second war began."

He looked dubious. "There's really some underground organization of just women who protect society?"

"Why is that hard to believe?"

He started to speak, but stopped himself. "No reason."

"Come on, Seth. Speak your mind."

He faced her, crossing his robust arms. "I don't see it. Women don't gather like that, outing crooked politicians and organizing bombings of terrorist nests. They don't kill people. They do a lot, but not that."

"What about all the women who served in the wars?"

"They served with us... not on their own. And a lot of them weren't in combat. Militaries have traditionally been all-male for a reason."

Even your generation of military men think women aren't made for combat, Steviansa. Some things never change.

Stevie, more surprised by Seth's opinion than she should've been, went on. "You don't believe women are capable of organizing in this way or protecting others without men involved?"

"Not really. I've never seen it. I don't know if it's because they aren't capable of it, or they just don't bother because there are plenty of men willing to. Like I told you before, I don't think it's women's character to take those kinds of risks or to be that violent. Maybe it's nature's way. Someone has to protect the kids, so nature gave women more caution." Seth eyed her. "Hey, you asked."

She nodded. "I did. So... you think men are more capable of murder or evil."

"Women can be evil too, believe me, but not like men can. Those goddamned wars weren't started by women, I can tell you that."

Stevie said nothing more. It was a viewpoint she'd heard before, from men and from women. She gazed at the mural again, at the three females standing tall above the crowd, wondering if Mobius's chatter about the DOA wasn't just chatter after all.

"What do you say?" Seth said. "You hungry for some of those Crocus dumplings yet?"

Stevie smiled. "Sure. There's a good place over on Specter. Hopefully it's still open for business."

"It is. That's one of the joints I checked before we came."

They left the Passage and headed east a few blocks, past old stone buildings and row homes interspersed with blocky new builds, and past little dives with everything from cannabis cookies to squash kabobs, from spiced teas to chicory coffee. Odors emanated from the dives, from the stimulating to the overwhelming. It was almost dark, and the thickening clouds told Stevie it would rain soon.

At the dumpling joint, Stevie let Seth scan the place for a seat he felt comfortable with. Once settled in, Seth gave her permission to order for the both of them since she was "a native Brownie." Soon, a smorgasbord of meat and veggie dumplings, carrot soup, and fried potato balls arrived, along with their spiced tea, which Stevie requested be caffeine-free for Seth's sake. They dug in.

"You've never talked about your ethnic background," Seth said, filling his plate.

"Care to guess?"

He studied her. "I'd say mixed black and white, maybe a little more white... like one white parent and one mixed parent."

She smiled. "Not bad. Although my mother was mostly black... the donor was white."

"So you know that going in... the sperm donor's race."

She nodded.

"Why'd she move you out of Crocus?"

Stevie hesitated. "I think... she feared that staying here would be a bad influence on me. Krokus wasn't as safe back then, and she wanted me near City University. But I think that decision lost her some friends."

"When I was a kid, my folks wouldn't even let me or my sister near the City without chaperoning us."

"You have a sister?"

She immediately regretted asking. Seth would've already mentioned her if she were still alive.

"Had. Died in the war. She was a nurse... they bombed her medical facility."

Stevie put down her fork. "I'm sorry. I shouldn't have asked."

He shook his head. "Trying to avoid reminders of the war is like trying to avoid those damned sidewalk holes... a waste of effort."

"You've done a pretty good job managing it, from what I've seen."

He shrugged. "Doesn't always feel that way. But I have it under control as long as I avoid the triggers. Like sudden loud noises... and rain, if it comes down hard. And this is the rainiest fucking year I can remember in this place." He paused. "When I was deployed, there was one year where it rained all the damned time. One of our worst skirmishes went down during a drenching... there were corpses everywhere, blood running in streaks down the streets..." He looked at her. "Sorry. You don't need to hear this shit."

"It doesn't bother me. It's just the first time I've heard you talk about it."

"I don't usually." He took a swig of his tea. "Good thing is... no rain up in the stratosphere. Not much noise either. Two of many reasons I like working at the Disc."

"There's less rain in the west..."

He shook his head. "I like my job. I feel like I'm making a difference... protecting our country." He paused. "Speaking of making a difference, did you hear the latest news, about Marigold Funds?"

"No. What happened?"

"One of their top guys, who started that financial education school for poor kids in Viola... he's been charged with fraud. He ripped off trillions from working folks and now the Feds have enough to take him down. It's making a big stink, especially since the Oakenfold Killer's been quiet lately. Even the market took a big hit yesterday. But at least they got him."

She shook her head. "It won't matter. He'll get a top lawyer, spend a couple years in the clink writing a book about the soul-searching he did... then he'll get out, start his own business teaching get-rich seminars, and spend the rest of his life hiding assets in foreign banks so he won't have to pay back what he owes."

Seth raised his eyebrows. "Fuck. I thought I was cynical."

She gave a half smile. "The laws protect them. You can't sell hard drugs, destroy paper books, or lie in court, but you can defraud your fellow citizens for trillions and people will still worship you for being successful."

He let out a sigh. "We live in a fucked up world."

"True. But people like you and me, we do what we can to make it better." She held up her mug.

"I'll drink to that," he said, clinking his mug with hers.

They moved on to lighter topics, until they'd finished everything on their plates.

"Dessert?" she asked him. "We can have some here, or there's a really good ice cream shop a few blocks away."

His eyes lit up. "I grew up on a dairy farm, and the ice cream in Salvia stinks. That's an easy one."

She giggled. "Ice cream it is, Captain."

When the total for their meal appeared on their console, Stevie pulled out her ID and scanned it before Seth could retrieve his, inwardly happy she'd beaten him to it.

Seth gave her a look. "You didn't have to do that."

"You bought lunch last time. I still think about that aged ham."

He chuckled. "Well... thank you."

When they stepped outside, rain had begun to fall.

Seth squinted at the sky. "It's gonna pour. I can feel it."

"We can skip the ice cream and get on the train right now..." She hoped Seth wouldn't feel embarrassed about taking the offer.

"You don't mind?"

"Not at all." She'd gotten her hopes up for strawberry shortcake ice cream on a sugar cone. But it would be there the next time she visited Krokus. Now, she cared only about ensuring Seth's comfort.

They made their way to the nearest stop and sat down on the train, the sound of pattering rain and animated chatter surrounding them as they headed back to the west bank. When the train approached her stop, Seth turned to her. "Do you need to stay at my place again, to catch up on sleep?"

She didn't want to impose on him again. Yet, the prospect of another night of Pomade and Girlfriend's poisonous interactions venting into her personal space, especially when she was still tired, was too unpleasant to consider. "Are you sure?"

"I wouldn't have offered."

"Thank you. One more night should do the trick."

"Do you need anything from your place? Toothbrush?"

She shook her head. "I keep one with me. I don't want coffee stains on my teeth."

The rain pounded as they headed toward Seth's. Stevie watched him for signs of trouble, but he seemed unbothered. Once at his apartment, he brewed her a decaf espresso and himself a decaf khaki. They sat on his gray couch and chatted more. Soon, Stevie was so relaxed that her residual sleep deficit had her yawning.

"I think it's time for me to hit the couch," she said, retrieving her toothbrush from her bag and heading to Seth's bathroom. She had no change of clothing, but could just wear her shirt to bed, removing her jeans when Seth ventured back to his bedroom to read.

When she emerged from the bathroom, she found Seth standing nearby... probably waiting to persuade her into letting him take the couch this time. But before she could voice her protest, Seth's face took on a strange look.

"What's wrong?" she said.

"Nothing." He walked closer to her and held out his hand. Unsure what was happening, but trusting Seth, she put her hand in his. He pulled her toward him, and leaned over and kissed her.

Sandalwood. And a hint of paprika.

No.

Stevie backed away, letting go of Seth's hand as her heart pounded in her chest. "I'm sorry. I... you surprised me." Stevie looked up at him, at his blonde lashes surrounding deep-set blue eyes that watched her carefully.

Don't do it again. Don't kiss me.

She looked away again, backing up another step. "I'm sorry. I can't."

"Why not?"

"I like you, Seth. I always have. But... I don't see you that way. And if... if my actions or my coming here led you to believe otherwise, I apologize."

Disbelief. That was the only way to describe Seth's expression. Like her words bore no resemblance to his own perceptions, or anyone's. Seth stared at her for several more moments, his eyes narrowed slightly, his ability to know what to say and to give his opinion freely at a complete standstill. "Okay," he finally said.

A torrent of unrecognizable feelings flooded her. "Maybe... maybe I should go home. I doubt it will be noisy tonight, and you can have your place to yourself." When she got no response, Stevie scurried off to Seth's living room and began gathering her coat and bag. When finished, she looked over at Seth. He stood there, silent. "Thank you for today. I had a great time."

"Me too," he said, quieter than she'd ever heard him.

Stevie left, trekking her way east as the rain tumbled from above and drowned out everything but her disarrayed thoughts.

The look on his face, the sudden wordlessness. But she knew... bewilderment would turn to anger, and anger to self-righteousness. That a woman with her attractiveness quotient, in a City where women outnumbered men, would reject a man of Seth's caliber. Even a decent man like Seth would feel a sense of betrayal at having the laws of probability work against him when they shouldn't have. Seth likely wouldn't give in to the anger, wouldn't let it leak out like the vapor that Pomade oozed every time he came around. But he would think it, let it permeate his thoughts for as long as it needed to.

Why did you go to his home, Steviansa, especially after a dinner date? What did you think would happen?

I don't know, Mom!

Once Stevie arrived at her building, she retracted her umbrella and went inside. Before reaching the elevator, she heard her name. Manny. She turned and waved, having forgotten to greet him as she normally would.

"You alright?" Manny asked her as he emerged from behind the desk.

She nodded, forcing a smile. When the elevator doors opened at the 34th floor, there stood Pomade. His expression soured when he saw her, his doughy face taking on a haughty look that was well-complimented by his wool vest, checked shirt, and perfect hair. Next to him stood a woman, a Yellow, slightly less tasteful than the last. Pomade stepped into the elevator before Stevie had a chance to exit, his new Yellow following him like an eager yellow dog.

She felt some relief. Not only had Girlfriend taken her advice, but the most noise she would hear that night was Pomade's squeaking bed and grunting finale. No need to fight with a new Yellow, when neither had witnessed the other's true character yet.

But such news didn't distract her for long from the smell of Seth, the grasp of his hand as he pulled her closer to him, the feel of his mouth on hers. She shut her door, the rest of it flooding back to her. Her backing away. Whatever conciliatory but ineffective words she'd bestowed upon him. And the expression on his face, as if betrayed by her, or perhaps by his own expectations, created by the numerous other women who would vie for Seth's touch. She pushed such thoughts from her mind, and turned on her computer. She began removing her clothing.

When fully nude, her headpiece and sensors on, a voice spoke to her.

"Scintillations, Artemis. Who is your pleasure today?"

"Lor, please."

When Stevie arrived at the Disc on Monday, she immediately looked toward Seth's workstation. She didn't know if she wanted him to be hidden within it, thus preventing the unknowns that would accompany their first interaction since she'd left his apartment... or if she preferred him in plain view, perhaps making a trip to Machine, forcing them to interact and allowing her to take his emotional temperature.

But she saw no sign of him... not then, nor the rest of the day. He was there, of course. He was always there. But he paid her no visit. His visits didn't occur every day, but they happened more often than not, even if just for a quick hello. She also didn't see him the few times she emerged from her workstation to use the restroom, to pay a quick visit to Herbie, or to conduct business with Machine. Machine did provide her the caffeinated version of her espresso that day. At least their relationship was back to normal again.

Later that afternoon, Stevie got a message. It was from Ronald, requesting that she come to his office. She pressed her lips together, making the journey upstairs to the executive floor, trying not to speculate unnecessarily about what Ronald needed from her. When she arrived, his yellow-haired assistant told her to go in.

Ronald sat at his desk, his expression giving away no clues. "Close the door."

She did so and took a seat in one of his plush, ergonomic chairs, the blue skies out his giant window giving the impression of fair, warm weather rather than the chilly, rarified air that surrounded their stratospheric place of employment.

"I hope you didn't take my recent interrogation of you too personally," Ronald began.

Of course I took it personally. That's what you wanted.

"I didn't, Sir. I understand how important a breach like that is, and I understand why my ties to the east bank would make me a logical candidate for suspicion."

He sighed. "It isn't merely your ties to Crocus, Stevie. Your mother... she had very strong objections to the Federal Watch program and was extremely vocal about those objections. And I know that without a father in the home, and without other siblings to occupy her attentions, she had a strong influence on you."

"She did."

He watched her. "Yet you work here, as a fundamental cog in the Federal Watch machinery."

"If you're wondering whether I have reservations about the program, I won't lie to you, Sir. I do. However, I spent a year getting vetted for this position, and I'm sure those who vetted me shared your concerns. They probably know more about my mother than I do. But they still hired me, and they've been happy with my work for all these years."

"There's no need to defend yourself, Stevie," Ronald said. "I was one of those who vetted you. Between you and me, you're not the only one who feels ambivalent about the program, about invading the privacy of our nation's citizens and justifying the invasion as a method of preventing more war. I had trepidations about taking this position, about putting myself on the chopping block. So did Miriam. Such a program... it shows our weakness, not our strength or resilience. I just hope..." he shook his head, his eyebrows knit together. "I just hope it does some good, and that someday we won't need it... that our City and our country will recover from the nightmares we experienced and that people like you and me can use our skills for something more positive."

Relief coursed through her. "I hope so, too."

He leaned forward and put his hands on his desk. "Well, let's put aside our darker musings about this program for now. I have an assignment for you. Herb knows I'm bringing you in on this, but no one else does and it needs to stay that way. Red light switched on for this one..."

"Got it, Sir."

That week, Stevie worked on nothing but her red light project for Ronald. The light would certainly prevent Seth from paying her any kind of visit. However, she knew he hadn't even come near her workstation. She wondered if she should talk to him, but couldn't bring herself to.

The following week, she finished several reports for Ronald, one of which yielded results that, at least to her, seemed intriguing. A trio of seemingly unrelated people—from different backgrounds and living in different parts of the country—somehow developed a thread that connected them and raised suspicions. When she brought it to Ronald, she expected him to show modest interest and tell her he'd run it by the other executives. But instead, his eyes widened. And within three days, an arrest was made in the northern region... at the location where the three individuals met and closed the triangle that the data had suggested. Ronald's brown eyes gained their warmth once more as he patted Stevie on the back before heading to the media room, where he would issue the public statement that would make national news.

Stevie decided then that it was time to move forward.

Nothing.

Surveillance footage from Ronald Carr's home, distilled down to only when he made an appearance, showed nothing. No inappropriate interactions with Miriam. No inappropriate interactions with 9-year-old Minnie. No inappropriate interactions with Minnie's neighborhood friends when they visited. Ronald wasn't home much; but when he was, he merely read, worked, ate with his family, and spent time with Minnie. Stevie had no father to compare Ronald to, but experience told her that Ronald's life was... ordinary.

Ronald even read to Minnie before she went to sleep. He read no silly or inappropriate books, instead choosing classics, books read by educated traditionalists and those with a finely-tuned understanding of the world. He held Minnie's hand, even kissed her forehead... but that was it.

Hours of this. Countless hours.

Stevie sighed. She'd taken a risk, getting that footage. She'd tested the Disc and those who potentially watched her before pulling the footage for Ronald's home. No one came to inquire about her test breach—a breach that should have set off an alert. They weren't watching her anymore, if they ever were. She had a duty, and she needed to resume it. And unlike tracking Ronald's phone calls, pulling footage was lower risk. Executive addresses were hidden from the search database... but Stevie had Ronald's address committed to memory.

Did the lack of evidence in Ronald's footage mean he was innocent? No. He could be molesting girls now, somewhere outside his home. But when? Ronald ate his breakfast at Larkspur Diner, worked long hours, and then he came home. Weekends were spent working or with family. She knew because she'd tailed him. Even if he'd taken Minnie into their home's dead zones, she would have seen him enter those places.

It was also possible he'd only molested the woman who'd accused him, back when she was a child herself. But if he'd engaged in such pedophilia in the past, it seemed unlikely that he'd cease such activities, especially with a potential victim easily accessible and under his legal guardianship. Pedophiles didn't "quit" their philia.

They didn't wane, cease, or find cure. They acted and justified their actions, seeking a new victim when their current one moved away or grew old enough to find methods of resistance.

Stevie sat there, shaking her head. Spying on her colleague and superior, a man she respected and who'd been a father figure to her... it made her feel disgusted, and ashamed.

And angry. There she was, invading the private life of a friend in his own home, with nothing to show for it but having wasted time on another fool's errand with an accused Federal bureaucrat. The irresponsibility of such accusations, by someone with a grudge against Ronald—perhaps a neighbor who didn't like Ronald's tone when he asked her to clean up after her dog, or someone who despised Federal Watch—irked her. Now, she would have to hunt down Ronald's accuser and monitor her, ensuring she wasn't a danger to their City. That would take time, time that should be spent on other things.

Stevie turned off her computer, changed into her running clothes, and left.

Ah, darkness. Fresh air and sweat. North she ran to Artemisia's green zone, spotting its skinny fledgling trees. It smelled like damp grass from a recent shower, and the epoxy benches were covered in droplets. She looped around the tiny respite and headed south, to the next one. As she ran her route that connected three different green zones, her thoughts returned to Seth. Recollections of prior conversations came and went—their talking about their backgrounds, Seth's reports from the news, their fetching one another coffee. The conversations seemed even more consequential now that they no longer occurred.

When she returned home, she made another espresso and contacted Mobius. *Need to talk, if you think it's safe.* After she'd showered and cleaned up, she saw that Mobius had responded.

Mobius: Scintillations, my lady. Are you okay?

140

She passed other Pansies in russet denim and thick cotton, their jackets sturdy and masking their thinness. Some looked at her, others took no notice. She turned right on 25th and made another immediate right into an alley. The alley stood only three feet wide, two stories of brick wall rising on either side of her. As she disappeared deeper into it, she heard music. Two burly men stood guarding the door, both in denim overalls, both with necks covered in Johnny Jump Ups.

They saw her coming. They watched for anyone who dared enter the alley, searching trespassers' faces and taking on a surlier air when the face didn't look familiar. One stared Stevie down as she drew closer. Stevie stared back. The burly man said nothing, waiting for her to offer up the necessities to gain entry. She pulled out a wad of currency from her pocket.

His eyebrows went up. Just a little, and just for a moment. Then he averted his eyes, as if trying to pretend he didn't place great value on the sum, when she knew he did.

"You a cop?" the other goon said.

A higher voice. And a smooth, hairless face. A woman. Her bulky build and bloodshot stare slightly unnerved Stevie.

"No."

"You a Fed?"

"No."

Not the kind you're worried about, anyway.

"Give me your bag," the henchwoman said.

Stevie feigned impatience and handed off her pack. Henchwoman searched the bag, finding only clothing. To them, a change of clothes, role-playing accoutrements perhaps... but nothing they hadn't seen before.

"Stand still." Henchwoman ran a scanner over Stevie, the device looking for weapons, surveillance, recording equipment, or other problematic paraphernalia. When her scan came up clean, the woman held out her hand. "How much?"

"Four hours."

Henchwoman counted the currency, noticing that Stevie had given her the correct amount, plus just enough extra to eradicate any remaining surliness from her expression. The woman nodded toward the door, where red light peeked out between the wooden slats. Stevie headed toward the light.

Inside, red light bathed her. A mirror hung near the door, allowing the guards to see who was coming from inside. The mirror reflected back a thin woman with a neck of pansies and a wary eye. Her strange eyes still bothered her, but she still liked the pansies.

Stevie walked the narrow hallway, past many doors, some open and some closed. The open ones were hers to take, where she could enter, hook into the equipment, and engage. She'd come there once before, years ago, to do recon. After a mere two minutes, she unhooked and never went back.

She passed the doors and continued upstairs, to where one requested in-person services. On a weekend, the range of services was extensive indeed. She continued down another hallway, past rooms with closed doors, music and muted human sounds seeping through each door's molecular structure. Finally, she arrived at one particular door, loud electronic music emanating from behind it. She stood for a moment, took a deep breath, and knocked.

"Not now!" came a male shout.

She knocked again.

"What is it?" called the same agitated voice.

She spoke softly into the com, not wanting to blast his eardrum through his earpiece. "Roses are red, violets are dead."

The music ceased.

After a brief delay, three scantily clad and violeted women opened the door and scurried out, after which a man appeared in the doorway.

More handsome than the average Financial. Dark hair streaked with gray, strong jaw, some semblance of musculature on his nearly nude body. And a chiseled, symmetrical face, the kind of face that pseudoscientific dolts assumed indicated greater genetic fitness and thus attracted fertile young women willing to donate a uterus and the rest of their lives.

"What's going on?" he said.

She entered the large room, not waiting for an invitation but knowing he wouldn't object. She closed the door. "Turn on the music."

He did so.

"You're in danger," she told him.

"From who?" he said, a bit of Pansy still on his tongue.

"From yourself."

Stevie took out her .357 and pulled the trigger, sending Marigold back a couple of feet. He didn't fall immediately, nor look scared... a holdover from his Viola roots.

Oh, Marigold. After serving your sentence and finding your "true purpose," you would've had the perfect rags-to-riches-to-fallen story with which to regale your future clients! You, the Pansy who rose from nothing to enter the world of Downtown Financials and become fabulously wealthy while the war raged on!

But there would be no story and no soul searching, because there was no jail time. Only celebration of having skirted justice, again.

When Marigold eventually tumbled, Stevie took her second shot. She checked her denim for errant back spatter. Upon finding none, she put her beloved Oakenfold away, shutting the door as she left.

Walk calmly. Down the back stairs, past two more henchpeople, and outside to a concrete-covered yard.

Remember: turn right, then right, then left, then down another alley. Gain your lead. Only minutes until the henchpeople discover the truth and begin pursuit.

Outside, rain crashed upon the concrete. Once beyond the yard, she began to run down the wet sidewalk, splashing as she dodged the cracks and holes. Right, then right, then left, peering behind her as she took each corner. Nothing and no one. Her raspberry hair and thick denim grew heavy with rain. She entered the alleyway, its narrow brick walls protecting her, shielding her.

Almost there. Almost out of the danger zone. Keep running.

Out of nowhere, something unforgiving slammed into her upper chest, clotheslining her and violently catapulting her onto her back. A dark figure loomed over her, ready to grab her.

I can't breathe!

Forget breathing, Steviansa! Use your legs!

Stevie scrunched her legs up toward her chest and thrust them at the dark figure. The first one or two attempts barely registered, but her desperate follow-up kicks knocked him back a little. Yet, undaunted, the dark figure came back at her and managed to grab one of her legs. She thrashed, kicking with her other leg as he dodged the assault and aggressively sought to subdue it too. Within moments, he did, binding both her legs and pressing them to the ground as he straddled her.

When he grabbed for her arms, his attack suddenly ceased as an explosive round grazed his chest. Pop. Even with her custom silencer, the pop bounced off the tall brick walls that enclosed them, announcing to the residents of Viola that something was wrong.

Pop. Pop. Pop. He fell forward, landing hard on top of her.

Go.

She shoved the heavy corpse aside while wriggling her legs out from under his. In a moment she was up and racing down the narrow alley, her heart pounding and her epinephrine-induced clarity of vision on alert for any other booby traps. She zigzagged through the streets of Viola, away from Johnny Street and west toward the Milagro, her throat burning from her anaerobic pace as the rain drowned her. At last, she reached the train line, her shallow breathing bordering on wheezing. She frantically looked around for pursuers. But she saw no one other than a few wet Pansies, who stared for a moment, probably wondering what her hurry was.

Eight minutes until the train arrived. She sprinted to the next stop, knowing she could be there in three, knowing that the farther she got from Johnny Street and its particular horrors, the safer she was. At the next stop, five minutes to go, she hurried into the restroom, stripped off her drenched denim, and donned her original outfit.

When she began rolling her coat and overalls, she realized they were covered in blood. His blood.

A moment of panic.

No, first things first. She pulled out her burner and called the emergency number.

"There's been a murder," she said in a high-pitched voice. "Down the alley, near the corner of Johnny Street and twenty-fifth. He's dead." She hung up, wiped it clean, and dropped the phone, crushing it under her boot and tossing the remains in the garbage.

The hum of the train, in the distance.

She hastily pulled out a small bottle, dumping its contents on the blood-soaked denim. The air filled with a caustic smell as the denim began to dissolve. With a glove, she picked up the burnt remains and stuffed them into the garbage. Donning a dark wig and a clown mask, she burst from the restroom as the train doors opened.

Stevie scanned the entire train car, spying for anyone who looked at her for too long. But she saw only a Pansy couple in conversation and a lone man who merely glanced at her.

She took a seat, putting her shaking hands between her knees to still them. She forced herself to inhale deeply, her hot breath building up inside her mask. The City had outlawed masks and their ability to thwart facial recognition software. But some still wore them in public, just for the sake of rebellion, until the cops took them away.

Pains began to emerge along her backside, particularly her tailbone, from her sudden collision with the concrete. Who was he? A drug trade minion? A citizen manning his territory? A random attacker? She was in no position to find out.

She shook her head. Imprecise shots. A location that transmitted noise. An unplanned casualty. Half-dissolved clothing left in the garbage.

Not good.

As her epinephrine levels began to dwindle, exhaustion set in. Everything wilted, except her mind, which still raced with images of her attacker. Suddenly, movement from the corner of her eye jolted her from her barrage of thoughts. Someone had boarded the train. Two people. When she saw a tawny mohawk, more adrenaline surged through Stevie's bloodstream.

Mohawk and her gray-streaked counterpart sat down, never giving her more than a cursory glance.

Get out.

At the next stop, Stevie exited the train. And with rain drenching her, she began to run.

EPISODE 8

NARCISSUS AND ECHO

Her teeth began to chatter again.

Stevie tightened her hood around her face, pulling her knees closer as she vigorously rubbed her legs. But the chatter soon returned. She would have to get up again and pace around like an overmedicated psychiatric patient, all with the goal of staving off hypothermia. The snoring from her two slumbering neighbors assured her they were no threat. Still, she kept her eyes open and her hand on her .357.

Five more hours. Might as well be twenty-five.

Don't complain, Steviansa. Complaining won't make it better.

You know I hate this place, these people. And you know why.

Deal with it. You have no other choice.

Stevie sighed. Her two feminine stalkers. They couldn't have recognized her in her scientifically altered state. Yet, there they were again.

After exiting the train to escape them, Stevie brandished the crudest of her skills once more: her ability to run at a brisk pace for as long as needed. Only then did she employ her emergency plan: find the nearest dead zone, take her B therapy, and brave the night until she no longer looked liked the Pansy who'd dashed through Viola in blood-stained denim. She skipped the run-down container buildings near the Milagro—too many potential witnesses—and found a lot near the Outer Rim, occupied only by a couple of snoring shanties.

Hours later, past daybreak, Stevie found a broken window and checked her appearance. She recognized her face again. Even her hair had darkened to its natural color. She put the wig back on anyway; she would blend in better with longer hair. When one of the shanties stirred in his dirty bedding, she donned her mask and left the hovel. A block away, she spotted a disheveled woman wearing a decent coat. But before she could say anything, the woman took one look at her clown mask and recoiled.

"Piss off!" she said, more scared than angry.

Stevie pulled out some currency and held it up. "I need your coat. And your shoes."

In shoes that were too small and a smelly black coat that covered her damp clothing, Stevie found her way to the nearest train stop, entered the restroom, and took off her mask. She didn't know every stop, but she knew roughly where each train line went because she'd ridden them all from one end to the other. Once seated on the train, its warmth overrode every other discomfort she experienced.

You're almost there. Almost to your steam shower and bed.

When the train crossed Pansy Bridge, Stevie felt calmer as her GABA levels increased. She wouldn't think about the events of the previous night. Not yet. Soon, drowsiness threatened.

Stay awake.

When her stop came, relief began to flood her, so much so that she started with surprise when someone spoke her name.

Mohawk and Gray Streak, appearing from nowhere.

"Scintillations, Stevie," Mohawk said, with just the right amount of irony. "Care to have a chat?"

Without thought, Stevie pulled out the cylinder from her pants pocket. She pressed the trigger, aimed the potent vapor at the women's faces, yanked a few tawny hairs from the mohawk, and ran off.

Stevie grimaced as the weed's trichomes stung her through her gloves. But with a little more digging, out it came.

Silvera vulgaris. The white-flowered but nettled plant originally imported to serve as decoy, to protect certain farm crops from being devoured by insects and other hungry creatures. Instead of offering such protection, it wound up spreading and choking out the crops, its opportunism only enhanced by the cool damp climate of its new home. Scientists had tried dousing the weed with herbicides and even altering its genome to be less hearty... the weed only adapted and kept spreading. Eventually, with her mother's help, the City discovered that the best way to conquer the invader was to yank it from the ground by hand. One by one.

And a good effort they made of it. With time, they'd eradicated most of the noxious weed and the crops began to recover. Until the wars came, and the pernicious plant began thriving among the ruin, in the cracks of the chewed up sidewalks, in the abandoned lots, in the charred farmland up north, where it spread to healthy farms. Once more, this time with no City money to pay them, volunteers stepped up to restart the eradication process.

Stevie sipped her water, strangely grateful to be hunched over in the soil of one of Artemisia's abandoned lots. It satisfied her to be part of a cause she believed in, to be outside among others who also cared, to get dirty and be near green things, even if it included prickly weeds. And it gave her the opportunity to sort through the previous night's events.

She shook her head, digging at another weed. *Care to have a chat?* indeed. As if asking permission to accost her would make her more amenable to arrest... or whatever activities they would subject her to behind closed doors. Four times now they'd appeared, in three different Hoods. They didn't recognize her the previous evening, but she didn't have the luxury of resting on that assumption.

How were they able to track her? Not through her phone, which she hadn't brought with her to Viola. If they'd found any useful evidence on her, they would have arrested her by now... if that was their goal. Heck, they probably didn't mind her efforts to help them clean up the City. They had some other motive: perhaps to scare her into submission or catch her in some act, after which they could lean on her for information, the kind only a Disc employee could get. Then, she would no longer be an independent agent. And that was something she could never tolerate.

Then, of course, there was her unknown alley attacker. Swift, unexpected, strong. She shook the sickening memories from her mind.

She bent over and grasped another *Silvera* plant. With every pull of the silvery weed—root and all, of course, otherwise they'd come right back—she felt better. Their world had one less destructive thing in it.

Always make the world better, Steviansa, not worse, her mother would say.

She couldn't make the world better if she didn't get those two goons off her back. A few strands of Mohawk's hair, with their obliging DNA-rich follicles, would help with that. She hadn't had time to get a sample from Gray Steak, but Mohawk's would serve as a good start. Such data wouldn't yield results overnight; but in the meantime, if they were stupid enough to bother her again, she would punish them with a vape that delivered far more discomfort than 30 minutes of burning eyes.

Fortunately, her B therapy had worked swiftly, allowing her to venture outside after a long shower and some sleep. The only remnant of her Pansy getup was her neck of violets, faded but still visible. A hooded jacket zipped all the way up solved that.

When the gray daylight began to diminish, Stevie stood up from the dirt, her back aching from crouching all afternoon. Her tailbone was sore and her legs stiff, leftover from last night's unexpected proceedings. She began gathering her tools, glad that the walk home would loosen her up.

"Calling it a day?"

Maria approached, her pants covered in mud.

Stevie nodded. "I need to get home. Early morning at the office."

"It's strange to think of that thing as someone's office," she said, glancing up in a southerly direction, where the Disc hovered over their City like a watchman.

"I know. I'm used to it now, but it felt strange when I started working there."

Maria brushed her dark hair from her face with a gloved hand. "Thanks for coming out again. And for bringing snacks."

"Happy to, Maria. Let me know where you'll be next."

"Probably Viola. Their urban micro-farms have reported some *Silvera* problems. We need to get at them before they spread. It's harder to get volunteers to go to Viola... but I suspect the place doesn't scare you."

It does now.

Stevie shook her head. "Of course I'll go. I want those farms to succeed, too."

She said goodbye to Maria and began her trek home. Before she knew it, she came upon the wood-paneled eatery, the one she'd eyed so many times but had yet to go inside. Her stomach grumbled, tempting her to cross the street and give the place her business. But then she remembered her appearance: the mud wedged under her fingernails, her grubby clothing. They wouldn't care... but she did. The couples sitting near the window, sipping their wine and eating their thoughtfully prepared meals... they didn't need her sloppy self ruining their ambience.

As she began to turn away, a man caught her eye. She realized it was Seth, seated with his back to a woody wall, dressed in an ironed gray shirt. Across from him sat a woman with long but undoctored brown hair. Seth's attention was focused on her, listening to her in the genuine way he listened. Stevie stared, longer than she should have, inundated by a confounding mixture of disappointment and relief. At last, she hurried off, not wanting to risk Seth seeing her.

Back at her apartment, cleaned up and eating a bowlful of spiced lentils, Stevie turned on the news. The familiar genetically enhanced anchors appeared.

"Top story tonight: the Oakenfold Killer has struck again. An anonymous call to police reported a shooting at an illegal services shack on the 2500 block of Johnny Street in Viola. The body of

Jonathan Seligman was found dead at the scene, shot with the same Oakenfold .357 Magnum revolver that has killed at least fifteen other victims. The Marigold Funds executive was recently released from house arrest after he agreed to a plea deal that would prevent him from serving prison time for committing securities fraud.

"In addition to Mister Seligman, the body of a second man was found only a few blocks away in an alley near 23rd Avenue. The victim is an unidentified male, killed by multiple gunshot wounds to the chest. City Police reports that the entry wounds were similar to those of the Oakenfold Killer's other victims, but that they are still investigating whether the bullets came from the same weapon or from a similar weapon. City Police also reports that a Viola resident witnessed someone fleeing the alley where the second murder occurred, and City surveillance footage has confirmed that a woman with red hair and flowered neck tattoos was seen running from the scene."

A brief video appeared onscreen. Stevie's heart began to race as she saw herself speeding through Viola in her rain-soaked denim. Despite the darkness, she could see the stains. Blood.

Chief Jansen appeared from a separate feed. "City surveillance footage has identified what appears to be an adult female running from the alley where the second shooting took place. This woman is now a suspect and we are in the process of identifying her. We have also detained several individuals from the shack where the first murder occurred, and we are talking with residents in the area. We expect to have more information by tomorrow." The Chief waited for the crowd of reporters to begin their inquiry.

One reporter spoke. "If the bullets for the two victims match, is it possible that the second shooting happened as a result of an unplanned attack on the shooter?"

"There are a lot of possibilities," Chief Jansen replied. "We can't speculate on the second shooting without further investigation." He paused for another question.

"The murder of Mister Seligman occurred only days after his

release from house arrest. Do you believe the shooter sought revenge for Mister Seligman's crimes?"

"We have no way of knowing the shooter's motives at this point. The previous victims had no record of criminal activity, so it's unlikely that the shooter sought revenge."

Another reporter spoke up. "Chief Jansen, is it possible that the shooter seeks some type of justice? The other victims include Financials with tremendous wealth, while many in the City struggle to get by. Is it possible that the other victims did harmful things but those crimes never got reported or were covered up?"

The Chief's jaw tightened. "This City still operates under the motto 'innocent until proven otherwise.' I'm not interested in discussions on vigilantism. Murder is murder. The Department is doing everything possible to close in on the killer and protect our citizens."

When the news anchors appeared again, the man spoke to his perfectly pretty co-anchor. "It does seem too much of a coincidence, Mary, that Mister Seligman was killed only days after the announcement that he would serve no jail time."

"Agreed, Tom. Yet, what about these other victims? These were good men: attractive and successful, who worked hard and served as good examples for our troubled economy." She shook her blonde head. "So sad."

Stevie turned off the news.

Take a few breaths. Their facial and iris searches will produce nothing. The footage of you sprinting through the streets of Viola will only lead them to a train stop. Even if they pick up your trail again, it will peter out once you approach the Outer Rim. And you destroyed the only useful forensic evidence they could use.

Henchwoman and Henchman hadn't sold her out to the cops, either. Nor would they. Like their fellow Pansies, they had no reason to trust the police or to help them in any way, especially for a man who'd given little of his immense wealth back to his native Hood. Talking to the cops would yield nothing other than finding themselves under the thumb of the authorities or, if charged with operating a shack, getting over-sentenced by the Judge Delaneys of their City. They knew the police had limited resources, that even if the cops shut down one of their shacks, it was only a matter of time before it reopened. Viola would always offer such services, as long as the west bankers came with their wads of currency.

The casualty. The shadowed attacker.

Not only will no one understand his death, those who investigate it won't care... because of where he called home.

That was the good news.

But once they discovered that both sets of rounds came from the same gun, they would have a prime suspect. They couldn't ID her, but they still had video footage of her, valuable hard evidence they wouldn't have gotten had it not been for a random attack by an unknown assailant. Stevie went to her computer, found the script for her raspberry-haired, violet-necked alter ego, and deleted it.

She opened her portal next. Only a handful of messages, one of which had a subject line that caught her eye.

Ronald Carr.

She rolled her eyes. The message had the same neat and well-worded prose, the same polite tone, the same attention to detail in following the portal's instructions as the first complaint about Ronald had. *Same accuser.* Most people used the portal only once, as the instructions made it clear that multiple submissions wouldn't be tolerated. But on occasion, the more diligent would visit the portal repeatedly, usually to offer up the same information supplied previously. This time, the message acknowledged the subsequent submission and apologized for it. The report included a synopsis of the previous, but with more emotion this time. She implored for justice, explaining that Ronald had molested her at his home during her formative years, and that he would do the same to Minnie.

Her formative years? She hadn't mentioned that before. If the accuser meant her teenage years, rather than those from childhood, Stevie would probably know her. She'd moved to Artemisia when she was 10, after which she spent time at the Carr home nearly every week. Between Kira's neighbors, friends, and cousins, there were many possibilities. Stevie pulled up both reports from the accuser; their net signatures shared the same location code. A brief search indicated that the messages originated from a building in Salvia.

She'd already decided to locate Ronald's accuser and monitor her. Now, such an errand would rise to the top of her list. Stevie frowned at the prospect of wasting more time on this. But doing so would allow her to move forward with the case or, hopefully, put it aside for good.

On a chilly Monday morning, Stevie walked to the shuttle grounds, passing the usual slew of vegetarian cafes and coffee joints before reaching Dianthus. There, the bars sat silent while young women disappeared into salons that would offer the thickened hair or the broader hips they sought. It seemed noisier that day, and when Stevie rounded a corner she realized why: there was construction activity in one of the few remaining vacant lots in Dianthus. Steel girders aimed for the sky, with the goal of creating another edifice with black glass and no balconies.

Seth entered her thoughts. Seth had a balcony, on which he probably sat from time to time, alone or perhaps with his brown-haired sweetheart. A small sadness came over her at the prospect of returning to the wordless void that existed between them. It was time to do something. She'd injured him, even if unintentionally. Thus, it was her job to repair the damage. And with that thought, she steered herself into a bakery.

Once at the Disc, Stevie worked for a while. When 10 am came around, one of the potential times Seth might crave a khaki, Stevie glanced at her bag of goodies. Her heart began to pound as she approached Seth's workstation and knocked.

Seth, his desk in a standing position, turned around. His long eyelashes blinked a couple of times, while the rest of his expression remained neutral.

"Good morning, Captain," she said, donning a smile, partially to placate him and partially because she couldn't help it.

"Hey, Stevie."

She produced the pastries. "Want one?"

He peered at the goodies for a moment. "Sure."

Stevie smiled to herself when he selected the chocolate croissant. "I'm heading over to Machine. Need some coffee?"

"Uh, yeah. Coffee sounds good."

"I'll be back," she said, picking up Seth's mug.

Stevie stood in line at Machine, feeling no impatience this time at the yellow-haired, pink-clad woman ahead of her, who always had great difficulty making up her mind on what she wanted from Machine. After her own turn, with two fresh coffees in hand, she dropped the lighter of the two at Seth's. She hesitated for a mere moment, preparing herself to leave if his body language indicated it was necessary.

However, Seth took his cue. "I don't suppose you've heard the latest."

"The shootings?"

"Yep. The Marigold Funds guy." He shook his head. "You called that one, didn't you? Fucker didn't even get jail time. Now we'll never know if he would've come out of the clink a changed man."

She smiled. "I suppose not."

Seth sipped his coffee. "The Marigold guy got all the press, but if you ask me, the other victim, whatever his name was... that's the real story. Same rounds, same gun, but different placement. They said one of the rounds grazed him, like it wasn't planned. Now they have this female suspect..." He shook his head.

"You still don't believe that a woman is capable of this."

"I think there's more to the story than they're telling us. They needed a suspect, now they have one. But the guy who took the bullets... he was probably hurting that woman and the shooter saw it on his way out. She had blood on her clothes... how'd it get there? If she shot him, the blood pattern would look different. And if the shooter's the type to knock off Marigold for being a crook, maybe he killed her attacker too and she ran off in a panic."

"Or... maybe she knocked off Marigold, ran away, and then got attacked by the second guy. She killed him and his blood got on her before she escaped."

Don't say any more.

Seth considered that. Then he shook his head. "I'm not buying it. I still think the killer's a man."

Back at her desk, Stevie felt relieved at having set things right with Seth. Yet, a nagging discomfort lingered. She disliked deceiving him. She'd done so before, of course, always out of necessity. But that day, it seemed... insulting. She shook off that thought and got back to work.

Later, when Ronald called her up to his office to discuss his latest assignment, she took a deep breath and headed upstairs, wishing she didn't have to face him.

"What do you see, Stevie?" he said, glancing over the reports she'd sent him.

"A couple of questionable IDs. In the south, near the coast. The third file has their details."

"That city... they have a small airport known for its lax security. A breeding ground for terrorists, much like the Outer Rim. Did you send these to Monitoring?"

She shook her head. "I didn't want to without consulting you first."

"You have the go-ahead. I want eyes on these two, twenty-four hours a day." He looked up, his kind eyes making contact with hers. "Good work, as usual."

"Thank you."

He checked his watch and stood. "I have to get going. Minnie has parent-teacher conferences tonight and Miriam wants us both there."

Stevie stood as well. "Is she doing well in school?"

"Yes. She's a bright child. She loves to read, and be read to. Especially classics."

Guilt stabbed at her as she recalled the image of Ronald reading at Minnie's bedside. "Let me know if you need anything else, and say hello to Miriam."

"Stevie."

She turned back around, suddenly feeling nervous.

Ronald began putting on his coat. "I don't mean to pry... but is something going on between you and Seth?"

If Stevie were capable of blushing, her face would have turned bright red. "What do you mean?"

"It's clear that you and he are friends, that he's the one you talk to here. I ask because you came up in conversation at a meeting with the other Army guys. Someone teased him about you, and he reacted with... more than just embarrassment. Has he harassed you or done anything to make you uncomfortable?"

"No. Never."

"Do you... I don't mean to be indelicate here... has he shown interest in you beyond friendship? I only ask because I've seen him with other women on a few occasions."

She shook her head. "No. We're just friends."

He nodded. "I wanted to make sure, with the way young men behave these days. He's a top notch employee, but I've detected a darker side to him, which I hoped was nothing more than the remnants of his war service." He glanced at her. "Pardon my intrusion... I suppose I still see you as one of my kids."

She smiled at that. "I don't mind."

Ronald nodded and left.

As Stevie stood on the shuttle back to the surface, her mind was occupied by thoughts of Ronald. Irritation nagged at her. She'd begun to feel like Ronald's accuser somehow knew that the best way to get attention through the portal was to do precisely what she was doing—follow the rules of submission, offer a well-written and organized report, accuse a high profile target of a crime that Stevie couldn't overlook, and, most of all, target someone she knew and could more easily research. It was as if the accuser knew just how to manipulate her, how to get her chasing Ronald for weeks or months and waste precious time that could be allocated toward those with a far higher probability of guilt.

Stop thinking about it. You know the next step.

Shouting.

Stevie opened her eyes, immediately knowing what had awakened her at 2:30 am. Pomade... and Girlfriend. Stevie let out a sigh. Girlfriend had returned.

"You were flirting with that girl with the blue drink! It was so obvious!"

"I was having a conversation," Pomade shot back with nasal indignation. "I never touched her."

"Did you see anyone while we were broken up?"

A pause.

Tell the truth, Pomade.

"You did, didn't you?"

"You said it yourself... we were broken up!"

"I can't believe you! If you really cared, you wouldn't treat me this way!"

"Treat you what way?"

"I thought it would be different this time."

"Oh, calm down!"

Their vapid, ethanol-induced exchange went on for some time, until they eventually settled into silence. Stevie fell back to sleep, but was again awakened by the inevitable squeaking of the bed, followed by Pomade's final grunt. Soon after, their fighting recommenced.

"I was really close!" she shouted.

"I'll get you next time, alright? Fuck!"

"We could do it again."

"I'm tired. It's 3:30 in the morning. Let's just go to sleep."

Oh, Girlfriend. How long did your attempt at self-respect last? A week or two? Did your friends chastise you for giving up on an eligible Financial? Did

*the fear of Yellow spinsterhood overwhelm you? Did your serotonin and oxytocin
withdrawals convince you that even a spoiled, lazy fop was better than nothing?
You should have come to me. I would have told you that the withdrawals would
cease, that balance would return.*

Their pointless squabbling continued Tuesday night. However,
Wednesday night offered relative quiet, with nothing more than the
squeaking bed and Pomade's grunt. Stevie barely acknowledged the
familiar noises and drifted off again... until she heard Pomade's whine.

"Where are you going?"

Indecipherable mumbling from Girlfriend.

"Oh, come on!" he cried.

Silence.

"Go ahead, leave," Pomade went on. "You're shitty company
anyway."

A door slammed. Stevie smiled as Girlfriend's self-respect meter
began its faithful march upward once more.

Wanting to ensure that Girlfriend's exodus occurred without
incident, Stevie jumped up and peered out her hall surveillance.
Girlfriend stood facing the elevator with her black coat and slightly
mussed yellow hair. Pomade followed her into the hallway.

"Why are you being such a bitch?"

When Girlfriend turned around, Stevie gasped. It wasn't
Girlfriend. It was another woman.

"I'll be sure to tell everyone what a lousy fuck you are," she said.

The woman stepped inside the elevator and the doors shut.

Stevie sat at her computer until late, looking forward to a night
of uninterrupted sleep. Even Pomade would need to recover from
multiple nights of discord. She crawled into her soft sheets, pulled
the covers over her, and fell asleep.

Shouting again. Loud. More worrisome.

She knew that voice. It was Girlfriend's voice. Anger surged
through Stevie.

"These aren't mine!" Girlfriend shouted.

"Yes they are!" Pomade insisted.

"No, they aren't! Don't you think a woman knows her own fucking underwear, you cheating asshole?"

"Obviously not. You aren't the brightest sometimes. You fucking forget everything."

"Fuck you!" she screamed. But her vehement protest got lost in the broken squeak of a woman who'd come to tears.

"Oh, come on! What are you crying for? They're underwear. They're yours and I've seen you wear them. Stop being such a Rosa queen!"

On the shouting went, rising in its intensity, until Stevie heard a bang against the wall. She sat up in bed.

Silence. Then wailing.

"Don't touch me! Don't touch me! Leave me alone!"

Adrenaline surged through her at the desperation in Girlfriend's cries. Then the screams became muffled, as if someone had silenced her. Then shuffling, struggle...

Stevie began pounding on the wall. "Hey!" she shouted. "If you hurt her, I will bear witness to the police! I will ruin your career!"

Silence. No more shuffling or muffled sounds.

"I want to hear her voice, now!" Stevie went on. "Or I will burn your door down."

Nothing at first. "I'm okay," Girlfriend finally said, strained and barely audible. "I'm okay," she repeated, louder.

Stevie dressed herself. Then she stood there, waiting for her body to offer a calming counterbalance to the adrenaline that coursed through her. Just as she considered calling the police, her door buzzed. It was Girlfriend on her hall surveillance, half-dressed, her bag over her shoulder and the remainder of her clothing bunched up in her arms. Stevie grabbed a weapon and opened the door. Girlfriend stood there, her body perfectly still but her eyes bright with the same adrenaline that raced through Stevie. Pomade hadn't pursued her.

Once inside, Girlfriend hesitated. Then she began to cry. Stevie put her arms around her as Girlfriend let her clothing fall to the floor, her body wracking with sobs.

"It's okay," Stevie said quietly. "You're safe."

After her sobs faded, Stevie pulled away and took a good look at her. Tear-stained face, red eyes, no bruising or bleeding... but her neck. It was blotched, and her sobs had sounded labored. "Did he choke you?"

She nodded. "Just for a moment."

"Do you want me to call the police?"

Girlfriend shook her head. "You know as well as I do that there's no point."

Stevie led her to the couch. Girlfriend picked up her clothing, sat down, and began dressing herself again. When she realized she'd put her sweater on backward, she sighed and turned it around. After smoothing her hair and wiping the tears from her face, she looked at Stevie with sweet brown eyes that reminded her of Ronald.

"I'm sorry we kept you up again." She paused. "I don't mean to bother you any more than I have, but do you know if he had another woman there?"

"He did. Last night."

She looked down, her eyes pooling up again. "You must think I'm such an idiot."

"Perhaps... before. But only because I saw what he is, and I knew you could do better."

She looked up, a tear raining down her cheek. "And now?"

"Now I'm impressed."

Girlfriend smiled a little.

"Did you want to sleep here?"

She shook her head. "I want to be far away from him."

Stevie nodded, somewhat relieved, given all the things she would need to hide. "I'll call you a taxi."

"No... I can't afford one."

"I'll cover it."

Stevie made the call and accompanied Girlfriend to the lobby. She waved at Manny, surprised at his being there so late.

"You don't have to wait," Girlfriend said.

"I don't mind."

Manny watched them, with eyes that seemed to indicate he knew something. When the taxi arrived, Stevie paid the driver in currency and waited until Girlfriend sat down in the back seat.

"By the way," Girlfriend said, puppy eyes looking up at her. "What's your name?"

"Stevie."

"I'm Amanda."

Stevie shut the door and waited until the taxi sped off. Back inside, Manny stood waiting.

"She alright?"

Stevie nodded. "Bad fight with my neighbor. It got physical."

Manny shook his head, crossing his arms over his stocky build. "That guy's such an asshole. He used to be this skinny pole with a million freckles and this bright red hair. Now he's making money and banging Yellows and thinks he can treat everyone like shit."

"You knew him before?"

"High school. Moved here from some shit town. He was an asshole then too... girls never liked him."

Ah.

Stevie said goodnight to Manny and headed back to bed.

A weekend of silence. No noise from next door. Not a single complaint from the portal. And no more outings or picnics with Seth.

Seth had other options, and always had. He never talked about them... it was what he didn't say that told her the most. He partook of the buffet available to him, much like Pomade did, as would anyone who had a buffet of options to choose from. She thought she'd injured him, but she hadn't. His kissing her... he'd merely gotten caught up in the moment, perhaps as she had, and a man like him was accustomed to women saying yes. If you spent enough time with someone you like, such a temptation could occur... and it was better for both of them that it didn't. And although she was grateful that they chatted with ease once more, she would miss their outings. She would miss him and the strange ease she felt in his presence.

Women and men can't be friends, Steviansa.

That never made sense to me, Mom. But maybe you're right in this case.

After a drizzly Monday morning commute, Stevie waved to Seth, who gave her a salute before he ducked into his workstation. She flipped on her red light and researched the location code for Ronald Carr's accuser. An older apartment building in Salvia, on Broad Street. Only twenty stories; fewer stories meant fewer apartments and fewer names to research. To obtain the rest of the information she needed, she waited until she got home and contacted Mobius.

Mobius: Scintillations, my old friend. How are you?

Artemis: Well. How's the Hood holding up?

Mobius: Still thriving, as always.

Artemis: I need a favor.

Mobius: Name it.

Artemis: I need a list of lessees for all units at 4105 Broad Street.

Mobius: You betcha. Give me a couple of days.

Artemis: Thank you.

Two days later, she came home to a message from Mobius. There it was... the list. She perused the document, which had the full names and ID Corp codes of the tenants in each apartment unit. None of names appeared familiar... except for one. However, it wasn't the name of someone she'd known growing up. When she cross-referenced it, she discovered why it seemed familiar. The name belonged to a woman who'd issued other portal complaints over the last couple of years, often aimed at Feds, none of which had led to anything worthwhile. She'd hunted down the woman's identity to keep an eye on her. Fortunately, monitoring her had yielded nothing that warranted action on Stevie's part. She would send the woman a warning, the kind of warning that would encourage her to rethink her abuse of the portal.

Stevie wanted to be angry at having wasted so much time on another dead end from a repeated rabble-rouser. Yet, any anger would have no chance against the relief that spread through her.

It's not you, Ronald. It's an empty threat, from a troubled woman. I'm sorry, my friend.

Stevie rounded the corner to Fourth Avenue, just south of the Circle, in the heart of the financial district and its shining, sky-high buildings. The smooth sidewalks teemed with men in dark suits, all striding here and there with confident expressions under their umbrellas, occasionally guffawing with their cronies. She ignored their stares.

She collapsed her umbrella and entered a bar, its walls black and sprinkled with ornate mirrors, the smell of musky cologne and aged whiskey overwhelming her. She passed several hordes of suits, the occasional Yellow in a tight black dress intermingling with the men. Stevie walked the gauntlet... where she saw him staring at her. She made eye contact—not the average kind that lasted a second or two, but the three-plus seconds kind that sent a message. Then she found a tight corner and sat.

Such a busy place. Friday night, the market's closed, and the Financials are out to release some tension after a grueling week of hijacking our economy.

She smiled at that. Mobius was correct about her occasional humorlessness, but even she saw the comedy in such thoughts. Even she knew that vilifying Financials was easy, that such men (and some women) had their virtues, that society needed sharks as much as it needed jellyfish. It just didn't need them to have more power than necessary, didn't need them infiltrating government positions with promises of economic growth, just to turn the law to their own favor while the rest of society suffered.

After boisterous discussion with his friends that grew louder and louder with each drink, he stood and stretched. Off he went to the restroom. She followed, watching him disappear into a stall.

Two men emerged from other stalls and looked at her, even hesitating, hoping her intrusion was meant for one of them, that she would share a stall for a few minutes of licentious pleasure. But when she made no move toward them, they left. Stevie locked the restroom door and approached his stall. The din of liquid pouring into liquid reverberated throughout the restroom as she waited.

When Pomade opened the stall, he hesitated upon seeing her, his soulless blue eyes growing large at her presence and what it meant. Smiling, she backed him into the stall, locked it... and got down on her knees. In a moment, Pomade undid his pants. But his expression changed when she stood and pointed the two-inch barrel pointed at his chest.

"What the f—"

When the round made contact, a pop echoed in the room as Pomade careened backward onto the toilet and slumped to the side, his pants crumpled around his ankles. Shot number two. She put her revolver away and crawled out from under the partition.

The restroom door jiggled. Voices. She closed her black coat, checked herself in the mirror, and wiped away bits of red spatter from her face and hair. She sprayed strong cologne to mask the acrid odor of gunpowder, unlocked the door, and stood aside as a couple of men filed in. She looked down, feigning embarrassment while obscuring her face. The men hesitated only for a moment before heading to the stalls. And she left.

Rain still fell. She opened her umbrella, another good way to obscure her identity from electronic eyes. One or two of the bar's patrons would tell the police they witnessed a Yellow in the bathroom around the time of Pomade's death. But they would provide no details, other than her looking like every Yellow in the place. Police would also eventually track her on their surveillance footage as she left and made her way out of Downtown. But soon they would lose her, they would have no face to search, and they would gain no more information than what they already had.

She headed to the Circle, the street noise drowning out the sound of rain pattering upon her umbrella. She didn't bemoan the pain of walking in the pointy tortures, the heaviness of her breasts, her dress chafing her skin, or the way her altered facial structure appeared in the mirrored glass she passed. She didn't even mind using up a sick day to prepare. She felt only relief. Soon, she spotted the tall ebony sculptures.

Into the Science Museum she went, where a large crowd of adults and children gathered. It was family night, plus the museum was hosting a black tie event in the Space Science wing. She elbowed her way through the crowds, grateful for so many people, until she arrived at the restroom. She changed into plain black pants and a sweater. Off came her yellow locks before they dissolved in the toilet, after which she donned a wig with mousy, matronly hair. And she left, getting lost in the mosaic of people and dead zones.

Under her umbrella, she crossed the street and approached the Circle's grass. She wiped the water droplets from a bench and took a seat. With a deep breath, calm came over her. The grass glowed in its verdancy, the fountain burst forth with water, the sages and pansies and crocuses offered their purples and yellows to any who would notice.

I used to take you on picnics here, Steviansa, when the weather was nice. Do you remember?

Of course, Mom.

Back at her building, when Stevie stepped out of the elevator,

Pomade's door sat quietly, as if knowing he wouldn't return. She hesitated for a moment before going inside her apartment.

After dinner, Stevie checked her portals. She had a message from Mobius.

That list of lessees I sent you, for that building on Broad... that was from almost a year ago. Sorry about that. The records around here aren't as organized as they should be. Here's the current one, and hope it helps.

M

Stevie pulled out the previous list and compared it with the new one. The names remained the same, but for one. Stevie's breath caught in her throat.

Kira Carr.

EPISODE 9

WASN'T EXPECTING YOU

Stevie sat on a furry chair in Kira's spacious, peach-colored bedroom. Clothing and other belongings were strewn about Kira's bed and floor. Stevie munched on salty potato chips, a treat she loved but one her mother carefully restricted. When she realized she'd eaten half the bowl of delectable spuds, embarrassment came over her.

"I ate too many of your potato chips," she admitted to Kira, who was crouched near her shelves, searching for a game she wanted to play.

"That's okay," Kira said, never looking at the bowl. "We have more. And I know how strict your mom is about snack foods, so I won't tell!"

Stevie giggled, relieved.

It was a sunny Saturday, when they should've been playing kickball at the park. But another bioterror warning had trapped them indoors.

Kira stood and flipped her honey blonde hair back. "I can't find it."

Stevie smiled. Of course she couldn't. Kira misplaced things all the time and her room was always messy. But Stevie never said a word. Her mother taught her it wasn't nice to make fun of people's imperfections.

"I have a better idea," Kira said, flopping down on her bed. "Let's talk about what we want our careers to be when we turn eighteen and get to live in our own apartments. You start."

Stevie hesitated. She'd considered such a topic many times. But she'd never shared her ideas with anyone.

"Want me to go first?" Kira said, peering at her. "You always need extra time to think."

Stevie nodded.

"I want to help people," Kira said. "The war... it's hurting us. People are losing their loved ones to the enemy, here and overseas. Some will lose their money and their homes. And my dad says that the City will run out of money too because of the war and because the Financials are taking all the money and spending it on fancy things. The people and the City will need help... and I'm going to help them. My dad says I'm good at helping others."

"You are good at helping others. You helped me when I moved here."

"You're nice! Just because you're from Crocus doesn't mean we shouldn't be friends. And you help me with my science homework." She grabbed a handful of chips. "What about you? You'll probably be a scientist, huh? That's helping people too, if you try to find an antidote to the poison that killed the dogs or if you make crops grow faster!"

"Maybe," Stevie said. "But... I think I want to help by stopping the bad people."

"What bad people? The enemy?"

"Them... but also the people here who take advantage of the war and people's fear, and hurt us."

Kira's face fell. "Like the Financials?"

"Some of them. Others too. How about this: I'll find all the bad people and make sure they're punished, and you help the good ones."

Her smile returned. "I'll agree to that!"

Stevie slouched on her soft couch and stared at one of her Peruvian Apple cacti, knowing she needed to get up and get ready for work. The long-forgotten memory had resurfaced upon waking that morning. She hadn't slept well. Vivid, nonsensical dreams had plagued her, images of Kira floating past, sometimes looking like Kira and other times not. But it was her. She could feel her, as if she knew her again, as if Kira slept in the same room with her.

The person who'd accused Ronald of sexual abuse wasn't the woman who'd issued those other complaints, or some other woman who'd spent time with the Carrs during her "formative years." The accuser was Kira herself, Ronald's own daughter.

Kira, her friend since she was 10. Her friend who'd "gone wild," as Stevie's mother put it. Stevie had disapproved of Kira's experimentation with drugs, her sexual adventures, and especially her association with certain groups that had her occasionally tussling with the law. Stevie didn't judge her friend, but she worried about Kira's safety and that she'd lost sight of her goals. It only took one or two legal entanglements or an unplanned pregnancy to derail one's life. Kira had even put herself in danger a few times, stories she would share when Stevie called. But any warning Stevie offered was brushed off. Eventually, Kira stopped returning her calls.

The Carrs looked down on me for not having a father for you, her mother would say. *But look how you turned out, and look how Kira turned out. This is what happens when you grow up too privileged, Steviansa. Only the privileged have the luxury to go wild.*

Stevie had always hated her mother's judgment of Kira. She'd hated her mother comparing them to the Carrs and using the comparison to feel superior, to justify her own questionable choices. However, she had to consider that her mother's arguments about privilege had at least some merit. Poor kids went wild too, but not in the way Kira did, with the panache and power of having grown up with plenty. Like the DeWitt students who'd vandalized the Passage... but worse.

Stevie sat for some time, her espresso cup only half-emptied and long cold. Who was Kira? Was she the girl who'd been victimized by her powerful father, who worked at Social Services to help others? Or was she the girl raised with advantage and luxury, who looked down her nose at the establishment she'd benefited from, who'd grown disgusted with their corrupt City and saw her powerful father as a key factor in that imbalance? Stevie's files overflowed with portal accusations against Feds, many of which came from people like Kira. And who better to do the accusing than a Fed's own daughter, who could provide the kind of information that would place him on a justice seeker's radar? Where even if that accusation didn't pan out, the detailed search for evidence might yield something else worthy of punishment?

It was as if Kira knew. Knew that Stevie stood at the other end of that portal, waiting to take advantage of the access she had to Ronald and to eradicate the bad from society, just as she'd promised. But Kira couldn't know. No one knew. Not Mobius, not even her mother, whose death served as the beginning of Stevie's real service to humanity.

Tired of trying to solve the unsolvable, Stevie stood and got ready for work.

On her way to the shuttle grounds, Stevie fingered her new cylinder when she encountered any corner, alleyway, or other place from which her two stalkers could make a sudden appearance. But despite her preparedness, she'd seen no sign of them since her eventful trip to Viola.

Once through security and on the shuttle, she turned down a rare offer to sit from an older man who worked in Maintenance. Gloom set in all around them, a dense gray fog that soon rendered their view of the shrinking City nonexistent. Up they went, rising above the earth, above the chaos and the noise, to yet another layer of clouds. Soon, they rose above the mist and the sun emerged. But its appearance had no warming effect on her.

She passed Seth's workstation, hesitating for a moment. She felt an urge to drop in, to tell him that Ronald had been accused of pedophilia, and that his own daughter had done the accusing and placed him in line for the guillotine. She didn't know where the urge came from. She only knew that Seth would somehow be the right person to tell, that he would offer some sort of blunt wisdom. But she could never tell him. She could never tell anyone.

She had to work that way... unhindered by others, whether worrying about their safety or worrying about them getting her pinched. Such freedom had its price: loneliness, no protection, no one to talk to when a job became difficult. But she'd accepted that. She was used to it. Even before she had so much to hide, she'd concealed her ideas and desires for years, knowing they wouldn't sit well with others.

There was another reason she couldn't tell Seth, even about her petty acts of service. She couldn't encumber him with the sort of garbage she dealt with, not when he still carried the residual burden of all those years of warfare. That burden pervaded his dreams and flashbacks, fueled his enduring vigilance. Seth was her friend, and she had to protect him. The same way she'd protected her mother.

After turning on her computer and screens, Stevie headed to Herbie's office. Before she got there, Seth emerged from his workstation.

She smiled. "Good morning, Major."

"Hey, Stevie." He had a crease between his brows again, and a tense look.

"What's wrong? Do you need more of the herbs?"

"No... I'm fine. How are you?"

"Good," she lied. She placed her hand on his arm briefly before continuing on.

She knew that distracted look by now. He'd had another bout of nightmares and broken sleep, his past hauntings only exacerbated by unmitigated norepinephrine levels. She didn't know if his reluctance to seek her help was due to their being at work, or because his involvement with the brown-haired woman made him feel uncomfortable talking to her on a personal level.

At Herbie's office, Marianne's desk sat empty. Stevie immediately knew why. She knocked on Herbie's door and entered when he shouted the okay.

"Did Marianne have the baby?"

Herbie looked up from his desk, his dark eyes without their usual sparkle. "Not yet, I'm afraid. She's had complications. I'm holding off on talking to the crew until I get some real news. Hopefully it will be good news."

A dread came over Stevie.

No. Not Marianne, not the baby.

"What can I do for you, Stevie?"

Stevie asked her questions and got them answered. When she left, she added, "Please keep me posted on Marianne."

"Will do, Stevie."

She worked until the afternoon, focusing on her data and pushing away thoughts of Marianne, Kira, Seth, and other problems she couldn't solve. All day her mental capacities felt sluggish, as if her concerns pervaded her work like they'd pervaded her sleep. But then she realized that, in her fogged mind that morning, she hadn't finished her espresso. To Machine she went, the dark beacon that she hoped would offer a sliver of muted joy.

She waited in line, the scent of coffee floating her way. She heard guffaws nearby and caught a flash of navy from the corner of her eye. She glanced over, and froze. Ronald Carr appeared only feet from her.

Turn around and walk. Or he'll see the truth. He'll know.

But before the message could reach her spinal cord and then her legs, Ronald spotted her. Soft brown eyes, the ones she'd always trusted, lit up just a little when he smiled.

"How are you, Mister Carr?"

"Well enough, Stevie. I was just stopping through for a quick hit of caffeine before my next meeting. I keep hoping we'll get one of these upstairs, but none of the others seem interested."

Stevie motioned for him to go ahead of her, to which Ronald gave his thanks. He placed a pink, flower-embossed mug under it, one Minnie likely made for him. "Coffee with two ounces of milk, please," he said politely, more politely than even she did when asking for the favor she valued so much.

Machine remained silent, and the pink chunky mug sat empty.

"Coffee with two ounces of milk, please," Ronald repeated, his tone more direct this time.

Still nothing.

Ronald did what anyone did when something that had always functioned in a predictable manner suddenly didn't—got a perplexed look on his face and stepped back to try and discover what he'd missed, all the while harboring a secret fear that he'd done something wrong.

"He must be malfunctioning," Ronald said, trying to hide his irritation.

Disappointment flooded her. "I'll let someone know."

Ronald thanked her, grabbed his mug, and left. Stevie left as well, wondering how she would survive the day on half an espresso from so many hours ago. But something stopped her. She returned to Machine, his stark blackness holding court before her. After eyeing him for a moment, Stevie placed her black mug under the spout.

"Double espresso, please."

She waited. And after a moment's hesitation, she heard noise. Machine began pouring the dark substance into her cup, a tan crema forming on its top. Perfect. She stood for a moment, almost afraid to take it, until she realized someone waited behind her. As she walked away, she heard Machine making his unique sounds as he served his next eager customer.

That evening, Stevie combed through all her data on Ronald Carr again: the portal complaints, notes from her recon missions, and the surveillance data she'd gathered. The evidence wasn't there. And Kira, who must have learned about the portal from the woman who'd used it too many times, couldn't offer the sort of details she needed to act.

Put it away and move on.

No. She can't level an accusation like that, after the other things she's done, and not face consequences.

Maybe she's telling the truth.

She read the portal directions. She knows I need evidence and there simply isn't any. I've watched the man who included me in his family read to his foster daughter on countless occasions. Surveillance doesn't lie. And he's not taking advantage of dead zones. I know the signs better than anyone and I would see them.

Maybe he only abused Kira.

That's unlikely.

Stevie held her breath for a moment, contemplating it all, trying to decide which voice to listen to. She exhaled, wishing again for Seth and his acute mind, his ability to sidestep equivocation and call something for what it was.

Then, an idea came to her. A useful idea, but one that crossed a boundary that should never be crossed.

She broke into the City's Social Services database, marveling at how easy it was to access private and confidential files that only a court order could unseal. Yet, nobody with her skills—and a penchant for blackmail—wanted such information, not when they could go after the City, the Feds, or the Financials and glean information with which to lean on them. And such lofty targets didn't use Social Services. Kira, despite having financial resources, had sought counseling at Social Services. She'd told Stevie that she couldn't afford to go anywhere else without using her father's "dirty money."

After boring deeper into the vast pit she'd already dug, Stevie found what she should never have looked for: session records from Kira's visits with her counselor. Kira's father would come into her room late at night and "spend time" with her, special time that only they knew about. Touching her, soothing her, teaching her. It was always the same, it wasn't that often, but it began when she was five years old.

Five years old.

Stevie's heart began to pound.

But why hadn't she seen any sign of such abuses with Minnie, their foster daughter? Had Kira lied? Or had Ronald ceased his nocturnal exploitations? He could have, but since when do such men cease? Stevie sighed in exasperation, once again wishing for Seth, but this time for his free use of expletives. She was back in the same place: without enough evidence to act.

She pulled up the surveillance data and reexamined all the nighttime activity from Minnie's bedroom. Nothing.

A Federal Watch executive, who allowed himself to be surveilled to serve as an example, would know to avoid any damning activity in his home. We had no home surveillance when we were kids, when he could have harmed Kira.

True. But if guilty, he would find a way. The urges of a paraphiliac will always trump reason, decency, and fear of getting caught.

Another idea.

She ran the data through a scan she'd never tried before. She'd never needed it before. The scan searched for evidence of tampering, if someone had cut or somehow doctored the digital data. But the scan produced no signs of tinkering.

Stevie pulled up the list of video files for Minnie's bedroom, each comprised of a 24-hour period of compressed data. She examined each file's size and date stamp, looking for anything amiss. The dates showed no anomalies. The files were close to the same size, but for two, which were somewhat smaller. Their decreased size wasn't enough to warrant concern, but she nonetheless spent some time analyzing them, her sense of exasperation nearly reaching its pinnacle.

And then, after writing lines of code and reading through all the "gobbledegook," she saw something. The two files were smaller for a reason: both contained less than 24 hours of actual data. That would happen if someone had doctored the data, but she'd already ruled out such a possibility. However, it could also happen for one other reason: if someone had disabled the surveillance at its source. Unlike disabling the hidden eyes at one's residence, shutting off the juice from the Disc wouldn't set off an alert. The file would merely come up short, which no one would detect unless searching for it, and even then could easily blame the shortage on a brief hiccup in the system. Few had the power to disable Federal Watch surveillance at its source. Even she lacked that power.

Stevie selected the first of the two shortened days, scrolling through it, watching the elapsed time crawl by. And sure enough, she found it: a time jump from 10:03 pm to 11:17 pm. After the jump, Minnie lay under her pink comforter, turning over on one side, then the other, before eventually falling asleep. Stevie examined the other shortened file... another time jump. And when she looked closely at the footage after the jump, she saw something she hadn't noticed previously, when she'd had no need to look closely.

Minnie wiped her face, twice. What had appeared like the random movements of a sleeping child was actually a young girl brushing away her tears.

The darkness came. It threatened to engulf her, to swallow her whole like a giant black whale in a vast black sea, trapping her within its giant stomach, where she would swim for eternity.

Stevie stood up, the urge to shout at the far-reaching capacity of her lungs becoming nearly overwhelming. But no one would hear her. It would be fruitless, purposeless, and in vain. Like everything. Their planet would keep rotating on its axis, plants and animals would persevere in reproducing their species, and humans would continue bludgeoning one another in tiny and gigantic ways.

The next morning, Stevie called in sick.

Stevie stood outside the Larkspur Diner, her bag slung over her shoulder and her hat and trench coat preventing the cold drizzle from seeping its way in.

He would take his time. It was Saturday... no need for Ronald to hurry off to the shuttle, to meet with other powerful suits about the safety and welfare of their county's citizens. She checked her watch. He should be done eating by now.

Unlike Seth, Ronald didn't spot her right away. He merely sipped his coffee with two ounces of milk and read his tablet, unaware of her presence until she stood at the other end of his table.

"Stevie," he said, his eyes widening in surprise.

She hesitated, her throat tightening so much that she didn't know if she could speak. She swallowed, gazing at Ronald's kind brown eyes, the blackness threatening again. "I need to talk to you."

"Of course." He motioned to the other chair. "Have a seat."

She shook her head. "Not here. We need to talk somewhere private, with no people... and no eyes."

"Are you in pain?" It was Disc-speak, to inquire if she were in danger. "No."

Ronald stood and swiped his ID for payment. Stevie followed him out the door and into a taxi, where she sat staring out the window, feeling Ronald's occasional glance but never meeting his eyes. They passed storefronts and glassy buildings and couples strolling to find breakfast. Soon, she saw tall black sculptures gleaming in the distance.

Once at the Circle, they stepped out of the taxi and stood among the towering ebony sentinels, the stone civic buildings, the green zone speckled with people despite another day of dense fog and icy drizzle. Ronald silently led them across the grass, the dampness creeping into Stevie's running shoes until they reached the Circle's focal point, where they stood in the middle of it all.

It was as she'd suspected. The Circle's center was a dead zone, for the Disc and for the City. She recalled Seth's tromping through the grass on their picnic day. Maybe he'd known that as well. She didn't know what Seth knew, any more than Seth knew what she knew. It had to be that way.

Ronald glanced around them. "What's going on, Stevie? Did you find something... in the data?"

She nodded.

"What happened?" The brown eyes reflected concern, and it was genuine. It was always genuine.

"You, Kira... and now your foster daughter. That happened."

Staring. A blink or two, as if flapping his eyelids would generate a coherent response. Until...

"I'm sorry?"

"You did it, Ronald. You molested Kira, and Minnie. And you utilized your position at the Disc to shut off the juice to Minnie's bedroom."

Ronald's eyes cooled just a little. "This is why you asked to meet with me?"

"Skip the denial, Ronald. I have the evidence."

He merely stared at her, the warmth in his eyes vanished.

"Tell me it's the truth," she went on. "Tell me you did this, during all those years I knew you and looked up to you like a father—" Her voice broke, the constriction in her throat returned.

The brown eyes watered, only to have the glistening disappear with another flap of his eyelids. Then he looked away.

You. You disgusting, ignoble, despicable pig.

"I..." he began. He shook his head, struggling to keep it all under an ever-loosening lid. "I've lived with this burden my entire life. I've tried to stop—"

"Don't."

This was why she never confronted those she hunted. She couldn't stand listening to their garbage, to hear the arsenal of responses that guilty people confabulated. She wouldn't tolerate them denying their behavior, despite clear evidence, as if repeatedly doing so would transform their words into truth. She wouldn't tolerate them justifying themselves, contriving some elaborate rationalization for their destructive behavior, conveyed in a studied tone as if they'd practiced it in front of the mirror every day after brushing their teeth. She especially wouldn't tolerate them bursting into tears and sobbing through an apology, begging for mercy or even promising to change, a commitment that would be quickly forgotten if she were foolish enough to believe it.

Mercy. What a pathetic excuse to avoid doing what was right, to avoid doing what was difficult. If these people felt any sort of real remorse, they would have turned themselves in or ended their own lives rather than continuing their destruction of humanity.

Drizzle fell upon her, upon Ronald. Electro-taxis whizzed in the distance, beyond the still of the grass. A high-frequency siren sounded, a medic's van racing to the aid of some ill person.

Ronald's face hardened, recovered from the other emotions that threatened to waylay him. "It was you. You leaked that surveillance data for the Passage of Truth. I knew it." When she offered no denial, he went on. "You lied to me, even when I offered you an out."

"I didn't trust you. Now I know why."

He let out a sigh. "Between you and me, Stevie, I thought what you did showed real audacity. I know you've engaged in other activities, those that challenge the establishment. As long as you weren't taking part in more questionable pursuits or putting the Watch at risk, I turned a blind eye... because I know you. I know you like I know Kira. I know who's benevolent in this fucked up world of ours, and who isn't."

"And are you benevolent, Ronald?"

He looked away, as if answering would waste his time, and hers. Across the grass, a couple with a toddler walked slowly, each parent holding a tiny hand as the child ambled about on unsure feet.

"What do you want from me, Stevie?"

"Everything."

"Everything? What... you're going to squeeze me for information? Or is it money you want?"

Stevie opened her trench and lifted her Oakenfold, just enough for Ronald to get a clear glimpse.

Any color on Ronald's face drained away. More eyelid flapping, this time more rapidly. "Oh no. No. Not you, Stevie. Tell me it isn't you."

She gave no answer.

He shook his head, his pallor remaining. "This is your mother's influence."

"My mother has nothing to do with this," she hissed. "It began after she passed away."

He glanced around nervously. "People will see. They'll hear, even with the silencer. They'll catch you. "

"Who said I'll do it now?"

"I have evidence, Stevie. You'll lose your job... and everything else."

"I have better evidence, Ronald. The world will know the truth about you, about Kira and Minnie and how you used Federal Watch to ensure you could molest your children without getting caught. The public will rebel against the program, and they'll assume Miriam tolerated your sick behavior... which means Minnie goes back into the system to wind up at a group home in Viola where she'll get manhandled by some other pervert. And I can hide, Ronald... better than anyone, for as long as necessary." Her eyes bore into his. "No matter what you do, I will find you."

Keep going, Ronald. Cycle through the stages of grief. When you've finished bargaining, you'll get angry, and then you'll accept the truth.

"How dare you involve my family," he growled.

"I didn't involve them. You did."

"And the service I've provided to our society, that I provided even to you and your mother... that means nothing..."

Don't. Or I'll open fire on you right now.

She braced herself for Ronald's next attempt at self-preservation. But then his face fell, as if the truth of it all had collapsed upon him. Tears welled up in his eyes, too many to blink away.

"This day had to come. I thought it would be a relief..." He took a deep breath and spoke again. His last argument, his last bargaining tool, spoken with the persuasive, genuine passion that Ronald did so well. Stevie didn't want to hear it, didn't care what he had to say. But she listened nonetheless, for reasons she couldn't grasp.

When Ronald finally went silent, Stevie stood for some time, the drizzle falling upon her hat and dripping down her trench. Reluctantly, unwillingly, morosely... she nodded. And Ronald walked away, disappearing into the fog.

Suddenly it seemed cold out, colder than their coldest months. She shivered as she tightened the belt on her trench coat. Then, she began to cry.

Don't you dare cry for that man, Steviansa.

Be quiet, Mom.

I won't be silenced. You know that.

Yes, you will. I won't listen to you anymore.

Stevie's tears flowed... her own personal rainfall, cleansing her like a downpour rinsed the City's streets. She stood in the Circle's center, in the midst of it all, and sobbed, not caring about the rain or the cold or what anyone thought. When her tears waned, she headed west through the fog and dampness, across the grass and past the old stately buildings and beyond the dark sculptures.

Home.

Stevie stepped off the elevator, her hat and coat still waterlogged, but her eyes dry. Pomade's apartment door gaped open. She peeked inside as she passed; two men in blue suits stood talking. One of them spotted her.

"Miss Maples!"

She sighed, pushing a curse from her mind, tempted to disappear into the stairwell and run, where no cop could catch her. But even in her upside-down state, she knew they'd find her. She halted as the burly detective emerged from Pomade's place.

"Good morning, ma'am. I'm Detective Stevens. You mind if I ask you a few questions?"

"No. Of course not."

He pulled out a recording device. "For the record, your full name is Steviansa Maples, and you live at 3315 Tarragon Street, number 3404?"

"That's correct."

He looked at her for a moment. "Steviansa Maples, huh? Your parents plant lovers, by any chance?"

Stevie stared.

"That's a joke, ma'am."

She nodded. "Of course. Sorry." She glanced at Pomade's open door. "This is all a little overwhelming."

"I can imagine. Do you know what happened to your neighbor?"

"I heard."

"Did you know him well?"

"No."

"Was he a good neighbor?"

She shrugged. "How so?"

"Was he quiet? Noisy?"

"Occasionally noisy. He had women over."

"You don't say. How many women?"

"I'm not sure. He was single, successful... you know how it is."

He nodded. "Of course, ma'am. Did you ever see anyone suspicious coming around here, or have any idea who would want to harm him?"

She shook her head. "No."

"What about his ex-girlfriend, this... Amanda Green. Ever meet her or get a sense for their relationship?"

"I've spoken to her briefly. She's very sweet. But I don't know the details of their relationship, Detective."

Detective Stevens nodded and turned off his recorder. "Thank you for your time, Miss Maples."

"You're welcome. Have you all found any clues yet, as to who's doing this?"

"We have, ma'am. I can't tell you the specifics... but personally, I give the Oakenfold Killer a month, two tops, before we have him or her in custody." He gave an emphatic nod. "Thanks again, ma'am."

A month, two tops.

After the detective disappeared into Pomade's apartment, Stevie entered her code and opened her door. The automatic lights came on, feeling abnormally bright on such a dreary day. She set her bag down and went to her closet, where she removed her .357 from her trench coat. She stared at its smooth sheen, at the grip that fit her hand perfectly, before stowing it away.

"Lights off."

Are you sure that was the right decision?

I hope so.

Late that evening, Stevie turned on the news. The caption read "Breaking News" as the familiar duo appeared onscreen.

"Tonight we have a stunning, tragic story here at CityNews. Ronald Carr, one of the executives in charge of the Federal Watch program, has been found dead in his home."

Fog enclosed them as rain pounded against the shuttle's windows. Up they went, away from the world until it no longer existed, to the place of her livelihood. The place where Ronald Carr would no longer exist.

"Did you hear? About one of the executives?" one man said to the woman sitting next to him.

"No. What happened?"

"He's dead. Looks like an overdose of pills."

She gasped, putting her hand over her mouth. "Oh my. How unbelievably sad!"

"He left behind a wife and daughter, and a foster daughter they'd adopted from the child welfare system."

She shook her head. "Which executive was it?"

"Ronald Carr."

"The nice looking one? With the big brown eyes? Oh, that's so sad!"

Stevie pulled out her headphones and put them on.

When they arrived at the Disc, it seemed far quieter than usual. Employees glanced at one another, looking for someone else to initiate conversation, unsure whether they should talk about it. Soon, Herbie would take her into his office and give her the news. A few would eye her, knowing she had a history with Ronald that reached back 20 years. She turned on her red sign, which remained lit for the rest of the day. No one bothered her... not even Herbie.

Wednesday morning, Stevie walked to an old stone church in Artemisia, the streets dry for the first time in days. When she arrived, an impressive crowd had already gathered, including many familiar faces from the Disc. She spotted Herbie's large build, a couple of other managers huddled near him. He let out a sob as one of the managers patted his back. Stevie looked away.

Miriam and Minnie stood near the entrance, both dressed in black, a pale-faced Miriam greeting the guests as Minnie watched all the unfamiliar faces. Miriam smiled upon seeing her, and Stevie gave her a hug. She didn't linger, knowing Miriam had many people to face. Before she could choose a place to sit, she saw something. There, at the other end of the church, so deep in a corner that one almost missed her, stood Kira. Kira looked right at her.

Stevie approached her, getting just close enough before stopping and removing her eyeshades. Kira stared, not making a move toward Stevie. After a long pause, Kira took off her eyeshades as well. Familiar, vulnerable, resilient eyes stared back at her. Stevie smiled, just a little. The shell cracked, Kira's stoic expression melted, and she began to cry. Stevie went over and put her arms around Kira, Kira's soft body leaning on hers as she sobbed. Stevie held on tight, the darkness finally lifting, the world in all its chaos beginning to make sense again.

When Kira pulled away, Stevie handed her a handkerchief to wipe her face and nose.

"Stevie," she whispered, clutching the handkerchief. "It's my fault."

"No, it isn't," Stevie replied sternly.

She shook her head. "Stevie, if you knew..."

"Let's go outside."

Stevie led Kira past the others and out to the street, where the whizzing taxis would drown their conversation. She made sure Kira stood at the proper angle, in the improbable circumstance that someone would observe their conversation over footage and read her lips.

"It's my fault," Kira said, her face wet with tears. "I called it in. They must have come after him, and somehow he convinced them to let him take his own life. He was always so persuasive..." Her face scrunched up again and more tears ran down her reddened face. "I know what you must be thinking, Stevie. To you, he's a father figure, but to me..." She lowered her voice. "He was a monster. A kind, loving, monster. If you only knew..." More tears. "You don't have to believe me. After the way I behaved toward you..."

Stevie placed her hands on Kira's shoulders. "I do believe you. I know you, Kira. *I know you.*"

Kira took a deep breath and wiped her tears with Stevie's handkerchief. "You once said it's just as important to destroy the bad as it is to create the good. Do you still believe that?"

"I do."

The din of passing taxis faded as the street gave them a temporary silence.

Kira heaved another sigh. "I thought I would feel better, triumphant. But I feel..."

"It will pass."

"I've missed you, Stevie."

"I've missed you, too."

When Kira's face crinkled up again, Stevie hugged her once more.

After a somber funeral and a slightly less somber half day at work, Stevie stepped off the elevator. She longed for the quiet of her apartment, for the soft couch, for a plate of vegetable quiche and drawn shades.

She glanced at Pomade's door again. It was closed. Soon, someone else would occupy the place, perhaps someone with more promise. Perhaps someone who would actually talk to her, or at least hold the elevator door for her. She entered her code and opened her door, already feeling better at the sight of its dark interior and smell of espresso beans. Just as she went to shut the door, she hesitated. The automatic lights should have come on. She waved her hand around, hoping to trigger the sensor. Nothing.

Something's wrong.

She turned to leave. But before she reached the threshold, someone grabbed her from behind, a strong arm surrounding her torso and arms, and another covering her mouth. The door slammed shut.

She stomped as hard as she could, aiming her heel at her assailant's foot, but it struck nothing more than air as she was easily lifted off her feet. She let out multiple screams, each muffled as she tried to pull her head forward to prepare for a head butt. Her assailant only clamped down on her harder, allowing her to do nothing at all but thrash about like a child engaged in a tantrum.

He carried her like a mere doll across the room and forced her upon a chair with a thud, pain shooting through her tailbone. Before she could do or think anything, he'd restrained her with twine and stretched duct tape over her mouth, forcing her to take shallow breaths through her nose. She strained against the twine, to no avail. At last she ceased her futile efforts, saving her energy for whatever would come.

The City. Kira. Seth. Who will look after them when I'm gone?

They'd found her. The two women... her two stalkers. They'd gone beyond what she'd believed them capable of, what anyone was capable of. Now, she would pay the price for underestimating their power, which was vast indeed if they could gain access to her home without setting off the warning system she had in place. And with all the damning evidence in her home, the price would be steep, indeed.

Yet, her assailant was male. Mohawk and Gray Streak's muscle, someone they brought in to make the sale. When her attacker's steps led him away from her, it only confirmed her belief. The two women stood in the shadows, waiting for their henchman to raise the lights and reveal their presence.

A tiny light appeared near her door. A flashlight. A gloved, male hand tinkered with her lighting control panel until the lights came on. Squinting at the sudden brightness, Stevie watched, waiting for the stalking duo to appear.

They didn't.

She saw only a muscular male figure in black field gear, from his black boots to his masked face. Stevie took in every detail she could.

If she survived, and certainly if he left any traces of DNA during his attack, she would find him.

But when her assailant removed his mask and stood before her, she blinked in disbelief.

It was Seth.

EPISODE 10
HOW YOU LIKE ME NOW?

Seth.

Seth, her friend. Seth, her colleague. Military man. And clearly... Special Forces.

Should have known.

Stevie sat still, staring at Seth, feeling a strange sense of relief at the sight of his blue eyes and tightly cut fair hair. Despite his angry expression, his tying her up, his invading her home.

Countless speculations ran through her mind like ideas being bandied about in a troubleshooting session. They ranged from the terrifying to the ludicrous. But she encouraged none of them. She waited, partly because it was up to Seth to make his intentions clear, and partly because her restrained body and duct-taped mouth gave her very few options.

"I'm going to take the tape off," Seth finally said, his voice quiet but measured. "If you make a fucking sound other than doing exactly what I tell you, I'll gag you again."

Her lips smarted when Seth yanked off the tape. As promised, she remained quiet.

"Quite a place you have here," he said, looking around. "Neat. Clean." He pointed to the bedrooms. "An interesting collection of clothing and wigs. And other things too, science-y things." His tone was mocking. "No wonder you never invited me over. Although... I guess you never had any reason to, did you?"

Disappointment, perhaps, in that last statement. But no bitterness. She could rule out the slight but real possibility of revenge for rejecting his advance.

"I suppose the place is pretty quiet now, huh? With your neighbor taking two bullets and being left to die with his pants down?" He shook his head, as if disapproving of the way Pomade parted with life, as if such a death was beneath him. "Well, Steviansa.... if I know you, you're probably wondering when I'll get to the point. And you'd probably rather walk right into the pain that's coming your way than listen to a bunch of bullshit."

Yes.

This was it. Seth knew about her misuse of Disc data. Someone had figured it out and sent Seth to handle it. Stevie held her breath as Seth reached inside his field jacket, ready to retrieve something. Surveillance footage? Usage data? A phone with which to call the Feds? She watched, waiting for the instrument of her destruction. But when he held it up, she gasped. From his hand dangled a handgun. Her Oakenfold.

Oh no.

Seth's eyebrows went up. "You weren't expecting that!" He walked closer to her, his jaw set. "Why the fuck else would I be here? So we can share another coffee and you can lie to my fucking face about knowing nothing about the Oakenfold Killer? So you can act innocent and tell me about your mom and growing up in Crocus, while in your spare time you've been murdering those men? Or so you can pretend to be my goddamned friend while you wait for the opportunity to put a bullet in my chest?" He shook his head. "How hard you must have laughed at me, at everything I said about women not being capable of real evil."

She shook her head in protest, but he didn't notice. He paced, anger shifting to agitation, more than she'd ever seen in him. After setting her gun down and attempting to compose himself, he faced her.

"Did you kill those men? Or did you just forget to mention that you too like collecting antique weapons?"

"I killed them."

"Every one of them?"

"Every one of them."

"And you lied to me, to my face, on multiple occasions."

"I did."

He turned away again, as if hearing the truth from its source was somehow more powerful than whatever evidence had sent him her way in the first place. He paced some more, his jaw set but his long lashes blinking a few times, as if trying to calm the storm that gathered within him. Suddenly, he sat down on her couch and put his head in his hands.

"Seth—"

"Don't talk. I can't stand the sound of your goddamned voice right now."

No, Seth. You don't understand. I can mitigate your pain, if you let me!

After several moments, he rose from the couch and approached her, his fists clenched. "When I got the tipoff, I didn't believe it at first. But the clues were there the whole time. I didn't put my ass on the line for seven years in that goddamned war just to have psychopaths like you infiltrate Federal Watch and inflict more damage on us. I swore I'd protect our people, any way I can." He shook his head. "I should've called it in already. I guess... I guess I had to hear it from you first."

When Seth pulled his phone from his pocket, Stevie didn't feel scared. She only felt lousy, for hurting Seth, for lying to him, and for the impact it had on him.

"Do you want to know why I do it?"

"No." He put the earpiece in.

"Seth..."

"Stop saying my goddamned name, you fucking bitch!" he shouted at her, his face reddening. He slammed his phone down and approached her.

She cringed and turned her face away. Anger flooded her, a heat spreading from her head to her feet as the twine seemed to grow tighter. Tears threatened... but she forced herself to think dark thoughts, the darkest of thoughts, to discourage their flow. Tears would never do.

"Look at me," he ordered.

But she couldn't.

"I said *look at me*."

When she still refused, Seth grabbed her face and forced it back toward him, fury engulfing her as her opinion of Seth began to disintegrate like a concrete building assaulted by an explosive device.

"It's your best bet to do what I say," he growled, still grasping her jaw.

"Or you'll what?" she spat, shaking his hand off. "You'll break into my home, invade my privacy, tie me up, and then parade around with your two hundred pounds of muscle and your Special Forces training and call me disgusting names? You're pathetic, Seth... drunk on your own power!"

Seth couldn't hide his surprise at her outburst. "I'm drunk on power? You skulk through the City at night, killing off Financials and leaving them for their friends and family to find them, and I'm drunk on power?"

"If you weren't, you'd have asked me why I do this, and why I lied to you—"

"Who gives a fuck why?" he cried. "Who gives a fuck? You murder innocent men! And yes, I checked their records, even more carefully than the reporters did. Even if they were assholes, or crooked, or immoral, they didn't deserve to die."

"They weren't innocent," she hissed at him. "They've done awful things."

"Oh yeah? Tell me about the awful things they did. Tell me what that Rosa guy did, the one who writes those books and teaches those financial seminars, to wind up dead in his own home, for his wife and kids to find him. Or that guy from the old library... did he reject you when you wanted a date, because your hair was too fucking short or because you look like some wannabe Brownie? Go ahead... tell me!"

She gritted her teeth, her dwindling respect for Seth taking another hit. For a mere moment she considered daring him to make that call, daring him to do anything that would get her away from him and the things he said. They would know she was responsible for the murders, but they would never know how she did it, not really. Any important information on her methods would be deleted the moment the Feds or anyone else broke into her system. And she'd find a way out of prison. There was always a way out.

But this wasn't some random creep. This was Seth, who, despite his searing comments and despite her diminished respect for him, had served their country, had been her good friend once. She owed him at least some of the truth. So she spoke.

"The financial guru who writes the books... he would pick up women in nice bars, lure them to his home, and then drug and rape them. The guy at the library... he'd meet up with women from those sites, then tie them up so he could torture and humiliate them."

He looked dubious. "And how would you know any of this?"

"I get reports, from victims."

"Reports? Women make claims about powerful men and you just believe them?"

"Of course I don't just believe them. I do my research."

"How?"

"I'm not telling you that."

"You don't have to. I already know. You use Watch data. You take what's supposed to be used to protect people, and use it to kill people."

"And what about you, Seth?" she countered. "How did you find out about me or discover where I live... or find your way in here? Maybe the Feds would find that interesting as well."

"You fucking threatening me?"

"No, I'm not. But don't you lecture me about abuse of power. Those dead men had plenty of power, and they chose to harm women because we live in a world that tolerates it and tells women it's their job to accept their powerlessness. I thought you were different than those men, but now you sound like one of them."

Seth's face paled. She wasn't sure if it was from anger or humiliation. Or both.

She went on. "Every one of those men I killed were detriments to society. They were guilty, they were carefully researched for evidence."

Seth shook his head. "I'm not buying it. Why would the Rosa guy need to drug women for sex? A guy like that could get plenty of women to spread their legs for him."

"Yes! He could! But that isn't what he wanted, Seth! He wanted power over women. He wanted them unconscious and showing no sign of resistance, disgust, fear, pain..." Seth shook his head again. "You don't believe me? Untie me. Untie me and I'll show you."

"Show me what?"

"The evidence." When Seth hesitated, she added, "If you don't trust me, just pick me up in this chair and take me to the computer. Let me enter all the passwords and I'll tell you what to do after that."

"No. You tell me the passwords."

She shook her head. "No one gets those."

"That's the deal, Stevie."

"Look, Seth. I may face punishment for what I've done, but no one will know my methods, including you. All I'm asking is that you look at the evidence I have. Then, you do what you feel is right."

Seth hesitated, a scowl on his face. Finally, he picked her up in her dining chair and set her back down in her office. He turned on her computer, untied her hands, and let her enter her passwords before tying her up again. With her instructions, he navigated to her evidence files.

"That folder, the one labeled 'Steeple'... open it." Seth shook his head when he saw the video files, knowing where they came from. "Go down to the fifth file, open it, and advance it to just before seven in the evening."

Seth followed her directions, and did so with enough ease that it was clear he'd spent time perusing surveillance data himself. When he finished, the footage showed Steeple entering his luxurious home with a smiling, golden-haired beauty on his arm. Stevie looked away, unwilling to watch it again.

Silence.

She glanced at Seth, a sadness coming over her. No matter what happened, their friendship would end. Seth would never tolerate such a betrayal of his trust, nor her methods of offering service to their City. He continued to watch, showing no reaction.

"Where's the rest... the rest of the evidence?" he said.

"What do you want to see first?"

"Start at the beginning."

Once they'd run through them all, Seth picked her up again and returned her to her original place. He untied her, relief coursing through her as the twine fell to the floor.

"Go to the bathroom if you need to," he said. "Leave the door open. Then get some food and water."

Stevie headed to her bathroom, relieving her full bladder while Seth stood aside, watching without watching. She glanced at her suit pocket, her cylinder still inside it.

Not yet.

In the kitchen, she drank some water and took out leftover noodles while Seth loomed over her, arms crossed. The food had no taste and she struggled to swallow the starchy noodles. After a few bites, she put it away again.

Seth pointed at the chair. "Sit down."

Confused, Stevie did as Seth asked. To her chagrin, Seth tied her up again, gagged her with something she couldn't maneuver off, and then secured her chair to her table. He gathered her Oakenfold and his other belongings, and left.

Noise. Stevie's head snapped up, her neck muscles seizing from having slept with her head nodded forward for too long. The door. Fear gripped her.

It was Seth, still dressed in field gear. His jacket glistened with moisture. It must have rained. She could see nothing through her window shades, other than light creeping in along the edges.

A strange relief filled her again. She knew the feeling was silly, if not foolish, given Seth's behavior the previous evening. But she couldn't help herself. If she must face beheading, she'd rather that Seth swung the sword.

Other than ensuring she hadn't escaped, Seth never looked at her. He seemed out of sorts, and the wrinkle between his brows looked deeper than ever. She'd given him nightmares, upset his sensitive neurochemistry. He took out a knife and approached her. She stiffened, until he began cutting the twine.

Sandalwood.

Seth motioned to the bathroom. Stevie stood, stumbling from having been trapped in the same position all night long, some body parts aching while others felt numb. Her neck hurt when she turned it the wrong way. She shuffled to the bathroom while Seth stood watch. When she pulled down her pants and sat on the toilet, she contemplated what rested quietly in her pocket. She left it there.

When finished, Seth motioned to the kitchen. She gulped down a glass of water and found some food, her appetite better that morning. She forced herself to eat as much as she could, not knowing how long Seth would leave her next time. But instead of tying her up again, he pointed to the couch. She curled up, pulling her white throw over her while Seth sat down on the other leg of the L-shaped couch. He leaned forward, his elbows on his knees as he rested his chin in his hands. But he remained silent.

"What's wrong, Seth?"

"You don't ask the questions. I do."

Still angry.

After several minutes of silence, Seth spoke. "Why do it this way? Why not do it legally, do the research and give it to the cops or the Feds?"

"The cops and Feds can't obtain the evidence that I can. Even if they did, they couldn't use it. And I tried that, giving other evidence to the authorities. It only winds up buried by some crooked insider, especially if you target Financials rather than common criminals. Or they don't have the money or manpower to solve it. Or, they make an arrest, just to have the perpetrator's lawyer get him off on a technicality. Then they go free, and go on to inflict their damage on our already vulnerable society."

"Why you?"

"Because it's my duty."

"Why?"

She shrugged. "It just is."

"How do you feel when you do it? When you pull the trigger?"

"Like I'm doing my job."

"And what about afterward?"

She hesitated. "Like how I feel when I yank an ugly, pernicious weed from a beautiful garden. You get dirty, the nettle burns you, but you've just rescued a small ecosystem from destruction, so it can flourish." She paused. "How did you know?"

He hesitated. "Your hair would be off, like you'd changed it... or your face would look a little different. And always on a Monday. You missed a few Mondays, just to look different on Tuesday. When I charted it, I realized it was always after a weekend that the shooter struck. Or you'd be gone Friday, and the shooter would strike that night. No one died on the weekends we spent time together."

"That's all circumstantial. You had more than that."

He nodded, still not looking at her. "Someone tipped me off... and asked me to do what they couldn't."

They. Mohawk and Gray Streak. That's how they'd known she'd be at Sage Bakery.

Seth went on. "Your neighbor, that asshole from Marigold... they weren't rapists or murderers."

"They're just as destructive, Seth. Only in a different way."

"And no one gets a warning, or a slap on the wrist."

"Some do, if their offenses are less detrimental."

"What happened... with that second murder in Viola?"

Memories of the terrifying dark stranger flooded back. She told Seth the truth.

He scoffed. "At least you were honest about that."

"I was honest about everything, except the obvious." When Seth gave no response, she continued. "I'm sorry, Seth, for deceiving you. But I had to. To tell you the truth would've put us both in danger. And you've seen enough violence in your life without me adding to it."

"What do you know about what I've seen?"

"More than you might think."

"Don't do that. Don't act like your choosing to murder people and seeing their bloody corpses is the same as being in a war zone. You've never served a day in your life."

"That's not what I mean, Seth. I wanted to enlist, but my mother begged me not to. She served in the first war, and she suffered years of war trauma. She hated violence, hated the news, hated the way we treat one another. I did all my research in secret, so she wouldn't worry or get exposed to any of it. And I didn't begin using the Oakenfold until after she died."

"How'd she die?"

"Crossfire, during a standoff between police and a group of shanties in the Outer Rim."

"Sorry," Seth said, his voice barely detectable.

After a few more minutes of silence, Seth stood. He went over to his pack, retrieved her Oakenfold, and tucked it away in one of her living room's dead zones. At last, his eyes met hers.

"I'm sorry... for the shitty things I said to you. It's just... you were the only woman I could be myself with, and..." He shrugged. "I can't be your friend. I can't be part of all this, and I can't know anything about it. Make sure I don't." Before he reached her door, he turned around again. "By the way, you made it too easy for me to capture you. You need a more secure entry... and you need to learn self-defense."

He left.

Stevie exited the shuttle station and embraced the cool, salty air. A good day, given her new metric for measuring such things. Seth no longer poked his head into her workspace to share news, and she no longer offered to fetch him his khakis. At only five minutes per day, in a day that included at least 480 minutes, her previous interactions with Seth comprised a mere one percent of her time spent at the Disc. Once again, she saw how much difference a single percentage point could make. Yet, she was safe, with the knowledge that Seth had deferred judgment and refrained from reporting her. And Seth was safe, without her questionable activities impacting his life.

Moreover, Herbie had come to her that day to bring good news: Marianne and her baby were going to be okay. Baby Mario had hovered too close to death for a time, but he survived and would recover. Stevie would also go home to an apartment with an enhanced security system, and tomorrow evening she would take another self-defense lesson. Three times per week she attended a group class to gain basic skills, with the goal of moving on to private lessons.

Back at home, Stevie changed into her running clothes, waved to Manny, and made for Blackwood Bridge. She looked forward to breathing the damp air and leaving the noise of the City, if only for a brief time. Stevie ran through Artemisia and then Rosa, her mind nearly at peace again after all that had happened.

Suddenly, just as she rounded a corner, someone grabbed her from behind. She cried out, only to be gagged. She attempted one of her new maneuvers, only to have it thwarted. Something covered her head as she was pulled off her feet, and she landed with a thud when tossed onto some surface. Unable to see anything, she thrashed until someone bound her arms and legs. A door slammed above her.

Motion. She was inside a vehicle. And it wasn't Seth this time. Whoever it was didn't smell like him, didn't have his strength.

She lay in what had to be the rear compartment of the vehicle, hearing nothing but the quiet whine of the electric motor. The vehicle jostled her as it sunk into holes in the road, stopping often for traffic signals. She reached back with her bound hands and felt around for a latch or some way out, but found nothing. The stop and go ended, and the sound of the road changed. The bridge. They headed to the east bank.

Fear finally set in. Last time it was Seth, but such luck wouldn't repeat itself. She brought her bound feet up and kicked at anything, to no avail.

Calm down, and save your energy. The moment they untie your hands, vape them.
Who are they?
Too many possibilities.

A short while later, the vehicle stopped and the door opened. Someone cut her ankle ties, hauled her to her feet, and pulled her blindly along until sitting her down on a cushioned surface. When her head covering came off, she blinked at the bright light.

Two figures stood before her. When her eyes focused, she saw familiar faces. Mohawk, and Gray Streak.

She closed her eyes for a moment and shook her head.

The denim-clad women pulled up a couple of chairs. Stevie stared at the chairs; they were made of wood... real wood. Thick, grainy, golden brown. She glanced around. They were inside a building, an industrial space converted into something livable. Shelves lined the walls, filled with artifacts... and real paper books.

"Sorry for the dramatics," Mohawk said, a gleam in her tawny eyes. Gray Streak sat down, eyeing Stevie suspiciously, while Mohawk patted Stevie down until she found what she was looking for. The cylinder. She retrieved it, removed Stevie's gag, and cut the rest of her ties. "You kept disappearing on us, refusing to talk to your fellow Brownies... so we forced you." She sat down, cocking her mohawked head as she studied the cylinder briefly. "Nice vape in Artemisia, by the way. Make that yourself?"

Stevie said nothing.

The two women waited. Upon seeing that she wouldn't talk, Gray Streak gave Mohawk an impatient look.

"Relax, Stevie," Mohawk said. "We didn't bring you here to hurt you and we didn't bring you here to lean on you."

"Then why did you?"

"We know what you've been doing... for the City, for the people."

Ah. You DO want something, and Seth's releasing me didn't let me off the hook.

"We know, for example, that you played the crucial role in catching the DeWitt garbage that defaced our Passage. We know you put your job and your freedom on the line for us."

"Us?" Stevie said. "Who's us?"

Stevie's question was met with a cop-like stare and a sour gaze. "The ones who provided the other players in the game," Mohawk said. "The ones who, like you, put themselves at risk for the betterment of our City."

"The people who confronted the DeWitt students were men," Stevie said.

"Men placed by us."

"So you're a watchdog organization, for Krokus."

"We're more than that." Mohawk ran her hand over her thick, tawny locks. "We also know about your dog rescue mission, your efforts to help an elderly man in Artemisia, your weed-pulling duty, and about numerous other elegant acts of petty vigilantism that make the Oakenfold Killer look like a cranky hack."

That's it? That's what you know? Then who ratted me out to Seth?

Stevie put on an annoyed face to mask her relief. "How do you know all this?"

"If you want that information, you'll have to earn it."

"How?"

"First, you have to do something for us."

"Such as?"

"A job," Mohawk said. "Not unlike what you've already been doing. But this time you'll have help."

Stevie shifted in her seat. "I appreciate the offer, but I work better alone."

"Working without a unit you can trust, in the world we live in... it's unsafe. We offer protection—from the cops, the Feds, and from evildoers."

"Sorry," Stevie said, standing up. "I assume I'm free to go, and that you'll quit stalking me..."

The two women glanced at one another. Gray Streak sullenly gestured toward the door. Stevie headed that way, feeling secure enough to turn her back on the two women.

"Stevie."

Stevie turned around. A third woman appeared.

Mobius.

She stared at her dark friend with the denim jumper and the beautiful afro, her anger flaring. Mobius knew the rules. She'd exposed her to these people she didn't know, and now she'd have to change everything—her alias, her portal, even her residence—to get them off her trail so they couldn't track her and find even more damning information.

"Don't be mad, Stevie," Mobius said, her expression contrite. "Leona and Awn, they found you on their own. I admitted I knew you to vouch for you and to prevent them from exposing you to others." When she got no protest from Stevie, she went on. "I've told you I don't like you out there alone. You'd be a fool to turn down Leona's offer."

"I'm sorry," Stevie told her. "I appreciate all you've done for me. But you know how I work. You know what I have at stake. All it takes is one leak to ruin everything. The answer is no."

Mobius cocked her head. "Imelda Jane wouldn't approve of you not considering an offer to be of service to the greater good."

Stevie shook her head. "Please don't do that. Don't use my dead mother to coerce me into giving you what you want." She turned to Leona and Awn. "If you get into a difficult situation, I'll help. But I can't be part of this."

Leona stood, striding closer to Stevie and crossing her arms. "You did the right thing by finding new homes for those couture collies, Stevie. What you don't know is that the former owner called it in to a detective she's slept with a few times. Fortunately, he got bored with the case and told her it came up dry. You came this close to getting cuffed."

"I don't believe you," Stevie lied.

"Come on, Stevie," Mobius said, taking a step closer, her dark eyes glimmering. "I know what you want, what you've always wanted. We can help you get it without risking your livelihood, but you're being more stubborn than—"

"Oh, for the mist in Hades!" Awn cried in a raspy voice. "Let the bitch go! She doesn't want to fucking be here."

The room went silent as all eyes turned to the gray-streaked woman with the sour face.

"Don't mind Awn," Leona said, offering a crooked smile. "She's always been challenged with regard to serotonin uptake, if you know what I mean." She paused. "Look, Stevie. What will it take for you to reconsider?"

"I need to know more. Mobius knows I can be trusted."

Leona glanced at Mobius, then at Awn, who scowled and gave a shrug. "Back when you were a kid, your mother probably mentioned an underground organization known as the Daughters of Anarchy."

Stevie nodded.

"Do you know what they stood for?"

"To some extent. Is that what you're doing here? Creating something similar to the DOA?"

"No," Leona said. "We *are* the DOA."

Stevie raised her eyebrows.

Leona gestured to Mobius. "So is your friend here... and so was your mother."

Stevie stared at Leona. "My mother? My mother belonged to the Daughters of Anarchy?"

"Oh, now she's interested," Awn groused. "You should've opened with that."

Leona waved a dismissive hand at Awn. "Yes, your mother belonged. So did ours, bless her soul." She and Awn crossed their arms over their chests and closed their eyes briefly. "The DOA could use someone with your commitment to our City and the people in it. It could also use someone with your unique knowledge and connections."

The Disc, and her access to a wealth of data.

"That's all we can tell you," Leona said. "Do a small job for us... see how it feels, see how we work. Call me anytime, as long as it's dark out. After that, if you still want to run solo, we'll go our separate ways."

The three of them watched her, out of arguments.

"What's the job?"

Stevie stepped off the train and headed north. She looked around with an especially careful eye, taking care to avoid Johnny Street or anywhere near it. She hadn't visited Viola since the Marigold job, nor had Maria called her for weed eradication. The spiny plants creeping up through the shredded sidewalks and the overgrown thickets in the abandoned lots told her that their manual labor was needed here. However, today, another duty called her to the misunderstood and unnecessarily maligned Hood. Duty toward those she didn't trust yet. Fortunately, she still had Leona's DNA sample. Leona had asked her to destroy it, and maybe she would... but not yet.

After purchasing a bag of homemade vegetarian tamales, she picked up some produce and a loaf of freshly baked bread. She went inside the local brewery, knowing she'd left just enough room for a few bottles of sarsaparilla. When she went to pay for them, she conjured up her best Krokusian. "Scintillations. I know you're all pretty busy, but could I score a tour of your facilities? Everyone says it's the best."

"Sure," the purple-haired clerk said, doing what she could to hide her irritation. "I'll see if someone's available."

After a few minutes, a hulking, inked-up man with brown overalls and no smile emerged. "Come on back," he said gruffly. "No pictures."

"No problem, fine sir. I don't even own a camera!"

He showed Stevie the brewing process, all the way from sowing seeds to bottling brew. Stevie feigned interest in her guide's flat-toned descriptions while surreptitiously taking images of all the employees, including her tour guide. Her black shirt hid the tiny lens that poked through her buttonhole, a trick she'd used many times. Once she got her images, her only other duty was to obtain their identities from the Disc and give it all to Leona. Leona didn't offer any other details, and she didn't ask.

An easy job, really. And she liked knowing that if something went wrong, a confederate waited nearby to run interference. But despite Leona's promises, despite Mobius and even her mother, she struggled with the idea of joining. There could be no sharing her petty acts of service while secretly engaging in her grander acts. Not without great risk. She had aroused Seth's suspicions simply by being his friend; the potential for trouble seemed exponentially greater when dealing with an entire organization.

Of course, the DOA had its own reputation. In the past, they'd done their share of anonymous community service, some of which was dangerous, illegal, and even deadly. For all she knew, the DOA would approve of her grand acts. But even so, she would always have to watch her back, always wonder if one of them would use such knowledge as leverage against her, when the time came that doing so meant her falling instead of them.

No. She couldn't join them.

A couple of days later, she contacted Leona.

"Scintillations," came Leona's steady, strong voice. "Did you pick up the dumplings?" she added, speaking in their prearranged code.

"I did."

"Middle of Blackwood Bridge, tomorrow night."

The next evening, Stevie ran to the bridge, arriving early and half expecting Leona to have beaten her there. But there was no sign of her. The Milagro's strong breeze cooled her as she peered out at the sparkling lights to the east and west, and the darkness that lay between them.

"Scintillations."

Leona approached her, her brown pleather zipped up to her neck and her mohawk whipping in the breeze.

Stevie handed her a small storage drive. "The images, their identities, and their data."

Leona stowed the drive in an internal pocket. "Thank you for this." She paused, looking out at the view. "I've always liked this spot. Halfway between the east and west banks, a place to escape it all."

"Me too."

"Have you given it any more thought? Joining us?"

Stevie pulled her hood up to combat the chilly wind. "I appreciate the offer, Leona. But I don't think it's for me. I'm sorry."

Leona nodded. "You aren't obligated just because your mother served. Others would argue differently, but things have changed since our mothers' time. Everything changes... we have to change too, to adapt to what life hands us. Those who don't... they wind up like those west bank suits standing in line for their daily dose of denial. Or worse." She shook her head, glancing at the west bank. "Take this Oakenfold Killer... he or she, probably a she, is no ordinary killer. She has a mission, a desire to polish up society by removing those who tarnish it from their towers of power. But she puts herself and her cause at risk by clinging to a cliched 'lone serial killer' archetype. She probably has a lot of power, but she doesn't have connections with the Feds or the cops, she can't protect herself if she gets attacked by multiple assailants, and she has no backup if a job goes bad."

"But none of that's happened yet, after numerous killings."

"It will. Without someone else to offer up new ideas, she'll rely on the same old methods, the ones she knows. And it's just a matter of time until it gets her cuffed." Leona faced Stevie again. "Take the Oakenfold revolver, for example. A signature, to be sure. But also a relic of the past, a crude device that will eventually fail her, and one that will lead the authorities right to her."

"I assumed the revolver was powerful because of its archaicness. They're simple machines and undetectable."

She shook her head. "Not anymore. Word has it the City has begun retrofitting security detectors across the City not only to recognize the metals and the technology used to mask them, but to recognize even the gunshot residue they leave. Then, surveillance will do the rest."

"How do you know this?"

"One of the benefits of being part of something bigger than yourself."

"But why would they go to such trouble and expense for one murderer, especially when they're hurting for money?"

"People are figuring out that the killer is getting away with it for a reason, and antique firearms are turning up again. My guess is the specs to print them will resurface, too. The cops have kept their plans under their hats... let the criminals get cocky. Then, judgment day will come, if you know what I mean. And, not that expensive. Some old vets with good tech skills have volunteered their time. Gives 'em a way to contribute." Leona patted her pleather jacket. "Thank you for this. Stay safe, and call me anytime... as long as it's dark out."

Leona turned and headed east, disappearing into the darkness.

Stevie dodged a hole in the sidewalk as she made her way west, her ankle boots clopping on the concrete. The drizzle had ceased and the clouds cleared, revealing a few bright celestial bodies that refused to be diminished by light pollution. She'd long wished the City would enact a lights-out period, where all but the most essential illumination would cease so everyone could look up and see what lay beyond their insubstantial corner of the galaxy. She strode past brick buildings with their enviable balconies, a few even populated by people conversing as they sipped their beverages. Soon, she arrived at his building.

"Can I help you?" the swarthy doorman said.

"Good evening. I've come to see Seth. He isn't expecting me."

But he's home. That she knew.

"I'll ring him." His earpiece already in place, the doorman scrolled through his list and pressed a few buttons. "Hey, it's Armand. You have a visitor." He looked at her. "What's your name?"

"Stevie."

"Says her name's Stevie."

Maybe this was a bad idea.

Armand hesitated for a few moments before glancing at her again. "Go on up."

Stevie took the elevator to the 19th floor, her heart beginning to pound as she knocked on Seth's door. Other than from a distance, she hadn't seen him in weeks. The door opened, and there stood Seth, in slacks and an Army t-shirt. He gazed at her for a moment before blinking a couple of times.

"Scintillations," she said.

He gave a reluctant smile at the jest, standing aside to let her in. His window shades remained closed, but the door to his balcony was partially ajar, like he'd been sitting out there.

"You'd better have a good reason for breaking my rules, Miss Stevie," he said, mimicking Herbie's name for her.

"I won't stay long. I have something for you." She set down her bag and retrieved her tablet. After turning it on, she handed it to Seth.

He read over the electronic document. "Is this what I think it is?"

She nodded. "Harry should get the approval this week. You can turn that lot on Charlie into a green zone."

Another tiny smile escaped him, his eyes crinkling a little. How she'd missed that crinkling. "That's... that's great. I'll let Harry know." He returned her tablet. "Thank you."

Stevie retrieved a box and handed it to him.

"What's this?" he said.

"Open it."

Seth unlatched the reusable box, flipping the lid over and removing the cotton fill. "Holy fuck."

He stared for a couple of moments before picking up the box's contents and tossing its packaging aside. Her Oakenfold .357 Magnum, freshly cleaned by her that morning, gleamed in his masculine hand. She resisted the urge to look above them. There was no surveillance here... not yet.

"It's still functional," she told him. "I made a few alterations to it so no one can link it to the deaths. I... I wasn't sure how you would feel about it. If you don't want it, let me know and I'll take care of it."

He glanced at her, then back at the .357, turning the sleek instrument over in his hands. He unlatched the chamber and spun it around a few times before closing it again and briefly aiming the piece. His expression darkened. "Why are you doing this?"

She looked back at his clouded eyes, still unsure if she'd done the right thing. "You told me once that you hadn't found an Oakenfold .357 for your collection. It's no longer safe for me to use, and I want you to have it."

He peered at the shining revolver again, before setting it down on his counter. "Look... I know I said I wanted nothing to do with this, but I gotta say something. What you've been doing... it's beyond reckless. I don't want to turn on the goddamned news one of these days and find out you've been cooked."

Stevie, surprised at Seth's confession, said nothing.

"Think about it," he added.

She nodded. "I will." She picked up her bag. "I promised I wouldn't stay long. Thank you... for seeing me." She headed toward the door, eager to leave. Not because she wanted to, but because things felt good between them and she didn't want to ruin it.

"Stevie."

She turned back around. When Seth approached her, her heart began to pound. To her surprise, he put his arms around her and hugged her. She reveled in his warmth as the smell of sandalwood inebriated her. She hugged him back, trying to quell the perplexing mixture of fear and arousal that threatened to overwhelm her.

Leave.

But she couldn't. She couldn't let go, not yet, not when it could be months before she talked to him again. Seth pulled away just a little, his long lashes unblinking as he gazed down at her. Then he kissed her.

The taste of him, his own taste with just a twinge of beer. He pulled away momentarily, as if waiting for her reaction, for her to back away. When she didn't, he kissed her again, this time more forcefully. Her trench coat slid off her shoulders and her hands found their way to his chest. Seth gently urged her backward until he had her pressed against the door, his lips buried in her neck as his hands moved along her sides and then under her shirt. Off it went. He backed away, taking her hand and leading her inside, into his bedroom. Into his bed.

The rest of their clothing in a pile on his floor, they lay on Seth's bed, his sage-colored sheets smelling of him. He hovered over her, kissing her breasts, her stomach, and then her lips as she put her arms around him.

To feel the weight of him. The heavy, muscled weight of a man. And then him inside of her. How glorious. She caressed his back, moving her body beneath him. How good he felt. How great he felt. And when she could no longer endure it, she exploded with bodily pleasure, unaware of all she did or said or thought. Seth followed soon after. They collapsed, his chest on hers, her arms around him, both catching their breaths.

Seth finally removed himself and lay down alongside her. They rested in silence, recovering and dissipating the heat that had built within each of them. Soon, Seth reached for the covers and pulled them over the both of them, nestling closer to her. And cocooned next to Seth's warmth, Stevie closed her eyes.

Stevie awakened, glancing around her. Seth's bedroom. She looked over at him, his eyes closed as the sound of rhythmic breathing came and went.

"You're a fool, Stevie."

Stevie blinked. There stood Ronald Carr, with her .357 in his hand. But it wasn't his voice she heard. It was her mother's.

Stevie sat up suddenly, her heart pounding. She scoured the room with her eyes—no Ronald. She turned to Seth, who lay on his stomach, his arm slung over the side of his bed as he slumbered. Thoughts flooded her mind. Too many thoughts. Serotonin and dopamine waning, norepinephrine on the rise.

What have I done?

She got out of bed, careful to avoid waking Seth. She felt around in the darkness for her clothing, finding her undies and jeans amidst Seth's garments. Where was the rest? She tiptoed out of Seth's bedroom and found her remaining clothing near the door. Her bag, too. She immediately looked for the .357... it still rested quietly upon the counter, where Seth had left it. Where it belonged. After dressing herself, she left.

Outside, the streets were deserted, only an occasional electro-taxi whizzing by. Damp air washed over her. Miraculously, the stars still shone in the night sky, not yet hidden behind another layer of clouds. Soon, her mind began to clear. She found her earpiece, tucked it into her ear, and spoke a name.

"Scintillations, Stevie."

"Likewise, Leona."

"A fellow creature of the night, I see."

"Sometimes."

"What can I do for you?"

Stevie hesitated for a moment. "When will you have your next dumpling feast?"

"Soon. Did you want to partake?"

"I do."

"To share our dumplings, you have to be with us, Stevie."

"Then I'm with you."

THANK YOU!

Thank you for reading the first season of *Daughters of Anarchy*! If you enjoyed it, please check out my other works on my website (5280press.com).

Also, if you want to be notified when I release new books or when I'm having a special deal or giveaway, please sign up for my email list (5280press.com home page, bottom right). Don't worry: I send out an email once a month *at most*.

You probably already know that book reviews mean the world to authors, especially indie authors. If you're up for posting an honest review on Amazon, Goodreads, or another book site, I would be very grateful!

And finally, if you want to delve more into the DOA world, check out my Author's Notes about the series at 5280press.com/blog, where I offer insight into the story and its characters.

ABOUT THE AUTHOR

C.A. Hartman specializes in writing science fiction. Recovering from her years as an academic scientist, she's refocused her overactive, analytical mind on creating thought-provoking sci-fi with memorable characters. A graduate of the University of Colorado, Hartman earned her PhD in Behavioral Genetics and worked as a scientist for 15 years. She lives in Denver with her husband and has a special fondness for good TV, the desert, aviator sunglasses, and dark roast coffee (decaf, of course, because you DON'T want to be around her when she's caffeinated). Doc Hartman is an introvert but she loves engaging with readers. You can find her on her website and blog (5280press.com), Twitter (@5280_SciFi), Pinterest, and Goodreads.

GLOSSARY

Artemisia: Neighborhood where Stevie lives. Her mother moved them to Artemisia when Stevie was 10.

Blackwood Bridge: Bridge that crosses the Milagro River, and connects Rosa and Crocus.

Brownie: Slang for someone from Crocus, referring to their tendency to wear brown pleather. Also refers to the citizens being somewhat "browner" in skin tone than other neighborhoods due to Crocus's ethnic makeup.

Brown Sugar: Slang for a woman with mixed black and white heritage.

Chem shop: A place where one can purchase legal drugs (e.g. Cannabis).

The Circle: An area in the heart of Downtown, where the Science Museum, the City Library, the Courthouse, and City Hall form a circle around a sizable green zone.

City University: Local public university and where Stevie did her undergraduate and graduate work.

Couture collie: A dog with a cosmetically enhanced appearance, regardless of breed. Enhancements are usually limited to the mane, where one alters the color and texture of the fur, but can also include other cosmetic enhancements such as size. Much like with women, the enhancements can be done cheaply through do-it-yourself means, or more expensively through your local cosmetic geneticist. Commonly, Yellows have matching yellow dogs.

Crocus: Neighborhood east of the Milagro River. Mobius's Hood, and where Stevie is originally from. A modest to blue collar middle class Hood that used to be poorer and more troubled. Known for its art, its murals, and its antiestablishment mentality.

Dead zone: A place where there's no video surveillance, or where the cameras can't quite reach.

DeWitt University: Expensive private university in Dianthus, often attended by the children of Financials who profited from the wars. Named after the former CEO of ID Corp, who donated a considerable sum to have the university's name changed. A major street in the City is also named after him.

Dianthus: An expensive, moneyed Hood that includes DeWitt University and lots of bars, clubs, and chem shops.

The Disc: A structure up in the stratosphere, named for its disc-like shape. The Disc was created as a satellite station, but became the headquarters for the Federal Watch program when it was instituted.

Downtown: A City neighborhood that includes the Circle and the financial district.

East bank: Within the City, any Hood east of the Milagro River. Includes Crocus, Viola, and the Outer Rim, among others.

Eyes: Slang for surveillance cameras.

Federal Watch program: A federal surveillance program, created after the second war, in which the government legally monitors its citizens' phone calls, email, and homes. The program is run from the Disc and is designed to detect terrorist activity. The data cannot be used for other purposes, including criminal investigation. Stevie and Seth are Federal employees who work for the program.

Green zone: A park or other green space within the City. What green zones and parks existed before the wars got destroyed during the second war, along with many of the natural areas outside the City. During the City's post-war redevelopment, many former green zones were developed into skyscrapers, with the rationalization that it would help their economy. As such, green zones are rare and highly valued.

Harry: A veteran who lives in Seth's building.

Herbie: Stevie's boss and a manager at the Disc.

Hood: Slang for neighborhood.

ID Corp: Large financial corporation that has a monopoly on the credit currency used by the country's citizens. ID Corp is known for its high fees, making it difficult for low income people to run their businesses.

Khaki: Espresso with enough milk to give it a khaki color. A commonly drunk beverage in the Army, where the nickname was inspired by their khaki uniforms.

Kira Carr: Ronald Carr's daughter and Stevie's best friend from age 10 through her formative years.

Krokus: See Crocus.

Manny: A doorman in Stevie's building who typically works swing shift.

Minnie: Ronald and Miriam Carr's 9-year-old foster daughter, adopted through Social Services.

Miriam Carr: Ronald's wife.

Mobius: Stevie's friend since childhood, who works for the City.

Outer Rim: The outskirts of the City on the East bank, where people live off the grid (and without surveillance) in abandoned buildings.

Pansy: Slang for someone from Viola, named after one of the flowers in the *Viola* genus.

Pansy Bridge: Bridge that crosses the Milagro River, connecting Rosa to Viola.

Pomade: Stevie's neighbor, named for his perfectly pomaded hair.

Ronald Carr: An executive for the Federal Watch program. Also, Kira's father and a childhood father figure to Stevie.

Rosa queen: A woman who embodies the new money opulence of the Rosa Hood. Often with long platinum hair, sizable breasts, and a curvaceous build, whether by nature or scientific enhancement. Can be seen wearing anything rare and unsustainable, such as wool or leather.

Salvia: An older, west bank neighborhood with a lot of war veterans and middle class folk. Seth's Hood.

Scintillations: A classic greeting among Crocusians, meant to be tongue-in-cheek.

Shack: Establishments in Viola where one can obtain illegal hard drugs, sexual services, and/or cyber-experiences.

Shanty: Someone who lives among the makeshift shanties of the Outer Rim, off the City's grid.

Viola: An east bank neighborhood, north of Crocus, and the poorest of the City's Hoods. Known for its crime, but also for tough, no-nonsense people who know how to survive, and its handcrafted food, drink, and goods made of sustainable products.

West bank: Within the City, any Hood west of the Milagro River. Includes Dianthus, Downtown, Artemisia, and Salvia, among others.

Yellow: A woman with long, yellowish-blonde hair. The hair is inexpensively bleached or dyed, giving it a yellowish appearance that looks cheap, dry, and over-processed. A contrast to the more attractive and tasteful—but far more expensive—genetically engineered golden or platinum blonde.

www.ingramcontent.com/pod-product-compliance
Lightning Source LLC
Chambersburg PA
CBHW021244260626
47155CB00004BA/1308